D0350421

CATHERINE HOUSE

CATHERINE HOUSE

a novel

ELISABETH THOMAS

This is a work of fiction. Names, characters, places, and incidents are products of the author's imagination or are used fictitiously and are not to be construed as real. Any resemblance to actual events, locales, organizations, or persons, living or dead, is entirely coincidental.

HarperCollins books may be purchased for educational, business, or sales promotional use. For information, please email the Special Markets Department at SPsales@harpercollins.com.

FIRST EDITION

Designed by Elina Cohen

Library of Congress Cataloging-in-Publication Data has been applied for.

ISBN 978-0-06-290565-9

20 21 22 23 24 LSC 10 9 8 7 6 5 4 3 2 1

For my friends

Year One

BILLIE JEAN

I ran a hand over my stomach. I was going be sick. The back of my throat tasted like sour wine and my ears rang with the echoes of a party: a smutty, fucked-up bass line reverberating through the floor; girls, a lot of them, slurring and yelping; a boy smashing a bottle and screaming to the crowd, "We're here! We are the kings of the castle!"

The castle. Catherine.

I opened my eyes.

I was lying naked in an empty bathtub. My arms, hanging over either side of the porcelain, had gone numb. Everything in the bathroom was a vague off-white, from the claw-foot tub to the high-tank toilet, the swan-patterned wallpaper, the greasy tiled floor. The only thing I could focus on, by my elbow, was a bar of soap. Its surface was incised with a brutal, flawless C.

Was I dying? Was I dead?

The bathroom door clicked open and a small brown face peeked in. It boggled as it saw me.

"You can come in," I said.

The girl hesitated. "Really?"

"Yes."

She stepped in and stared down at my naked body with pursed lips. Her mouth was white and moist at the corners, like an old woman's, and she wore thick plastic-framed glasses that were much too big for her face. Her hair was brushed into four strict black puffs.

"You're my roommate," I said.

She nodded. "We met on the stairs, remember? You were going to a party."

Her voice was so low, flat, and abrupt that it almost didn't sound like English. She held her right hand cupped awkwardly against her chest.

"I don't remember your name," I said.

"Barbara. Barbara Pearce. Everyone calls me Baby."

"Like." I burped, covering my mouth with the back of my hand. "*Dirty Dancing*."

She sighed.

"I'm Ines," I said.

"I remember."

"Do you want—a towel?" she said.

"Sure."

She pulled a towel off the rack and handed it to me. I draped it over my lap.

She sat down and leaned against the wall, still cupping her hand. Her pajamas were thin hospital-blue cotton, identical to the ones I had found in my own dresser, and like her glasses, they were much too big for her. They bunched around her dark, skinny ankles and wrists.

"Do you think you're going to be much longer?" she said. "I—wanted to take a bath."

"Did you go to the party?" I said. "The one in the Harrington cellar?"

"Only for a minute."

"Why?"

She picked at the sweater sleeve. "Was it fun?"

I put a hand to my head.

The party had packed the basement gallery, a narrow space crowded with heavy oaken tables, humid with the smell of sweat, stale mouths, and vinegary alcohol. Boys and girls pressed against each other as they shook hands and clasped shoulders. Some glanced around the room with wide, nervous eyes as they took it all in: the high coffered ceiling and faded tapestries on the walls, the unlabeled wine and brass bowls of oranges and kumquats. Others tugged at their new uniforms, white T-shirts and jeans, as they shuffled to an old Tears for Fears cassette blasting out of the boom box. A boy folded his arms, chewed his lips, and spoke too loudly as he tried to casually work his SAT scores into a conversation. A girl, her T-shirt tucked in tense and tight, seemed to be trying to shake the hand of everyone in the room. She was so excited to meet us. She was so excited to be here.

Had I been excited, too? My heart was beating fast, like I'd been running. Too fast; I couldn't stay there and pretend to be normal.

I'd grabbed a bottle of wine and slipped into the hallway. There was a window of colored glass that looked out onto the gallery. I sat on the windowsill, drank the wine, and watched the party distort. Faces blurred in and out of each other. Laughter pitched higher as a girl shrieked. A tapestry of a naked woman riding a bull was pulled from its rod and crumpled to the floor. The image contorted psychedelically as it fell.

No, I wasn't excited to be here, at the house. But I was relieved. Just this afternoon I'd twisted around in my bus seat to watch the Catherine gate lock behind me. I couldn't see anything, though; the gate had already disappeared into a copse of heavy black pines. The trees scraped against the dense, leaden sky.

At the party, only hours later, I could barely remember how I'd gotten to the house. I'd taken another easy swig of wine. I didn't care. It didn't matter. All that mattered was that in here, no one knew who I was or what I'd done. I could stop running. I was safe.

I'd drunk until the night blurred and my heartbeat slowed. Soon I couldn't feel my heart at all.

And now I was here.

Baby was still clutching the sweater in her lap. She stared at me without blinking.

"What are you doing?" I said.

"What?"

"Why are you here, in the bathroom?"

"I told you. I want to take a bath."

"You do not."

She glanced down at her cupped hand, then back at me. "Promise not to tell?" she said.

"I'm not going to tell anyone anything."

She opened her hand.

She was holding a snail with a handsome marigold-yellow shell, which he was just peeking out of now. He waved a shy tentacle.

Baby placed the snail on the floor. Shocked, he retreated back into his shell, and then hesitantly poked the tentacle out again.

"I found him on my lawn," she said. "As my mom was packing up the car. Under the azalea bush in the driveway. I took him. I carried him the whole way here." She poked one of his tentacles. "Do you think he'll be okay?"

I twisted over the tub for a better look. He was sliming across the floor now, toward the sink.

"He'll be great," I said.

A mucus trail glimmered on the tiles.

"Promise not to tell?" Baby said. "I shouldn't have—I don't even know how I got him past the gate. Pets are not allowed. Of course."

"It's a snail."

She blinked, apparently not understanding what I meant.

I said, "I won't tell."

She breathed a sigh of relief.

I climbed out of the tub. Baby's eyes dashed away from me, and I remembered I was naked. I covered myself with the towel she'd given me as I lay down on the floor.

"Anyway," she said, "I came here because I thought—I might run the hot bathwater for him. Maybe he would like the steam. I don't know."

The cool tile felt good against the side of my head. The room throbbed.

The snail had made it to the sink. Now he was climbing the pedestal, tentacles still timidly wavering. He was the sweetest creature I could imagine.

"I love him," I said.

"I do, too."

"Does he have a name?"

She shrugged.

"We should name him."

She touched his shell. "Billie Jean," she whispered.

"Billie Jean is a girl's name."

She lowered her hand.

"Is he your boyfriend?" she said.

"Who? Billie Jean?"

She pursed her lips again. "No—the guy you were with. I heard you, in the hallway—going back to his room."

"Oh," I said. "Right. No."

"He's not your boyfriend?"

"I don't know him at all."

She pushed her glasses farther up her nose.

"I'm going to be a really bad roommate," I said. "Sorry."

Billie Jean was retreating into his shell.

"Are we friends?" Baby said suddenly.

"Of course," I said. "Best friends."

"I've never had a best friend before."

I put a hand to my mouth.

"Do you need to throw up?" she said.

"I'm not sure yet," I mumbled.

"What?"

"I—"

I crawled to the toilet. I heaved.

❧

Catherine House. No, it wasn't a college, exactly, though it was accredited as such, my second interviewer had explained as she waved steam off a mug of hot lemon water. We were sitting in her sterile white marble kitchen. As she spoke, she tapped her mug with a sapphire-ringed finger.

"You went there, right?" I said. "To Catherine?"

She inclined her head in a gentle assent.

"So you know," I said. "If it isn't a college, what is it?"

She kept tapping her mug. I couldn't read her expression.

What was Catherine, exactly? Let's say, a community of minds. A crucible of experimental, reformist liberal arts study. Research-and-development institute for the most radical new materials sciences. A postsecondary school more selective than any Ivy League, and so terrifically endowed that tuition was free to any student lucky enough to be accepted. A tiny, pioneering, fanatically private place that by some miracle of chemistry produced some of the world's best minds: prizewinning authors, artists and inventors, diplomats, senators, Supreme Court justices, two presidents of the United States. A school, and an estate: a complex confection of architecture and design, a house—a magnificent house—miles off the highway, in black woods, behind a long iron gate.

Orientation was held on Friday in the house's grand auditorium. I sat in the back of the balcony, my legs slung over an armrest. The chairs were upholstered in faded navy velvet, the same velvet as the stage curtains and peeling carpet. Water damage darkened the walls and rococo giltwood ceiling. Loose electric wires snaked in front of the curtains into the shadows.

Down below, about a third of the seats were filled with our class of first-years, all in white T-shirts and jeans. We'd only been here two days and already it seemed everyone else had clustered into cliques.

A woman stood in the shadow of the balcony, her arms folded and legs crossed at the ankle. She wore a slim oyster-gray dress that seemed almost to glow.

Viktória Varga. She wasn't just Catherine's director; she was the school's public face. Years before I came to the house, I'd seen her on the *PBS NewsHour*, debating the integrity of Catherine's plasm research or something like that. Mostly I remembered the way she sat so absolutely, impeccably still. She'd had a benevolent smile on her lips, but her eyes were cold and severe.

I mouthed her name to myself. *Viktória*. She had appeared almost mythic there on TV, yet here she was: a real woman, in a silvery dress, in the same auditorium as me.

I wished I were close enough to get a good look at her face.

Beside me, a girl with a strict haircut sat on the edge of her seat with a notebook in her lap. *Catherine House Orientation—Policies and Procedures*, she had written across the top of the page. She had also written a number: *09041996*. I stared at it awhile before realizing it was the date.

The lights dimmed. Everyone quieted. The curtains parted to reveal a black screen, which then flickered to life.

A woman in a pale pink skirt suit was walking down a dimly lit hall.

"Hello," she said. "Welcome to Catherine House. My name is M. Day, and I'm the dean of student life here at Catherine. It is my immense pleasure to welcome you to your home for the next three years."

I sneezed. The girl next to me shot me a glare.

Catherine House, M. Day was saying, hand resting on a wooden telephone booth, is not just a school, but a cloister—an environment of total concentration and retreat. We encourage students to treasure these three years as a very special private time in their lives. But we understand that some may wish to stay in touch with their families and friends back home. Such students may do so by spending what we call "points," which are earned by excelling at program assignments, contributing meaningfully to the Catherine community, or through trades, which are assigned in your second year. Students are then welcome to spend points on phone credits and postage stamps. Your Blue Book explains the points system in further detail.

The film skipped to a spacious room lined with shelves full of toiletries. M. Day gestured toward them with a hostess's delight.

At Catherine, it is our pleasure to provide our students with everything they need: a healthy breakfast, lunch, tea, and dinner; formal and everyday dress; pencils, notebooks, and other school supplies; toiletries to nourish your hair and skin; and medications as prescribed. Other accessories and vanity items, such as fashion clothing or cosmetics, may be purchased with points at the commissary.

A flash of light and a pause, as if someone had fiddled with the camera. Then M. Day was in a dorm room, running a hand over a tidy bed.

Whether you live in Molina, Ashley, or Harrington, your hall is your home for the next three years. And while we do have a staff of aides to help keep the house in tip-top shape, we expect our students to clean up after themselves and manage their living areas with respect, just as they do their minds. Begin your day by making your bed and taking a bath. Floss and brush your teeth. Treat your bodies and your spaces with pride.

M. Day was walking across the yard, into a cluster of trees, approaching a squat white building.

If we believe you have wandered from the path of learning, we may send you here, to the Catherine House Restoration Center. The Restoration Center is not a place of punishment. It is a place to readjust your relationship to Catherine and your environment. Each of our students has been selected by Viktória and the admissions committee as someone who belongs here at Catherine. You will give to Catherine, and Catherine will give to you. We will not let each other down.

I glanced at Viktória when M. Day said her name. I would have thought she'd raise her hand or smile to the crowd to acknowledge the mention. She didn't move.

M. Day continued on, wandering through various rooms at Catherine. Here was how we registered for fitness activities; this was what to do in case of a medical emergency; these were the holidays, festivals, and feasts that would mark the passage of our time. Ballrooms, parlors, and dining rooms flashed pink, white, and gold.

Should we have any questions, we may refer to the Blue Book for more details.

"It's a lot, I know," our usher said as we gathered in the Molina parlor after the presentation. The usher, Kimmy Tannenbaum—

"Three *n*'s, one *b*, yes, write that down, there *will* be a quiz . . . Oh, don't, *don't*, I'm kidding, I'm kidding!"—was a frizzy, chirpy upperclassman tasked with adjusting us to life at Catherine, and to Molina in particular. She had already given us a quick, high-spirited tour of the Molina courtyard, bedroom halls, laundry pickup and drop-off, and handed out a flurry of registration forms and schedules. "Once classes begin next week," she was saying now, rocking back and forth on her heels, "you'll get the hang of things before you know it, lickety-split, like that." She snapped her fingers. "I promise."

A girl coughed. We all glanced at her, then away.

"Anyway," Kimmy said. "Any questions?"

The parlor was tense with quiet energy. There were about thirty of us first-years in Molina, which, Kimmy had explained, was the newest hall and had the smallest number of students. We all stood crammed together among the parlor's fussy divans, card tables, and spindly pink satin sofas, eyeing each other in tight-lipped silence. The air was heavy with the smell of dead roses.

"How do we get more wine?" the girl next to me blurted out.

The room tittered, and the girl blushed. I could smell her sweat. It smelled plasticky, like the cheap shampoo we'd found in our welcome kits. Kimmy's smile hardened.

"Guys," Kimmy said, "listen. I get it. Obviously, Catherine is not your average school. You're not going to get carded here. Your parents are a billion miles away. And"—she lifted her chin—"Catherine has always been a house in which discipline and disorder are both valued as part of the learning experience. We want you to work hard, but we also want you to have the best years of your life. So go ahead, drink yourself stupid. But remember—this is not an easy school. If you don't want to fail out, eventually you're going to have to do your homework. And you *really* don't want to fail out."

She stared around the room, chin still lifted, as if daring us to say something more. No one did. The room watched her in anticipation.

Kimmy sighed.

"You can pick up bottles during tea service," she said. "New shipments come in on the truck every week."

Kimmy rubbed at her neck. She wasn't looking at us anymore; she was staring up at the parlor chandelier. It hung heavy with glittering crystals and beads.

"You are so lucky," she said.

Her voice had become distant.

"So lucky," she said, "to be here—at the beginning."

❧

Back in our room, Baby flipped through the Blue Book and paced from one wall to the other. I lay on my bed and stared at the ceiling.

"Here," Baby said finally, stopping on a page. "No cassettes, CDs, or books from home . . . no personal letters . . . and no pets. Pets of any kind are strictly prohibited."

She gave Billie Jean's tank a significant look. We'd found the tank on our first trip to the commissary, among a wreckage of grimy latex gloves and broken safety goggles, the ruins of some canceled chemistry lab. We filled the tank with moist dirt and sticks scavenged from the yard and fed Billie Jean bits of lettuce sneaked into our napkins after lunch. Neither of us was sure how to take care of a snail, but he seemed pleased enough. He was curled up in his shell now, perched on the side of the tank.

"If you're so scared, get rid of him," I said. "Put him out on the lawn. No one cares."

Baby was breathing hard.

"Or don't." I twisted on the bed, pulling the blanket up and over my head. "We could run away, you know. Us and Billie Jean. Climb over the gate, jack a car, head down to Miami Beach. Sun and sand. Nightclubs. Casinos. How about it?"

"I'd rather die," Baby said. "Anyway, we could never make it past the gate. We'd just end up in the tower."

"The what?"

"The Restoration Center. From the video. 'The tower'—that's what everyone calls it."

"How do you know?"

Baby was still staring at Billie Jean.

"It was mentioned in that article last year," she said. "The one in *New York* magazine, about Catherine graduates in government?"

"I don't know what article you're talking about."

"Seriously?"

"Yes. Seriously."

Baby sat down on her bed.

"I read everything I could about Catherine," Baby whispered. "I always did, ever since I was a little girl. Every little newspaper article, every stupid exposé. Even the mean ones—the ones after Shiner. Those writers didn't know anything, I could tell. I didn't know anything, either. But I wanted to." She lifted her chin. "No one thought I would get in, but here I am. The only girl from Lubbock admitted in years."

"I thought we're not supposed to say where we're from," I said.

Baby shot me a peevish look I barely noticed. A strange calm had settled over me.

We could never make it past the gate, Baby had said. Of course we couldn't. That was the Catherine experiment: give the house three years—three profound, total years—then become anything or anyone you want to be. Watch all your dreams come true.

So what had M. Day called the house? *A cloister—an environment of total concentration and retreat.* Meaning nothing and no one was getting past that gate. No one in, and no one out.

Three years trapped in this house.

"Do you know what you're going to concentrate in?" Baby said.

I rubbed at the dry skin on my lips.

"Ines?"

"What?"

"Do you know what you're going to concentrate in?"

"Oh. No."

I didn't have any dreams. Not anymore. Maybe I did before I applied to Catherine, but that was during junior year of high school. I'd been a completely different person back then. Someone much better behaved.

Baby was still watching me with shrewdly narrowed eyes. She seemed to be waiting for something.

"I," Baby finally said, "am going to concentrate in new materials. You know—plasm studies?"

I put a hand to my throat. My heartbeat was dull and low. I couldn't tell if I was relaxed or panicking.

"You're probably wondering how I know I'll get in, if it's so selective," Baby continued, her voice higher now. "It—has a pretty hard application process, obviously. They've had enough trouble with people who don't respect the work. But my second interviewer said I'd be perfect for it. She even said she'd recommend me to the department. So."

"Flowers," I said.

Baby blinked. "What?"

"Flowers," I said. "Botany. I'm going to concentrate in botany."

"Botany?" Baby said. "Are you serious? Why?"

I didn't know why. I'd suddenly thought of an illustration

from a book I'd read as a child. In the illustration, a fairy princess bride with glimmering white wings stood barefoot in a garden. She wore a white lace dress and a white lace veil and carried a big bouquet of gardenias, roses, and freesias. A wisteria bower arched overhead.

I hadn't thought of that illustration in such a long time. I couldn't believe I even remembered it.

"I don't know," I said. "It seems like a nice thing."

"Well," Baby said with disinterest, "too bad, because there's no botany concentration."

She was staring at Billie Jean again.

I stood up. "Let's go to dinner."

She continued to stare. I touched her shoulder.

"We're going to be okay," I said. "We're going to dinner."

She nodded at me. I took her hand and walked her out of the room.

❧

The next Monday, I woke up stale-mouthed and hungover in a silent bedroom. The tea tray that was delivered every morning had already been placed on our table, and one of the cups had been used. Baby's bed was made, its thin, sun-bleached coverlet tucked in tight and the pillow fluffed. She was gone.

I hated waking up alone.

I got up and looked out the window. The house was too quiet today. I tapped the glass.

Our windows faced the Molina courtyard, which was vaguely Mediterranean in design. Overgrown fig trees with broad, sallow leaves shaded potted shrubs and herbs, and tangles of weeds choked the paths. Glazed mosaicked tiles flashed eerie tones of ruby, amber, and peacock-green. In the center of the courtyard stood a long-dry fountain with a stone sculpture of a little boy cradling a turtle. His eyes were empty. Nothing moved in the windows of the surrounding buildings. No one stood on any of the green-shuttered balconies. No one was here.

Far above Molina's walls, the Ashley tower loomed, battlemented and black as a rook. Six black birds flew past it toward the sun.

I tapped on the glass again, then turned from the window.

The tea tray had already become familiar to me. It was hand-painted oily green and laden with a dull silver kettle, two mismatched porcelain cups, a canister of gray-brown coffee powder, and two tea bags in a glass jar. Some days the tray held a small blue dish of crumbly yellow cookies that tasted like margarine. There were no cookies today, but there was something else. An envelope tucked underneath the clean teacup. It was addressed to me.

I opened it with my thumb.

I must have registered for classes one day over the summer. I could picture that afternoon: a rumpled motel bed and muddy sneakers by the door, footsteps in the hall, my dirty hands folding open a brochure. But now I didn't recognize any of the class names on the sheet in the envelope: Introduction to Philosophy, Introduction to World Religions, Calculus I, First-Order Logic. They were listed with room numbers like AT46 and HW15 that also meant nothing to me.

I glanced out at the rising sun. It looked to be about midmorning. Introduction to World Religions had probably started a while ago.

I got dressed in blue jeans, a white T-shirt, and white Keds. Though we had been allowed to bring a small amount of outerwear from home, casual clothes were the same for everyone at Catherine. Our dressers had already been stocked with the T-shirts and jeans when we'd arrived, along with three identical pairs of Keds lined up in the closet, beneath a yellow slicker, a wool coat, and one black satin dress.

I eventually worked out that AT meant the Ashley tower, and found Room 46 up four flights of dim, dank stone stairs, at the end of a skinny hallway, and through a crooked door that ached and creaked as I pushed it open. I slid into one of the empty seats in the back of the small lecture room.

The professor glanced my way, then turned back without a reaction. She was writing on the blackboard.

"The *atman*," she was saying as she wrote, "is the individual self. The essential. That which travels through cycles of birth and rebirth. The *brahman*, that is, the Godhead, the ground of all being, the Universal absolute—Yes?"

She was looking a girl in the front row who had raised her hand.

"I thought Hinduism had, like, hundreds of gods," the girl said. "I used to know this guy—"

The professor raised a halting hand. The girl stopped.

"I'd like to take this time to remind you that here at Catherine, speaking of our past lives is discouraged," the professor said in a low voice. "This experience is about moving forward. Becoming new. We are informed by our pasts, of course. But we must also learn to let these things go."

The boy in front of me was eating a sandwich. A ham sandwich with mayonnaise, lettuce, and cucumbers, crusts cut off. He took a crisp, crunching bite.

I tapped him on the shoulder. He twisted around to look at me, wiping mayonnaise from the corner of his mouth.

"Can I have a bite?" I whispered.

He gave me a long look up and down. He handed me the sandwich.

I took a bite. The ham was salty and deliciously cool.

The professor was writing on the board again.

"Hey," the boy hissed, "give it back."

I took one more bite, a big one, and handed it back to him.

"We'll continue with Hinduism over the next couple of weeks," the professor was saying, "before moving on to Buddhism. Please pick up your packets from the library by noon tomorrow and do remember, the first essay—"

The girl in the front row had raised her hand again.

"Yes?" the professor said.

"Which of these articles are we supposed to read?" she said, gesturing to the list.

The professor blinked. Then she said, louder, to everyone: "I realize that for some of you this is your first class at Catherine. Until today, your time in this house has been one of unending revelry."

She twisted the chalk between her long fingers.

"Revelry does have a place in your education. This house may have been founded as an experiment in discipline, but that was a long time ago. We know now that if we want our students to learn and grow, and come to understand themselves in any real, happy way . . . we have to give you some degree of freedom. But artists and poets and presidents and justices are not born out of three years of *partying*. This school will teach you how to think. How to make well-considered, rigorous associations between peoples, objects, and cultures, across centuries and across the cosmos. Associations that occur not just because the drunken mind sees associations everywhere, but because our world is one of patterns. We are here to find ourselves, but ourselves as one with everything. This is what we believe in this house. This is what you will learn and trust and love for its sublime truth. But in order to understand this truth . . . you are going to have to *work*."

She turned to the girl who had raised her hand.

"I expect you to have read all of those articles by our next meeting," she said. "And I look forward to hearing your thoughts on them. After that, I will assign a new list."

She straightened.

"Welcome to Catherine," she said.

I tapped the boy on the shoulder.

"Can I have some more?" I whispered.

"Oh my God," he said.

❧

In those first weeks at Catherine, as fresh September days turned into bitter black October nights, I would lie in bed for hours memorizing our room. The maple beds with their sagging mattresses and chipped, stained headboards; the mismatched dressers; the desks, Baby's covered with insane piles of notes in strict rectilinear piles, mine strewn with hair ties and socks. The windows with their ripped screens, the yellow tea table. My clothes, tossed on the floor, and the closet full of Baby's neat T-shirts and coats, all hung like ghosts.

"Why do you have a Brandeis sweatshirt?" I asked once, staring into her closet as I munched on a pear. Billie Jean was eating his snack, too. He slimed up the cabbage leaf in his tank with merry little chews.

Baby didn't look up at me. She was folding her laundry and stacking it in the dresser. She hesitated before saying, "It's my sister's."

"Do you like your sister?" I mumbled through the bite.

"She's dead."

I swallowed. "Sorry."

Baby kept folding her T-shirts. Our laundry was already folded when we picked it up, but she always redid hers.

After a long moment, Baby said, "Do you want to know how she died?"

"Sure."

She straightened her stack of shirts.

"It was a car accident," she said. "A really awful one. She was driving back to her dorm at Brandeis and got hit by a drunk driver. When the rescuers came, she was already dying. The last thing she said was that she'd been missing me."

Baby's face was expressionless as she slipped the shirts into her drawer.

I took another bite of pear.

❧

One day, over a lunch of anchovy salad, I overheard a third-year trying to impress a pretty girl with his knowledge of Catherine's history. According to his whispers, the original mansion had been built as a home for the eccentric magnate who founded the school. The grim, baroque fantasy rooms of that man's home now made up Harrington, which housed most of Catherine's common spaces: the great hall, auditorium, main library, and classrooms, and in the basement, the aides' warren of operations.

Since its founding, the house had grown like a disease, and now there were three residential halls—Harrington, Molina, and Ashley—all interconnected but distinct in architectural style. I always knew when I had crossed the threshold back into my hall, Molina. I recognized its aspects: its lacy wrought-iron balconies, Spanish red-clay roofs, shutters painted slick, theatrical green. The cavalcades of marble urns lining the corridors. I found myself wandering its distorted landscape even in my dreams. I would follow our bedroom hallway to the left, down a creaking spiral stairway, which wound down to the dank, cobwebbed laundry and cellar; to the right, the hallway led me to the parlor and morning room, and onward to a broad, liver-red travertine staircase. That staircase guided me up to a series of dusty atriums and upperclassmen bedrooms and farther, to the pavilion of windows that led to Ashley.

Ashley was by far Catherine's biggest hall; every time I found myself wandering its labyrinthine corridors, I felt like I might never escape. Its crooked rooms echoed with the noise of creaking panels and radiators and insane buzzing lights. But I liked making my way to the top of the seven-story Ashley tower, where I could look out over Catherine's yard. In the northeast, browning grass rolled down to the aides' and faculty's towers. To the southwest were the Catherine gardens, concealed by a crumbling brick wall. Supposedly, there were storage silos and a loading dock hiding farther southeast, but that was too far for me to see.

In every direction, everywhere, we were surrounded by woods of dense black maples and pines. The woods obscured the gate.

I had an idea of the house. But I still didn't see it clearly. The rooms left only hazy impressions as they sequenced one into another, parlor to dining room to stairwell to yard. I got lost. I lost things, too, like my umbrella and my class schedule. I tried to make my way to First-Order Logic and instead found myself on a bench in some blue hallway, staring out the window, feeling the house's architecture dividing and subdividing all around me. I was haunted by the monster spread of spaces, hallways, and doors.

Baby and I had very different schedules. Her classes, in advance of the new materials concentration, kept her in labs all day, whereas I had lost track of when and where my classes met. I spent most days in bed deliciously bored, reading Betty and Veronica comics from the Molina library, waiting for Baby to come home. When she opened the door those afternoons to find me still nestled underneath my coverlet, she would look me up and down, lips firmly pursed, but say nothing. She set to studying or brushing her hair or rearranging her collection of pencils without a word.

The two of us, we liked not talking together.

During the day, Baby worked hard, really hard. I had never seen anyone study so much. And at night, she cried, a lot. I wondered if she was thinking about her sister.

Once, when Baby was crying, I crawled into bed with her. I held her as she sniffled and wept. Her body felt very human in my arms, warm and damp, but she didn't react to my touch. It was like she didn't feel me at all.

❧

I could see myself in the mirror hanging on the wall in the doctor's examination room. I was slouched and skinny, yellow-skinned and bruise-eyed, my lips swollen and bitten-up raw. My hair slunk over my shoulders in slutty waves that were dark with grease; I hated washing my hair in the tub, so I didn't. I looked beautiful. Like a rotting fruit.

The doctor opened the door and closed it behind herself with a click. She wasn't wearing a doctor's coat but a black dress and black pumps, her hair wrenched into a strict chignon.

"So," she said as she flipped a sheet on her chart. "Ines Murillo de los . . . are all these names yours?"

"You can just call me Ines."

She snapped the folder shut. "All right, your first annual. Any particular questions or complaints? How are you feeling?"

"Really great," I said. "Fantastic."

"How are your classes going?" She looked at me with cold, dispassionate eyes. "Are you studying?"

Our midterm grades had come in. I didn't even remember taking the tests. "Yes. I'm acing everything. I'm a star."

The doctor unwound the stethoscope from her neck and breathed on its head.

I examined her face as she moved the stethoscope over my back. Her nose was sprinkled with pale freckles.

She wrapped a blood pressure cuff around my arm. Its squeeze felt warm and dear, and I had the sudden embarrassing urge to cry.

"Feeling okay?" she said.

"Yes," I said.

She unwrapped the cuff and jotted down some notes. "One-oh-five over eighty. Did you smoke before coming here?"

"Just now?"

"No, before you came to Catherine."

"Sometimes."

"Have you had trouble, with the quitting?"

"No."

"How are the meals treating you? Have your bowel movements been good?"

"Yes. Really great."

"Sex, protected?"

"Yes."

"Lean back."

I did.

She palpated my lower stomach. The pain there felt like dread.

"So, aren't you happy to be here?" she said.

"At the doctor?"

"At Catherine."

I stared at the ceiling.

Was I supposed to be happy?

"I know it can be hard for you kids," she said as she touched me, "to be so isolated from your friends and family and everything you've ever known. But don't worry. You're going to have so much fun here, soon you'll forget to even think about the past." She patted my knee. "All right, let's get you in the stirrups."

I put my feet up.

"Scoot up."

I scooted.

One of the supply cabinets had been left ajar. The bottom and middle shelves were lined with canisters of cotton balls, tongue depressors, Band-Aids, and gauze. But the top shelf was empty except for a tray fitted with a series of slender metal rods standing on end. The rods were of various sizes, each topped with a plastic digital reader, like thermometers.

"What are those?" I said.

"What's what?"

"On the top shelf of the cabinet."

She deposited the sample in a bottle, then followed my gaze. "The plasm pins? We use them for plasm repair. You've never seen plasm pins before?"

I'd heard of plasm pins, of course, but I'd never seen one in person. I craned my neck to get a better look. The shelf was too high up.

"Do you use them here?" I said.

The doctor's lips were set in a firm line. "What do you mean?"

"I mean, I thought that the pins and everything—I thought it was all a hoax. And Catherine was supposed to stop experimenting."

She snapped off her gloves. "You can sit up."

I kept staring at the plasm pins as I sat up.

The doctor jotted down notes in her pad. "Anything else? How are your cramps?"

"I need thicker pads," I said. "The supply ones are too thin."

"Change them more often."

"I have a very heavy flow."

"The pads are fine. You'll get used to them. Get dressed."

I shimmied back into my underwear and skirt. I grabbed cough drops and condoms from the jars on the counter as I left.

❧

I stepped off the path to walk across the yard. The sky was weak gray today and fat clouds hung low on the horizon. My whole body felt heavy. I walked for a long time over wide stretches of wild grass before I reached the trees. Blackberry brambles clustered around trunks that were dark and sticky with sap. As I moved on, I crouched to pick up a maple leaf. It smelled like sweet decay. Pine needles crunched beneath my feet and masses of gray weeds snagged at my legs.

I closed my eyes. I tried to imagine I was in the fairy garden, the one from the picture book I'd had as a little girl. I tried to smell the wisteria bower; I tried to see the crystal dew beading on peonies and roses.

I opened my eyes. A spider was creeping toward my feet.

Had I ever been able to imagine it right? Had I ever really believed the world so lovely and full of magic?

I wormed my way through the brambles and around the trunks, feet unsteady, until I found the gate. I ran my fingers over the iron bars. I clasped one, as if to test its weight. I peered through.

Past the gate, the woods grew deeper and denser. For a moment I thought I saw something dart between the tree trunks. Then a beam of sunlight flashed and I couldn't see anything at all.

I still remembered who I was and where I had come from. I was someone before Catherine, of course. I'd had a neighborhood, one with clean, bright houses and clean, bright lawns. I had friends—though I realized now they weren't exactly the kind of kids who kept you out of trouble. I had a home, a white apartment with white leather furniture and violent art on the walls. I even had family, a mother. When I thought of her now, I usually remembered her hand dangling from the arm of her favorite chair, the ugly Prouvé fauteuil she'd brought all this way. Her fingernails dragon-red, her cigarette trailing blue smoke, her voice murmuring into the phone, *Maman, we are never going back to him. We are happy here. We are so very, very happy.*

But the only part of my life I had really liked back then was my chemistry teacher. Mr. González had long, beautiful eyelashes, a diamond stud in his right ear, and he always laughed at my stupid jokes. And he could always tell when I didn't want to go home from school. He let me hang out with him in the teachers' lounge and shared his macadamia nut chocolates with me. As I ate, he would tell me stories about his adventures hiking in Peru or clubbing in London. I imagined he danced with men who were all gorgeous, exciting, and smart, just like him.

Mr. González was the only person I had ever loved. So when he told me—my hand clasped in his—that I should apply to Catherine, I did it. I filled out the forms, submitted the project essays, and eventually attended the interviews. I wouldn't have gone through all that for anyone else. But he asked, so I did it. I was pretty good, back then—good at school, good at friends, good at everything. I used to be pretty nice.

The application process took months. By the time all my materials were in, it was the winter of my senior year. I was spending very little time in school and hadn't spoken to my mother in months. I'd swung loose from all that. I was staying out late, swallowing magic pills, and laughing so hard I threw up. I was following teachers down hallways and slipping notes into strangers' pockets. I was still good sometimes. But mostly, I was bad. And it wasn't long before neon highs lurched into gruesome black lows.

As I lay there under the blackberry bushes at Catherine, the smell of the earth became something else—the smell of starchy bedsheets, vomit, and strawberry ice cream—and my throat ached with a scream. I remembered everything.

Mr. González was the only person I spoke to after that night in the hotel room. I found his address in the school directory and showed up at his condo a few days later. I was sure he'd read the news and figured I was involved; he knew the terrible people I was tangled up with then. But when I appeared at his door, he didn't ask any questions. He just reheated me a bowl of lasagna, turned on an *I Love Lucy* rerun, and let me sleep on his couch.

And then he let me disappear.

When I heard I had been accepted to Catherine, I'd been running for weeks. I got the admissions office call in a brassy motel lobby, heart beating fast as I cradled the reception desk phone against my ear. I didn't know how they had tracked me down; I hadn't been in contact with anyone besides Mr. González. I didn't even know if I'd actually graduated from high school; I'd left a month before commencement. I didn't know anything, and I didn't care. I got the call and I went to Catherine because that's what I was doing then: I was going. I was a going person. That's the only thing I was.

Catherine promised its students a golden future, if we gave up a few things in return. Three years of no mothers, fathers, brothers, or sisters. No newspapers, no new music, no television. No football games or mascots, no vending machines, no weekend trips to Philadelphia to see plays or ballets. No world except Catherine.

That's what everyone else gave up. But I didn't give up anything. I was already a ghost.

Baby and I ate breakfast together in the morning room every day. We never talked much, usually because neither of us had slept the night before. We drank our seltzer, sucked on hard-boiled eggs, and slurped up porridge in sleepy silence. Baby had a funny way of peeling her eggs. She would pull the shell apart with ruthless precision, and then pile the shards as if they were bits of gems. I liked watching her do it.

Baby had just finished this process and was beginning the surgery of pinching off the egg's membrane when a girl dropped a card onto our table.

I picked up the card. It was notebook paper, the kind we were all supplied with, cut into a handsome oval. It read, in loving script, "You are cordially invited to the birthday party of Yaya Osmond."

"Gifts," said Yaya Osmond, "are highly encouraged."

I looked up. I knew her, Yaya. Her room was down the hall from Baby's and mine. She swanned around the Molina hallways in costume jewelry and, most recently, a shabby faux-mink coat, which meant she must be sleeping with an upperclassman with enough points to buy things from the commissary. Today she was barefoot in pajamas, hair swept up into a samurai bun and ears weighted with plastic gold hoops. Her skin shone dark bronze.

"You can't have a *party*," Baby said in her vicious little voice. "It is the middle of finals period."

Yaya folded her arms and leaned back on her heels. She eyed Baby up and down.

Baby looked down at her egg.

"Is it really your birthday?" I said. We weren't supposed to be celebrating birthdays. Birthdays were part of our lives before Catherine.

Yaya shrugged. "It's something."

I put down the card. "Happy something."

Yaya's smile flashed on me.

She said, "See you at the party."

That night, I sat in my bed drinking wine out of a teacup as I watched the moon's slow, quiet rise. Everything in the house was slow and quiet.

I set my teacup down on my desk, wiped my mouth, and stood up.

"What are you doing?" Baby said.

"I'm going to Yaya's birthday party."

"But—what about finals?" Baby tapped her flash cards on her desk. She had been going through them for hours, fervently muttering to herself.

"What about them?"

"Aren't you worried about failing?" She shifted in her seat. "You—you don't do any work. You stay out all night and sleep through class. And now you have a final in two days. Aren't you worried about your grades?"

Baby was right; I did skip a lot of my classes, and I didn't study. And the class program at Catherine was confusing enough. According to the "syncretic curriculum," as our professors called it, even the survey courses were meant to be wildly interdisciplinary. I hadn't expected that in First-Order Logic we would be mapping out the fundamental relationships between objects and their names, truths and their consequences. Introduction to Philosophy had tasked itself with an overview of art, science, and the history of the world. Units leapt backward and forward across centuries according to some radical pattern I couldn't identify or follow.

The classes were hard. But I might have done better if I had paid attention. Instead, all my classes were scrambled with one another. Philosophical theorems warped into logic proofs, calculus into religious origin stories. Nothing made sense. And now it was finals reading week, and the whole house was tense with primitive panic. When students weren't crouched over textbooks in the library or taking tests in cold, silent classrooms, they were wild, dancing in the hallways and fucking on the stairs, crying in the bathrooms and sleeping in the halls. But I wasn't panicked. I wasn't worried at all.

"It's not like you're that smart." Baby's voice was saying. "No offense. But you're not—you're not one of those girls who don't study and can still get A's. I mean, if you don't study, you're going to fail."

I poured more wine into my teacup.

"You really aren't scared," she whispered.

I sipped.

"How did you even get in here?" she said. "If you don't care?"

I shrugged. "I used to care," I said. "A long time ago. It only ever made things worse."

Baby stared at me in that big-eyed way of hers. Like she was watching me perform some wild, deadly magic trick, wondering how I could possibly pull it off.

I wasn't pulling it off. I'd already received a warning from Kimmy. She had appeared in my room one Thursday afternoon with a bright bag of chocolate macaroons—"Just a mid-semester treat!"—and a singsong description of what it meant to be on academic probation.

I knew I should care. Of course I understood that I was supposed to be studying, doing my homework, paying attention in class, and worrying about finals. But I couldn't work up the energy. In some abstract way I knew that if I failed my finals, I would have to leave Catherine, but leaving Catherine didn't seem quite possible. I had to stay at Catherine because I had nowhere else to go. There was no other future for me.

"You don't need to go to another party," Baby mumbled. "You're always going to parties."

"Am I?"

"Yes. You always—leave."

Her voice had grown small.

"Do you want me to stay?" I said. "You don't like me very much."

That was true. But maybe Baby was used to me now, the way I was used to her. We spent hours together, nights, mornings, meals. I knew what she smelled like when she needed a bath, and she pushed me awake when I snored too loudly. She'd memorized my clothing sizes so she could separate our laundry, and I'd memorized her noises: her toothbrush shushing against her teeth, her throat clearing as she read, her snuffling as she dreamed.

"I think best friends go to parties together," I said. "Come with me. It'll be fun."

"I can't have *fun*," she said. "I have to *study*." She tapped the flash cards again. "And I heard they might do a room inspection tonight. I want everything—good."

"They're not going to do a room inspection in the middle of the night."

"Yes, they will. That's how they *do* it."

"But everything here is perfect."

She gave Billie Jean's tank a pointed look. He was munching on a bit of banana with one tentacle out, jauntily akimbo.

"Just leave him," I said. "Or hide the tank in the closet. They won't care. Come with me."

She said again, "I can't."

There was a little bit of food stuck at the corner of her mouth.

I grasped her shoulders and kissed her cool, stiff cheek.

"I love you," I said.

"You do not," she said. "Stop saying things you don't mean."

I petted her neck.

Before I left, I grabbed the bowl of blackberries I had left on the windowsill. I cradled the bowl against my stomach as I walked down the hall.

Parties had a way of echoing through the house. Floorboards creaked as students scampered across upper floors, stairwells resounded with their shouts—"Should I bring cards? Did you? Oh, I don't know! Okay! I'll bring them, I'll bring them"—and bathrooms clanked with the clamor of girls crowding in, gossiping, giggling, playing with their faces. Slinky synth-pop, years out of date, pounded from the cassette players we rented from the commissary. And the next day, scraps of conversation slipped across dining hall tables: "Man, someone threw up in our bathtub." "Oh my God, I think I fucked Richie last night." "Fuck, I need some Chinese food. If I call up Hunan Express, do you think they'll deliver to rural Pennsylvania? Like, if I give them a really, really big tip?"

But as I walked down the hall to Yaya's room that night, I didn't hear any music or noise. And when I pushed open her door, I saw the party was over. The dim room was littered with teacups and empty bottles, and only two people were there: Yaya, perched cross-legged on her desk, and a fuzzy-haired boy lounging on her bed. The boy was watching Yaya with gleaming eyes; she was busy examining the ends of her ponytail as she brushed it with long, languid, disinterested strokes. She wasn't wearing pants. Her underwear was pink.

Yaya looked up at me as I came in. Moonlight moved over her features.

She said, "You're late."

"I have a present for you," I said.

The boy's eyes followed Yaya as she took the bowl from me.

"Blackberries," I said. "The last ones of the season."

Yaya stared at me as she tapped a finger against the bowl. Her fingernail clicked against the porcelain.

"Ines, right?" she said.

"Yes."

She turned to the boy. "Hey," she said. "I'm going to bed. You should probably go, too."

"Ha ha," he said.

Yaya didn't laugh.

"Really?" He sat up. "Just like that?

"Uh-huh," Yaya said. "Just like that."

The boy huffed, but loped out of the room.

Yaya's room was the most decorated one I'd seen at Catherine. Cheap Chinese beaded necklaces dangled from pins by the window, gaudy satin scarves swathed her bedposts, and a tiny photograph of Mariah Carey stood framed on her desk. A plate of half-eaten strawberry tarts lay forgotten on the floor.

Yaya uncrossed her legs as she undid her ponytail. Her hair was long, stiff, and royal black, her eyes as dark as an Egyptian god's.

"What," she said, "should we do with these?"

The blackberries glimmered.

"I know," she said.

She took out two teacups and filled each one with a handful of blackberries. Then she splashed something from a wine bottle over them. It wasn't wine, though; the liquid was clear.

"Grain," she said, seeing my confusion. "Some Harrington third-years brew it."

She muddled the blackberries into the corn liquor. As she mushed, she said, "You're down the hall, aren't you? We must have met during orientation. I thought you were gorgeous. Except for your teeth."

She poured grain over the muddled berries.

"Is that why you're so quiet?" she said. "Your teeth?"

"I'm not quiet."

She laughed. "God."

We clinked cups. We drank.

I nodded at the photograph framed on her desk. "How'd you get Mariah in here?" I said. "I thought we weren't supposed to have personal photographs."

Yaya reached into the bottom of her cup to pick at a blackberry. "I can't be sharing all my secrets, now, can I?"

I swirled my glass. "Did you have a good birthday party?"

"Sure. It was fine. Everything here is fine."

Yaya wiped the side of her mouth with her fingernail.

"You don't like it here," I said. "In the house."

"No," she said. "I hate it. It makes me sick."

I could imagine her somewhere else. Spain, maybe, and wild, dangling off the arm of a baron, on a yacht cruising over a hot blue sea, smoking a cigar in a long white dress.

She was staring down at her drink.

"Man, this really needs ice," she mumbled. Then she said, "But did you hear? Four first-years have already been asked to leave. Gone. They'll be out tomorrow."

I had heard that. One of the first-years was in Molina, a tiny, white-faced girl. She had thrown up in the morning room yesterday at breakfast. She must have heard the night before.

"No way am I failing out, even if I hate it here," Yaya said. "I'm not going to get sucked into this house's shit, but I *will* graduate. I'm not fucking this up."

"I always fuck things up," I said.

"Yeah, me too. But then what? We end up at some normal college, applying for scholarships every day and doing, what—*keg stands* every night?"

Yaya shook her head.

"I mean, I guess it'd be nice to drink better shit than this." She lifted the teacup. "Wear normal shit, fuck around with normal guys. But if we wanted to be normal, we wouldn't have applied to Catherine. And if we weren't supposed to get in, we wouldn't be here." She shrugged. "Anyway, shit. Free tuition and room and board for three years? If I lose that, my mama will slit my throat."

"My mother doesn't care about me," I said.

"Really? What'd you do to her?"

"Nothing. I think we kind of just forgot about each other."

"Man. Sounds nice."

I said, "I don't know why I came here."

She glanced up at me. "I don't believe that."

A cloud moved over the moon.

"Have you heard from your family?" I said. "Your mama?"

"Oh please," Yaya said. "This house isn't going to give us any of our mail. When I tried to make a phone call the other day, it cost four hundred points to dial out. Literally impossible to afford. We're not going to be hearing from anyone for a long time."

Her eyes were dark.

"Remember those ridiculous pamphlets they mailed our parents? No worries—if we're 'well ordered' we can call our loved ones any day of the week." Yaya rolled her eyes. "My mama read that and laughed. She's not stupid. I'm not stupid, either. She taught me a long time ago that if I want to be big, I'm going to have to do big things. Big, strange, ugly things."

Something about Yaya's words made me think of the boy—the man—who'd been lying on her bed.

She yawned and ran a hand through her hair.

"I've got to cut this off," she mumbled. "All the other black girls want to keep up with the salon, but, man, I don't have time for that."

"Shave it," I said.

"You're funny," she said, without laughing. She crossed her arms. "Why do you hang out with that weird girl?"

"Baby?" I said. "She's my roommate."

Yaya stared at me as if waiting for more of an explanation. I said nothing.

Yaya reached into the bottom of her cup again. She stuck a mushy blackberry into her mouth.

❧

When I went home that night, I didn't go back the way I came, down the passage from Harrington through to the Molina parlor. Instead, I walked out the entryway, past an avenue of windows, and onto the yard.

The grass stretched before me, colorless and cold. In the distance, the towers and jagged pine trees loomed, vicious black and sharp. The yard smelled icy, like a long winter coming, and the night was gravely still. The moon, high in the sky, was white as a ghost.

I crouched on the grass, hugging my knees.

Some students had dreamed of Catherine their whole lives. Maybe they'd heard it was one of the most secret, wild, beautiful houses ever built and knew they had to come here someday. Maybe they'd watched an interview with some movie star, heard the reverent way she mentioned her alma mater—*Catherine*—and yearned to go wherever she had been. Maybe they longed for Catherine because they longed for anything miles and miles away from their dull, gray homes and dull, gray lives.

Or maybe it was the only school they could afford.

For whatever reason, they dreamed of Catherine. They hadn't spent their childhoods playing kickball or pretending to be princesses. Instead, they had bent over problem sets and Latin textbooks, writing practice essays until their fingers bled, sleeping in the car on the way to ballet studios and concert halls, swim practices, science fairs—anything to shape them into the type of person Catherine wanted. Whatever that might be. And who really knew? Who knew how Catherine sized up hundreds and thousands of smart, accomplished, charitable, perfect children and decided who was in and who was out?

Even the most insane parents, admissions officers, and overachieving students couldn't decipher Catherine's admissions standards. But the kids who came here, studied hard, and graduated—kids like me, if I didn't get kicked out—went on to live lives of sublime power and prestige. And everyone else spent their days wondering what sweet secrets lay here, behind Catherine's gate. How special we must feel, and how secure, here inside.

I hadn't cared about the prestige. It hadn't even occurred to me to apply until Mr. González told me I should. I definitely didn't think I would be accepted. But somehow, I was in. And I should have been happier than anyone to be sheltered by Catherine's gate. After all, here in the house, nobody knew where I'd been or the things I'd done. I was brand-new.

Except wandering Catherine's dark, too-silent halls didn't make me feel new. I felt as crooked and perverse as ever. Like one of the house's many shadows I saw reflected in its dirty windows and mirrors.

Hadn't I heard somewhere that Catherine was one of the most haunted houses in America? I didn't believe in spirits. But in that moment, crouched there on the grass, I could feel the house behind me: its deep, dark, infinite body as twisted and corrupt as a forest.

When I climbed the stairs to our room, a gray morning was dawning. I closed the door softly, sure that Baby was asleep. But she was awake. She was sitting cross-legged on her bed with a napkin in her lap.

"Baby?" I said.

She sniffled.

I sat down beside her. I touched her hand.

"Baby, what's wrong?"

She hiccupped.

I lifted the napkin.

The shards of Billie Jean's broken shell glistened in the moonlight.

"They came," she said. "They came to do the inspection. And I knew they would find him. I knew."

I set the napkin back down.

"And you weren't here," she said. "You were away. You were at a party. I needed you. I knew they were going to find him. And you weren't here."

I rubbed her wrist.

I didn't wonder why she had done it. Why she couldn't have just hidden the tank and kept our secret. I didn't care. It didn't matter.

"Tomorrow," I said, "let's give him a nice funeral. We can bring cookies and wear our black sweaters."

She ran a hand over the napkin.

Footsteps echoed outside the door, then something clattered. The tea tray had been delivered.

COMING IN

Days at Catherine operated by a clockwork of meals. Tea trays arrived at gray daybreak, then, precisely two hours later, the halls served breakfast in their morning rooms. The dusty windows in Molina's morning room faced west, so the sunlight shone sideways on the spread of eggs, gray biscuits, half-peeled oranges, and pitchers of Five Alive and seltzer. The halls served afternoon tea in their respective parlors, too. Afternoon tea, the Blue Book explained, was a cherished time of rest, a break between classes for a drink, a snack, and some warm conversation amid our busy days. I liked napping in the parlor during tea, but I didn't like the cookies. Every time I ate them, my stomach filled with unsettled dread.

Lunch and dinner were served in the Harrington great hall. The meals there were kingly, rich and hideous, and not very filling. We spent hours listlessly picking at game hens with fatty skin, boiled hams braised in wine, consommés and onion soups and eggs poached in sour cream sauce. The fruits and vegetables were shrunken and strange. Our digestion was always upset.

The only day we didn't eat dinner together was Friday. Or rather, the rest of the house ate dinner then, but first-years weren't invited. I didn't know why. We ate as many cookies as we could during tea and went to bed with throbbing stomachs.

Days became weeks. Night fell earlier and earlier. A chill entered the house and didn't leave. Wind beat at the windows, whistled through the stone bricks, and sneaked under doorways. Radiators let out pools of dank heat that never spread far enough. I bundled myself in the itchy wool sweaters I found in my wardrobe. They made me feel sweaty but somehow still cold. My bones were cold. My brain was cold. I had a new schedule for the semester—Art History Introduction I, Calculus II, Marriage and the American Family, Ancient Philosophy—but I rarely went to class. I stayed in bed. I slept for hours.

Outside, the yard browned and died.

When I wasn't in bed, I wandered the Harrington library, the hub of the house's academic wheel. The library's stained-glass doors opened into a three-story kaleidoscope crammed with desks and noise and books, professors arguing with crying boys, girls napping on couches. Past the front desk, where student workers gossiped as they organized course packets, were shelves upon shelves of books. They almost hid the winding staircase to the second floor. On the second floor stood more shelves of books, along with the house's only computer lab: ten machines lined up in a dull, low-lit row. I browsed the *Encarta Encyclopedia* there. It had a good article about Aztec sacrifices. Most of the computers were damaged; some wouldn't turn on at all. None had access to the Web.

On the third floor, behind one of the bookcases, I found a forgotten reading room, a tiny alcove with one green lamp and a dusty, sunken blue couch. A print of a dark man driving a chariot hung on the wall. He was wielding a bolt of lightning and baring his teeth. His skin glistened with sweat.

I lay on the couch and closed my eyes. I touched myself, dreaming of him and me and a fragrant garden.

When I opened my eyes, I was still in the house.

❧

That winter I was sleeping with a girl I'd met in the bathroom outside my philosophy class. Mandy had ferociously straight, long black hair and tiny teeth. We had little in common, but we didn't talk much. I would go over to her room at night when I couldn't sleep. The smell of her deodorant, a stifling, woody, churchy scent, darkened my mind so I couldn't think of anything else.

One night, I ran my hand over Mandy's back. The moon had slipped from behind a cloud. In its white light, I saw she had a scar, a long pale scratch from the top of her shoulder down her spine.

I felt, in that moment, that I saw Mandy clearly for the first time. Usually when I came to her room I was drunk. But I was sober enough now to notice her bitten nails, her pin-straight eyelashes, and her scar.

Mandy turned to me. Her eyes, in the moonlight, were shiny and fierce.

"Don't," she hissed.

I dropped my hand from her back.

There was a silence. Mandy opened her mouth, then closed it again, as if she realized she should say something more but didn't know what. She lay back in the bed. Our bodies weren't touching.

"It wasn't her fault, you know," Mandy finally said. "It was mine, too. We both hurt each other."

I don't think I had fully realized it until right then: I wasn't the only one at Catherine on the run. None of my classmates spoke of their pasts, but I sensed them—all their misshapen histories—at dinner, as they chewed their carrot salads in silence, or when their voices laughed too loudly at a stupid joke, or later, in the many feverish hours they spent studying in the library. Everyone here was here desperately. All of us, for one reason or another, had nowhere else to go.

So, here we were. Christmas must have come and gone. First-years whispered about what we might be doing if we were home: trimming trees, lighting chapel candles, getting drunk with cousins, sledding down silvery hills. Some tried to make phone calls home, but Yaya had been right, none of us had earned nearly enough points. So Christmas was gone, and New Year's, and nothing happened.

Nothing ever happened at Catherine.

Mornings, after I peed and brushed my teeth, I grasped the sink. I stared into the mirror.

Days. I could see them all, all the days, reflecting into each other forever. Mirrors repeating against mirrors.

Baby had passed Chemistry I, but now she had Chemistry II, which was even harder. Sometimes when I walked by the lab I heard her class chanting like an order of monks or sketching diagram after diagram in tense silence. At night, in our room, Baby paced and muttered formulas to herself. She didn't eat. She left flash cards in her bed, by the bathtub, under the dresser. She cried more.

Baby did have a way of calming herself down, I learned. She picked Master Locks. She'd brought a whole stash of them and a lock-picking kit in a little leather pouch. When she was stuck on one of her worksheet problems, she'd spread them out on her desk and pick them one by one. When a lock finally popped open, she didn't smile. She just set it aside and moved on to the next.

"Who taught you how to do that?" I asked once while I watched her. I had been trying to do my calculus homework, but all of my answers were checking out wrong.

Baby worked for a while longer, fingers twisted around the lock, before she said, "My sister."

"Your sister knew how to pick locks?"

"My sister knew how to do everything." She had a proud lift to her chin.

I imagined her sister's car crash, sometimes. Shattered glass, thrilling heat.

"I'm going for a walk," I said.

I went outside. I walked in circles around the brown yard. I picked up a stick and put it down again. The sun disappeared behind the trees. I went back inside.

❧

I watched the first snowfall of the season from my couch in the library. The skylight had been opalescent gray all morning. By afternoon, the first flakes fell. They multiplied like a cancer on the glass, shrouding the light. Soon the whole window was dead white.

I arrived back at our bedroom to find Baby standing by the window, watching the snow with her arms folded. She was wearing our formal uniform of black tights and a black dress that fell stiff to her knobby knees.

"The winter festival," she said when she saw my confusion at her outfit. "Did you—did you really forget?"

Yes, I had forgotten about the festival. We'd received a notice about it on one of last week's morning tea trays. I hadn't understood whether it was in celebration of the solstice or the new year or some obscure midwinter holiday.

"Well, get dressed," Baby said. "And in something appropriate, please. We are going to be late."

After the library, the Harrington great hall was the most expansive room in the house. Long oak tables ran from wall to wall, and the high-pitched, barrel-vaulted ceiling echoed with the noise of crazy laughter, feverish conversation, and chair legs scraping against stone. One wall was an open bank of windows that looked out onto the yard; the others were hung with faded tapestries of Roman myths. The tapestries fluoresced with turquoise and magenta light from the stained-glass clerestory. The professors and administrators sat on a raised dais in the back of the room. Behind the dais hung another tapestry, this one woven with the cryptic patterns and figures that formed the Catherine House insignia.

Baby and I squeezed our way to the table with the other Molina students, all in similar black formal dress. I sat down and spread my napkin on my lap. I poured myself a glass of wine.

Baby was staring at me, sharp-eyed.

"Yes, sweetie?" I said as I poured.

"You have a bruise on your throat," she said.

I touched my neck. It was probably from Mandy. I'd gone to her room the night before.

As I sipped my wine, I looked for Viktória at the professors' table. She always sat in the center, and there she was now, head turned in conversation. Her profile was vase-like, elegant and strange. It was hard to tell her age; her hair was streaked with gray, but thick and long, and her skin was unwrinkled, but thin, almost spectral. Her white chiffon shirt was so sheer I could see the outlines of her breasts. She wasn't wearing a bra.

"Vanilla pudding," said Theo Williams, another Molina first-year, as he slid into the seat beside mine and plucked up the menu card. "My favorite."

I glanced over his shoulder at the menu. It described a four-course meal of desserts. To start, vanilla pudding, then cream cheese pie, then a selection of Jell-Os, a palate cleanser before the final course of white cake. I could see the cake now on the service table. It was tall and proud as a bride, encrusted with thick icing and dripping with fondant lace.

Baby looked like she was going to be sick.

"Dessert for dinner?" said Nick, across the table. "Oh, good. All we need are some martinis and passive-aggressive quips and it'll be just like home. My mother would be so proud."

"Would she?" Theo said. "Would she really be proud of her little Nicky boy?"

"Of course she would. She loves me so. I'm her greatest investment."

"Man, what about last night?" Theo said.

Nick tucked his napkin into his collar. "What *about* last night?"

"When you were throwing up in the fireplace?" Theo said. "Would she have been proud of you then?"

"Oh yes." Nick straightened the napkin. "That's a Townsend signature move, really."

Theo grinned. "Fucking doofus."

Theo Williams and Nick Townsend had formed an instant, easy friendship. They didn't look a thing alike: Theo was a shortish, scrawny black kid with shaggy hair and an eager energy, while Nick had the broad shoulders, princely blond curls, and beautiful manners of someone who'd gone to expensive private schools and summered on various shores. But they were both the kind of boys who felt at home everywhere. Nothing ever bothered them. When a pipe burst in the second-floor hallway, or last month when bad chicken cassoulet left the whole house with food poisoning—every misfortune just made them laugh.

"Ugh, is that what I saw in the fireplace this morning?" Yaya said, wrinkling her nose. She slid into the seat next to Theo's. "You are *foul*."

"Mad you weren't invited to the party?" Theo said.

"That was not a party," Yaya said. "And those girls were skanks."

"Takes one to know one," Theo said.

She gave him a wedgie. He cursed and grabbed his crotch.

A hush fell over the hall. Our attention shifted to the administrators' dais. Viktória was standing.

"Welcome to our winter festival," she said.

She smiled over the assembly.

"I am so pleased to gather with you all on this cold evening," she continued. "Here at Catherine, we've always believed in the power of rhythm. The rhythm of the day—classes and teas, work and sleep. The rhythm of the seasons. The rhythm of our voices and hearts. These rhythms bind us to ourselves, to each other, and to our environments. And these festival nights, the nights when we take a special moment to drink and eat and laugh together in celebration of these vital rhythms—well, they have always been my favorite nights in this house."

She was looking down at her hands. Her face barely moved as she spoke.

"Tonight, we celebrate the precious quiet of wintertime," she said. "And how lovely is this time of silence and work and anticipation and decay?" She looked up. "Here at Catherine, we know not to fear death. Because even in death, there is life. Death is not the black night, but its white moon. The honeyed egg of rebirth."

Her voice was low. She had a slight unplaceable accent.

"So please," she said, "let us praise tonight, this room, and each other. Let us feast and be glad in the darkest of times."

She raised her glass.

"To winter," she said, "and to tonight."

We sipped.

As she sat down, M. Neptune, the director of the new materials concentration, placed his hand on her arm. I couldn't see his face, but I could tell from her expression that he was whispering in her ear.

"At least it was a short speech," Yaya said as the aides distributed tureens of vanilla pudding. She spooned some onto her plate.

"Short now," Theo said. "But wait until our coming in. That's when things get crazy."

"Our—coming in?" Baby whispered.

"Yeah. It's . . . I don't know. Something we do in a couple of weeks."

"Why hasn't Kimmy told us about it?"

"Kimmy doesn't tell us anything," Yaya said, stirring at her pudding with a disconsolate frown. Something seemed to have upset her. "No one tells us shit."

Baby wasn't eating her pudding, either. I touched her shoulder.

"Well," Theo said, soft enough that we all had to lean in to listen, "according to Crystal—"

"Hold up," Yaya said. "Who's Crystal?"

"One of the skanks," Nick whispered.

Theo gave him the finger. "According to *Crystal*, our coming in is in a couple of weeks, in, like, the middle of the night. She made it sound like some kind of ceremony. And apparently it's what separates us from the upperclassman. After it happens, we'll start going to sessions."

"Sessions?" Yaya said.

"Friday-night dinners."

"So it's an initiation ceremony," Nick said.

"An initiation ceremony?" Yaya said, raising her eyebrow. "We've been here four months. Isn't it a little late for that?"

Theo shrugged. "Crystal wouldn't tell me anything else."

We all looked at each other. None of us smiled.

Baby pressed her palms tight against the table. She looked like she was going to be sick.

The pudding tureens were whisked away.

❧

That winter, I would find myself staring at something—a bottle of shampoo maybe, or a crisp stack of T-shirts, or, through a cracked door, two aides laughing as they waxed a classroom floor—and it would hit me: I was inside. The shampoo, the T-shirts, and the aides' murmurs were all secret, private things. I was inside. And the rest of the world was out.

The outside world had always had a vulgar curiosity about Catherine. Every few months some magazine published a "Catherine CULT: EXPOSED!!" editorial or a conspiracy theorist on TV raved about how the Catherine graduate network controlled Chinese money market rates. I didn't remember the details of their speculation. Why would I? I didn't think any of it was true. And even when I'd applied, I was sure I'd never be accepted.

Now that I was here, I wished I remembered the specifics. What was Catherine's secret?

"There is no secret," Henry Vu said over a lunch of radishes and salmon salad sandwiches. Henry, a nebbish Ashley first-year, had slunk to our table for the day. He blew his nose into a napkin. "It's only a *school*," he mumbled as he finished, wiping away the snot. "The only reason our graduates are so impressive is because they worked extraordinarily hard to get into Catherine, they worked hard while they were here, and they worked hard afterward. Catherine is . . . secluded, yes, but it's not like we're stuck in this house forever. We do graduate eventually. Professors publish from their research here and aides come and go. This isn't, like, Area 51. Tabloids want some—some sexy story of what goes on here, but the truth is we're just studying. A lot. That's it."

"Nah, that's not it," Anna Montgomery said. I liked Anna. She was a frank, casual girl, sunny-blond and muscular. She looked like she spent her summers hiking mountains and building boats with her dad. She was leaning back in her chair now, balancing on its two back legs with boyish ease. "No way is this a normal school. Sure, aides come and go, but have you ever seen of one of them give an interview? I bet they sign ironclad confidentiality agreements. And yeah, Catherine kids graduate and go on to live successful, normal, happy lives. But in those successful, normal, happy lives . . . none of them ever talks about what actually happens in the house. I mean, did you see Gardner on Barbara Walters? He wouldn't shut up about the

Norfolk disaster or Rengate, but as soon as she started going for his college years, zilch. That's nuts."

Henry shrugged, poking at a radish. "It's a different kind of school, sure. Obviously, with all the, um, racial diversity, the progressive admission systems. And the syncretic curriculum. This is what happens when a school is founded by Transcendentalists instead of Puritans. You end up with a very special student body, and an administration that likes getting those very special students stupidly, transcendentally drunk. But really, the house and its history, it isn't some big secret. You could read about it in any book on higher education in America. Yes, Catherine is a somewhat radical school. But it's just a school."

"Maybe," Anna said. "But remember how the grads spoke about the house during our admissions interviews? The way our graduates feel about Catherine, and the way we'll feel someday—the way some of us feel already . . ." Anna stopped. She chewed on the inside of her cheek, thoughtful. "Listen," she finally said, "we don't have a football team. We don't have any grad schools, so most of our research is pretty pedestrian. This place is gorgeous, but the admins obviously care more about luring us here with free tuition than keeping up the house—did you hear there was another leak in the Ashley parlor? We don't have old colonial history like Harvard or Yale. And even if we did, like you said, we're not supposed to *fetishize the past* or whatever. We don't even invite our graduates back for reunions or anything. Really, we have no idea why we do half the meals and festivals and other shit we do. But doesn't it seem like everyone who goes to Catherine leaves . . . just . . . in love with this house?" Anna shrugged. "I don't know. But you don't know, either. There's something here. Some special kind of power."

Henry's face twisted in a delicate sneer. "Everyone's sentimental about their college years," he said. "The 'shortest, gladdest years of life.' There's nothing special about that."

Anna took a bite of her sandwich. "We're not mentioning the obvious thing," she said with her mouth full.

"What's that?"

She nodded at the students clustered on the other side of the hall.

I'd already come to recognize the new materials concentrators. There were only about twenty of them; Baby was right to say that it was Catherine's most exclusive course of studies. The concentrators stuck to their own, as if by spending so much time together in the lab they forgot how to socialize with anyone else. They wandered the halls in a hollow-eyed pack, whispering as they rushed between classes and labs and huddling together at their own table in the great hall. That's where they were now, murmuring over something I couldn't make out. I craned to look. It was a toy, a blue wooden spinning top.

"If you want to study new materials, if you don't think the whole thing's a joke, you come to Catherine," Anna said. "That's why I'm here. That's why a lot of us are here."

"Are you applying?" I said. "To the concentration?"

Anna looked at me as if she had only just realized I existed. She was braiding her hair into a thick plait. "Well, yeah. I could study, like, American literature or whatever at a much easier school. One where I could go to the movies or call my parents on the phone. But ever since I was a little kid, and I saw those videos from the Shiner report . . . I knew it couldn't have all been faked. And I knew that's what I wanted to do. Plasm. That's the magic ingredient. That's what makes Catherine special." She nodded at Henry. "It's like you said, Catherine was founded by Transcendentalists, not Puritans. This school has always been about plasm study, even if we were calling it something else back then—pneuma or chi or telesma or whatever. *Cosmo-electric energy.* And maybe nobody was taking us seriously back then, and certainly no one takes us seriously now. But if you do believe in the future, in future materials, this is where you belong."

Henry was still poking at a radish.

I stood up.

Anna turned to look at me. "What's up?" she said.

"I," I said, "am going to calculus."

As I left, I glanced over at the new materials concentrators. They weren't more attractive than everyone else; their eyes were shadowed with fatigue and their hair was greasy. But there was something powerful and electric in the way they hunched together. They were laughing now at some joke I couldn't hear from our side of the room. The top lay forgotten on its side.

Could my stiff little Baby really become one of them someday? One of those powerful, electric boys and girls?

I'd heard the concentration was so selective that they usually chose only two or three students per class. So there should be about five of them at that table, not twenty. And some looked older than twenty-two.

I remembered, suddenly, a nine o'clock news story from months or years ago. Parents claiming Catherine had kidnapped their children, teary-eyed mothers pleading, begging someone to care. Catherine was supposed to be a three-year school. But those families said their children were never coming home. I guessed they must have been in the new materials program.

Plasm had never interested me much. I knew that it was once thought to be a revolutionary discovery, some incredible future of materials, chemistry, life, whatever. But it all seemed so vague. Was plasm even visible? Was plasm anything? It'd been years since Catherine released the Shiner report, though, like Anna, I remembered watching the footage during a TV special. I remembered the demonstrator's careful hands as she pressed the thermometer-like pins along the shattered porcelain vase; I remembered the porcelain's spectral hushing noise as it fused itself back together.

But that was years ago. Since then, there had been some scandal about M. Shiner and his research, something that put the whole project into question. I wasn't sure what it was about. All I knew was that the Shiner report was now considered a joke, and Catherine was supposed to have stopped its experimental program. I'd heard other research clinics had tried to reproduce his results, and none were successful. Whatever magic material Catherine had discovered was gone. If it had ever been here at all.

I grabbed a plum from the dessert service on my way to Calculus II. I ate it in class as the professor wrote out differential equations on the chalkboard. The sound of his chalk clicking sounded like soothing rain. I laid my head down and closed my eyes.

It was too early in the morning. I clenched my hands against my head. The hallway throbbed with professors scuffling in from the snow, shuffling between offices with mugs of tea. Everything smelled like mildew. I hadn't slept. I was still drunk.

"Ines," M. Owens said.

I looked up. He was standing over me with a steaming teacup, his lips twisted into an elegant frown. He was a gray, aristocratically ugly man with thick, jowly cheeks and pinkish eyes that turned down at the corners. He always looked a bit morose.

"Hello," I said.

"Please," he said, "come in."

I stood, knees creaking. I swayed.

"Are you feeling all right?" he said as he set down his tea. Most professors didn't get their own offices, but advisors were afforded special privileges. The luxury suited him. He'd lined his windowsill with three snowy white orchids and covered the floor with an Oriental rug that must have been plush at one time but was now threadbare in patches.

"Never better," I said, sitting in a drab crimson velveteen armchair. "I like your tie."

He glanced down at the tie. It was navy and patterned with tiny flamingos. "Thank you. My wife gave it to me."

I curled up my legs. "You must have a nice wife."

"I think so, yes."

"I bet she cooks you nice soups. Like minestrone."

"Corn chowder, generally."

I could imagine her. She was an art teacher, probably, with skinny arms, a braying laugh, sandy graying hair tied under a kerchief. The kind of woman who did jigsaw puzzles and watched *Jeopardy!* and took their chocolate Lab for twilight walks on the beach, and, every morning, sat down with a cup of coffee and wrote M. Owens a letter.

I knew faculty jobs at Catherine were coveted positions. And they were usually just two-year terms. But I couldn't imagine being a grown-up and choosing this life.

I leaned my head in my hand and stared at his tie. "I like flamingos."

M. Owens sipped his tea as he pulled a file from the stack on his desk and flipped it opened. He spent a long time on the page, eyes sliding down the sheet, then back up again, finger pressed against his lip.

I rubbed my temple.

"Ines," he said, after spending what felt like an eternity paging through the rest of the file.

"Yes?"

"My dear . . . what happened?"

I shifted in my seat. "What do you mean?"

"What do I mean? Well, let's see." He flipped back. "You had a very interesting high school transcript. Not perfect, and I see your grades took quite a dip senior year, but still interesting, promising. I can certainly see why M. González recommended you. Your project essays, your interviews . . ." He flipped through more pages. "All lovely, really, very lovely. But now. You failed two classes last semester, and barely passed the others. And judging by your midterm reports, this semester will be even worse. So, Ines, please." He looked up. "What happened?"

I couldn't answer. My brain was swimming.

M. González. Not "mister." That meant he'd attended Catherine himself, maybe even been a teacher here. I hadn't realized, though now it seemed obvious. His creativity and genius for chemistry, his fierce concern over everything and everyone, even me. The way the other teachers always spoke of him with either savage jealousy or strange, extraordinary reverence. Of course he'd gone to Catherine.

Why had he never mentioned it? Or had he, and I'd forgotten? No, I would have remembered if he'd shared something so personal. He enjoyed talking about his travels and nights out dancing, but always skirted over anything intimate and specific. Once, walking past the teachers' lounge, I'd overheard someone say that his mother had been diagnosed with pancreatic cancer, but he'd never mentioned it to me. Were his years at Catherine as private as that?

And why had Mr. González recommended me? I couldn't imagine. He probably regretted it now. As soon as he'd opened his condo door to find me there, after that night in the hotel—when he looked me up and down and saw me, really saw me, for the first time—he must have realized what a mistake he'd made.

At least he hadn't told Catherine what I'd done.

M. Owens leaned back in his chair. "What do you want out of this experience?" he said. "Out of being here, at Catherine?"

A freezing rain pittered against M. Owens's window. He stared at me with his hands folded.

"We see this often," he finally said. "When young adults are so isolated, so removed from their parents, friends, and communities. It is a change. A total structural change. Of course that has its effects. We do expect some growing pains." He tapped my transcript. "But this . . ." He shook his head. "This is a truly disappointing performance."

I scratched my knee. He was still staring at me.

"You are antisocial," he said.

I nodded.

"You are unproductive."

"Yes."

"And you are lazy. Do you disagree?"

"Yes. I mean, no. I don't disagree."

He swirled his tea.

"You could do well here, Ines," M. Owens said. "You must know that, somewhere deep inside. You applied, didn't you? You wrote the project essays, you sat in hour after hour of interviews, you told us your whole life story, however reluctantly. And you were accepted. And you came. You could do well here. But to succeed at Catherine you're going to have to do more than pass through the gate."

He had stopped swirling his tea.

"You must choose Catherine," he said. "Not just once, but every day. Choose to be here. Choose to study. To make friends. To succeed. To wake up every day and be alive, and go to work. It's not an easy thing to do. It can be very hard. But you can do it. I know you can." He leaned forward, eyes unblinking. "The question is, do you want to? Or do you want to spend the next three years stupid and drunk?"

"I don't know," I said.

He closed the file. "Well, I can tell you, at this rate you won't make it to three years. In case it's not obvious, dear, if you don't do any work, you won't be staying here. In fact, if you fail two more classes, you'll be asked to leave the school."

My throat squeezed.

"Ines," he was saying.

"What?" I breathed.

"I was saying, Ines, if you don't want to be here—"

"I can't leave," I said.

He stopped talking. He was staring at me again. I couldn't read his expression.

"I can't," I said again.

He leaned forward.

"All right," he said, lower now. "This is what you're going to do. For the rest of the semester, show up to your classes. That is all you have to do: show up. And show up to finals, too. Write something in the test packet. Anything. You've no great mind, but it's enough. If you are there, just *there*, you will pass. I promise. And next semester, with a fresh start, we will work on changing your attitude in a meaningful way. But for now, please, show up. Can you do that for me?"

"For you, M. Owens? Anything."

He leaned back again. "I like you, Ines."

"I like you, too, M. Owens."

He was watching me closely.

"Everyone likes you, I bet," he said. "Everyone likes bored, pretty girls. Your classmates and your teachers, I'm sure they all look at you and see"—he waved a hand, smiling a little—"whichever fearless hero used to drive them wild. The new girl who ignored them, the most gorgeous golden boy. You are attractive because you can be anyone or anything . . . because you are nothing. You are empty. Or at least, you want to be empty." He touched the paper again. "That's what this transcript says. You are trying to disappear, whish, into smoke. And if you're not careful, you will succeed."

I was picking at my fingernail.

"I want to see you become something, Ines," he said. "I want to see you graduate."

I had never really considered graduating. I hadn't thought that far ahead.

"Ines," he whispered.

"Yes?"

"You're a good girl," he said. "Nothing's wrong with you. You're fine."

I nodded. I nodded again. I rubbed at my eye.

M. Owens looked down at the transcript. "Now, concentration. In your application, you showed promise in physics and chemistry, but you aren't taking any now. Do you have any interest in plasm?"

"No."

"History?" He raised an eyebrow. "Literature?"

Literature was M. Owens's specialty. He was teaching a seminar on the Victorian Romantics this semester. "I tried to register for your seminar but didn't make the lottery," I said, which was true. "I was heartbroken."

He smiled. "I'll make sure you get in next semester. I'll discuss it with your grade dean. Which is who?"

"M. David."

"Ah yes. All right. But for concentration? What do you want to do?"

I kept picking at my fingernail.

Empty. That's what M. Owens had called me.

In my art history class, we were studying Old Masters still-life paintings. Woven baskets crowded with pears, peaches, and duck eggs, shadowed memento mori, crystal vases with grayish glows and luminescent beads of condensation. Those vases weren't empty, but full, wildly full, of peonies and roses, tulips and bluebells. The flowers reminded me of the fairy bride's bouquet from my book.

"I liked the art history survey," I said. I didn't recognize my voice; it sounded almost shy.

"History of art. A beautiful discipline." He closed the folder and pulled out a concentration application form. "You won't be officially accepted until next summer, but it shouldn't be a problem." He started filling out the form. "Isn't your coming in soon?"

"Next week, I think. That's what I've heard."

"Are you excited?"

"No."

"Scared?"

"No. Why, should I be? Is it scary?"

He shrugged. "There are worse things." He signed the application with a flourish.

I opened my eyes to a harsh February morning. Wind shuddered the windows. I crawled out of bed and pulled a sweater off the floor.

Something was different about the tea tray today. I stared at it as I dragged the scratchy knit over my ribs. There was the kettle, the coffee, the packets of tea. But there were no snacks, no cookies. Had Baby eaten them all?

It didn't matter. I wasn't hungry. I didn't even go to lunch that day, or tea. I only went to Ancient Philosophy class, then to

Calculus II. I even tried taking notes, though I didn't recognize half the symbols on the board. Since meeting with M. Owens, I was trying to be good.

But as I walked into the great hall for dinner that evening, a third-year student aide touched my elbow.

"Hey," she said, "you're not getting dinner tonight."

Her lips were set in a stubborn frown. She had a hole in her eyebrow where a ring must have been once.

"Yes, I am eating dinner," I said.

She shook her head.

I looked over her shoulder. Students sat around the Molina table, hunched over their pale salads—was that endive?—but, I realized, none of them were first-years. In fact, I didn't see any first-years here at all.

"But I'm hungry," I said.

Her hand hadn't left my elbow. She squeezed it now.

"It's going to be fine," she whispered.

Her eyes, staring at me, were wide and watery pink. Was she about to cry?

"You'll see," she said. "It's going to be so great."

I turned. I walked back through the halls to our bedroom.

It couldn't have been past six o'clock, but our room was full of shadows. I turned on my bedside lamp, then turned it off again. I got under the covers. I hugged my empty stomach.

The great hall had been serving flounder last night. It wasn't very good, but I would've eaten more if I had known it would be my last meal.

I slipped in and out of dreams. Baby came into the room eventually. There she was, swaying in front of me. Was she sleepwalking? Was she a ghost?

No, she was in her bed. I was asleep. We were both asleep.

Someone knocked on the door.

I sat up. Baby sat up, too. We stared at each other.

I opened the door to M. David, our grade dean, clasping his hands behind his back and rocking back and forth on his heels. He looked neat, tailored, and alert.

"Please," he said, "get dressed and join us in the parlor."

"I'm already dressed."

He glanced down at the jeans I had slept in.

"Just meet us in the parlor," he said. "In ten minutes."

The parlor, when we shuffled into it, was filled with Molina first-years. They leaned on walls and lounged over chairs, stifling yawns with the backs of their hands. No one was talking.

"What time is it?" a boy mumbled. He stood with his hands tucked into his armpits, eyes sleepy and dark.

We glanced at one another, but no one answered. The parlor didn't have a clock and M. David had disappeared. It was still black night outside.

"Man, I would murder for a big bowl of real Texas chili," Yaya said. She was perched on the arm of a sofa. "Real good chili, hot, with cornbread and butter. Or, no—a *cheeseburger.*"

"Oh," a girl said, laying a hand on Yaya's arm. "Yes."

M. David appeared again. Then he led us in a drowsy, shuffling mass down one hall and up another, down a stairway, and then farther, down another. We must have been in some Harrington subbasement when we arrived at a long, dim hallway wallpapered in cerulean faux-silk. The hallway led to two white doors with golden handles.

Most of the rooms at Catherine didn't have locks. But this one had not just a lock, but a black box—a keycard reader—that beamed a steady red light.

Baby slipped her hand into mine as M. David drew an ID from his breast pocket. He waved it in front of the lock.

The doors opened onto a ballroom. Oak parquet flooring,

warped and pocked by the years, swept up to a stage framed by olive-brown velvet curtains. The walls recessed into alcoves decorated with flaking plaster sculptures of dolphins, lobsters, and crabs. Three chandeliers dripped from the ceiling, buzzing with electric light.

The Harrington and Ashley first-years had already arrived and were pulling green exercise mats from piles in the center of the room. Apparently by some instruction, they were arranging them in a giant circle.

The room had no windows. We were underground.

"Please," said a voice rising over the noise of our shuffling, "try not to sit next to your roommates or closest friends. We want you all to get to know each other better."

The voice was Viktória's. She stood with balletic grace in a raw silk dress, legs crossed at the ankles. Her eyes drifted over the crowd of students.

She murmured something to M. Neptune, the director of the new materials concentration. He, too, watched us curiously, a notebook and pen folded in his hands. He nodded at what Viktória said, then waved and winked at someone he recognized across the room. M. Neptune was shorter than Viktória, and he was not a handsome man; his eyes were too small, his hairline receding into a witchy peak. But there was something charismatic about his face. It was hard to look away from him.

Baby turned to me with panic in her eyes.

"Don't listen to them," I said as I grabbed a mat. "Sit next to me."

Baby and I sat cross-legged on our mats. Altogether, our class must have been around a hundred people. We couldn't manage a perfect circle, but we tried. We made a lot of mumbling and squeaking noise as we settled. Then we were silent.

I glanced around. Now that we were seated, I could see that it wasn't only first-years here in the ballroom. A few upperclassmen waited by the stage, along with a handful of aides. I counted seven upperclassmen in total. And they weren't just any upperclassmen; they were all new materials concentrators.

They were watching us. I couldn't read their expressions, but I recognized the cool comfort of their bodies as they lounged against the stage. They didn't seem bothered by all of the first-years staring at them. They were relaxed. They were waiting.

Baby didn't even try to hide her ogling. Her eyes on the concentrators were wide and bright with desire.

Viktória walked to the middle of the circle.

"Welcome," she said, "to Catherine." She gave a little smile. "I know you've all been through a lot to come here. To come inside."

She turned to look around the circle. Her eyes were soft.

"The path into Catherine is not an easy one," Viktória continued. "You've had to be intelligent. You've had to be creative. You've had to work hard—very hard. But you've done it. You are here."

M. Neptune was seated in one of the alcoves now, notebook closed in his lap. He was watching her.

Viktória folded her arms behind her back.

"I respect you enough to be honest," she said. "These three years will not be easy. You will need to be more intelligent, more creative, and harder-working than ever before. There will be times when you will question whether you truly belong here, in this house. You will wonder, Am I strong enough? Am I good enough?" She turned. "There's no way to predict when these questions might come to you. It could happen while taking a particularly difficult test, or during your forums, or at a party with friends. Or it could come to you in this room, tonight."

She turned.

"Because this is the truth: To be unsure here is to belong. To be unsure but present and eager and open to a heroic new past, future, and today—this is the Catherine project. This is how we research the most profound relationships between our bodies, minds, and worlds. The unsure place is where you are now and where you are meant to be." She smiled. "This is your new home. And I am happy—so happy—to be here with you, at the end of one stage of your life and the beginning of a wonderful new one."

The boy next to me was crying.

"You have suffered to come to this point. Suffered through high school"—a few small giggles—"and through teachers, friends, and family who weren't supportive of all the things you are. People who hurt you. And you have suffered through your own selves—your own critical eyes, your own standards, your own minds. Your spirits are beautiful, but they are not easy.

"But tonight," she said, "we will say goodbye to your pasts and enter into a new house. The house of your eternal future."

By the end of the sentence, she spoke so softly it was almost a whisper.

I coughed.

"So," she said. "Let us begin."

The aides over by the stage had arranged trays of plates and cups. At Viktória's nod, they began circulating among us. When one arrived at where Baby and I sat, I saw that the plates held little round white cakes and green clay cups filled with wine.

I took two cakes and swallowed them whole, even though I didn't feel hungry anymore. The cakes didn't taste like anything except almost sweet, like honey. The wine was even sweeter.

I was in the middle of swallowing when Baby whispered, "Ines."

I turned, wiping my mouth.

One of the new materials concentrators, a willowy girl with a long black braid, had appeared at the side of the boy next to me. She also held a tray, like the others. But instead of cakes or wine, her tray held a set of plasm pins.

I had never seen the pins this close before. And something about how slender they were, and how dark, made me feel like I still couldn't see them clearly. I only saw that they were lined up in order of size, and that the digital readers on their ends were all unlit at the moment. At the other end of each pin was a tiny flat pad.

I bent toward the tray for a closer look. I wished I remembered more from that special about the Shiner report, but it was so long ago. I'd been too young to understand the science. I'd thought it was a hoax.

The boy waited, cross-legged and blank-faced, as the concentrator ran her hands over the pins and selected one. She fitted the flat pad to the boy's skull, then curved the body against his head. I hadn't realized the metal was flexible.

The concentrator did something to the pin I couldn't see. The pin beeped as its reader lit up.

I had been watching her so closely I didn't realize a different concentrator stood behind me until he tapped me on the shoulder. I looked up into a face full of fervid acne.

"Turn," the boy said.

I did. I could see Baby watching me out of the corner of her eye.

Wasn't Catherine supposed to have stopped experimenting? Should this be happening? Did the pins even do anything, really? The doctor hadn't answered me when I'd asked.

I looked all around, but no one was objecting.

"Lie down," the concentrator said.

I did. He lifted up my shirt. I could feel him fit the pins on either side of my belly button. I had braced myself for some kind of cold pricking sensation, but they were the same temperature as my skin. As he pressed them into place, I felt something warm shift beneath my skin, and then a hazy sense of relief. The feeling sparked a sudden and specific young memory of peeing in the ocean.

I started to smell something faint, warm, and animal, almost like milk.

"Turn," he said again.

I turned.

He pushed through my hair to touch my skull. He fit a pin to the skin there. One pin, then another, and another.

I closed my eyes.

When the concentrator was gone, I opened my eyes again. All the other students were lying, like I was, with the pins buried along their hair and beneath their clothes. We looked like little aliens.

I touched Baby's hand. "Hey," I said.

She turned to me. The pins flashed.

"Don't worry," I said. "This'll be fun."

She nodded. Her eyes were blank, her lips set anxiously tight.

The chandeliers had been turned down, almost off.

Many minutes passed before Viktória said, "Breathe in."

I breathed in.

"Out."

I breathed out.

As the minutes passed, any curiosity I had sank into boredom. I breathed, in and out, until I wished I weren't breathing. I wished I were up in the library reading my Betty and Veronica comics.

But then, I couldn't imagine what it would be like to stand and leave the ballroom. It seemed I might never leave. Something was weighing me down.

"In," Viktória said, "and out."

Darkness moved behind my eyelids. My breath rose through my stomach, through my throat, out, then back in. Pressure squeezed my skull.

In, and out.

I don't know if I slept, or if my eyes were open or closed, or how much time passed. It could have been minutes, hours, or years. My body floated away from me but I was still here. We were all here.

That's what Viktória was saying. "You are in the house."

Her voice was low, so low it almost felt like it was coming from my own mind.

"You are in the house and the house is in the woods. The woods are in the house. The stairs are in the house. Down the stairs is the hallway, and at the end of the hallway is the ballroom. You are in the ballroom. The ballroom is in the house. You are in the house and the house is in you."

Her voice was slow and rhythmic as a prayer.

How had I ever felt sleepy? Every part of my body was turned on to everyone and anyone, all of us here together, in the ballroom. This ballroom in the house.

I could feel myself. Yes—really feel myself, like I hadn't in a long time.

I was here.

I blinked.

I lifted my hands and put them down again. I couldn't look at them. I couldn't.

How could M. Owens have said nothing was wrong with me? How could I have almost believed him?

The walls of the ballroom were closing around my head. The room was growing dark. I was thrusting forward—

I was crashing into the hotel room. I was slumping down. I was staring into a face.

"The house is the woods," Viktória said. "You are in the woods."

I tried to turn my head but couldn't. Vomit rose up in my throat. I was choking.

A girl said, "I am in the house." Her voice seemed to come from the ceiling.

"But before, you were somewhere else," Viktória said. "Where?"

"In a white house at the end of a street," the girl said. "We moved in last year, my mom and me. It was a big house. Too big. All the rooms had carpets. My mom vacuumed every day. I hated the sound of the vacuum."

One of my pins had come loose. The pad had fallen from my skull. I touched my hand to the space where it used to be.

I rubbed my eyes. I felt as if I were emerging from a daydream. I wasn't choking anymore, and I couldn't see anything except the ballroom.

"You were in the house," Viktória was still saying, "and what was in you?"

"The sad thing," the girl said. "I was sad. I was sad like the vacuum was sad. I was sad, and I couldn't stop being sad."

"Yes," Viktória said. "The sadness was inside."

I lowered my hand from the loose pin. I blinked again.

I said nothing as I felt my heartbeat slow.

"Does anyone else," Viktória was saying, "have bad things inside?"

I could hear the aides shuffle among our bodies. Pins beeped as the concentrators made small adjustments.

I felt a flash of panic. They were going to realize that one of my pins had fallen loose. They were going to bring me deeper into the dark daydream.

One of the concentrators stepped over my head. I looked up. It was the same boy with the acne.

He frowned as he glanced over the detached pin. But as he bent to fix it, his eyes flashed onto mine.

Please, I mouthed, don't.

His face was impassive.

I didn't know why he listened to me, but he did. He stood and let his hands fall. His footsteps echoed as he walked away.

I breathed.

The room was becoming clearer.

"My parents didn't want me to go here, to Catherine," a boy was saying in a lisping voice. "They wanted me close to home. But every other school was so expensive. My dad said we could have made it work, but I knew he was lying. Catherine was my only chance. My only chance to be everything they want me to be." His voice wavered. "But I don't want to be here, so far away. I miss my parents. I miss my church. I was in a group there. I miss hanging out with them after school, with my friends. I miss TV. And—what if my mom gets sick again? What if it comes back? And I don't even know?"

Viktória slowly paced the room.

"I understand," she said. "Yes. Fear. We have fear inside. But that is not you anymore. You don't have to be afraid. Your future is here, in this house. You are here. You are in the house."

"In the house," we said.

"In the house, down the hall."

"In the house," we said, "down the hall."

The stories drifted, and my mind drifted, too. Until Baby was the one speaking.

"Last year," Baby said, "I was at the Macy's parade. I went there alone. I had—we'd gone to New York to visit my aunt for Thanksgiving. Her apartment was ugly and hot, and all my cousins hate me. So I went to the parade. And next to me, there was this pretty little girl. She had the longest pretty curls, really nice brown, chocolate-brown. And pretty eyes, and dimples. She was sitting on her dad's shoulders and she was laughing. And—I hated her."

Baby's voice was stronger now.

"I hated her. I really did. I hated her so much it hurt. I could see how nice her life would be. She was going to be invited to sleepovers and pizza parties. She was going to go on dates with pretty boys. She would have nice, pretty children. And then she would die, and she would be happy. She would be happy. And I was angry—so angry I cried—at the parade, because that will never be me. I will never be someone happy. Because I am someone alone. That's what I thought."

Her voice was strong, though softer now.

"But now I see I'm not alone. Because here, in the house, I have everything. I have teachers who care about me. I have books. I have the lab. I'm still not pretty or sweet—but I don't care. Because I have work to do. There can be something good in me. Something mine."

"You can be good," Viktória said. "In the house."

"In the house," Baby said, and we all echoed, "In the house."

"In the house, downstairs, down the hall, in the ballroom."

I could see Viktória more clearly now. She stepped around us as she spoke.

I touched my throat and felt the vomit still there, rising in waves as if pumped by my heart.

The chandeliers hummed.

"You are in the house and the house is in today," Viktória said. "Today is not a moment. Today is not a point. Today is an infinite area. Today is forever. Everything that has happened and that will ever happen is now. Everything that has been and will be is here. And everything is good. Everything is fine."

I closed my eyes again.

"You are not sad. You are not afraid. You are not hateful. Because you are here. You are here. You are inside. And you are ready."

Some of the students' eyes were open, others closed. But all of their faces were slack with pleasure.

"You are here," Viktória said.

No, I thought lightly. I'm not here. You can't catch me. I'm too gone.

Footsteps echoed near my head.

"You are in," Viktória said. "And doesn't it feel good?"

I turned to the sound of her voice.

The eye contact hit me with a shock. Viktória was watching me with a slight smile. Her eyes drifted to my skull.

She knew I hadn't fixed the pin.

THE TOWER

In the days following the coming in, I attended my classes, like I had promised M. Owens I would. I raised my hand and sometimes gave right answers. I did the readings, or at least sat in front of the textbooks and turned the pages.

But as I turned those pages, my mind drifted, and I remembered Viktória's smile. Her clear gaze, eyes steady on me, and her little teeth. The slow click of her shoes as she'd walked away.

She knew. She knew I'd felt the pin come loose and done nothing to fix it. I thought I had disappeared in the crowd of students, that I was invisible, but she saw me. She knew.

What was she going to do? That kind of resistance had to be a serious offense. Was she going to throw me out? Or pull me further in—into some tight, airless room where she could properly examine me?

My stomach squeezed at the thought. I couldn't let her see my insides. I couldn't.

No one talked about the coming in afterward. But I could feel the weight of it everywhere, in the quiet way students picked at their breakfasts or how they slunk quickly back to their rooms after class. Even generally open, sunny people like Nick avoided the topic. I was sitting with him in the great hall once, a few days after the ceremony, chatting about breeds of dog, when he suddenly stopped mid-sentence, stood, and left the room without a word.

I'd watched his retreating back in shock. Then I dimly remembered someone telling a story about a dog during the coming in. Had that been Nick? What had he said?

I couldn't understand it. So I tried to forget about the coming in. I concentrated on my finals.

In the end, I passed every class. My grades were awful, but I passed. That was enough. I decided to concentrate in History of Art, as I'd told M. Owens I might. It was as good a concentration as any, and I'd already registered for the second half of the survey course.

Diego Jimenez, a small, serious boy who lived upstairs, was applying to the concentration, too. According to him, I should start working on my chronological and geographical distributional requirements, and Black Visual Cultures was supposed to be a good course this semester. Also, I would need to take German.

"I don't need German," I said. "I already speak French and Spanish."

"Well, you need German, too." Diego shuffled the cards with a dignified *shwip* before dealing a hand to himself and Yaya. They were playing gin rummy. "Art history was invented in Austria."

Diego flipped over a card from the deck. His fingers were short and tidy, with buffed, clipped nails. They made everything he did appear elegant and correct, whether it was slipping on gloves, draping a napkin over his lap, or peeling a grapefruit and arranging the slices in a starburst on a saucer. He wore his chin-length, otter-brown hair neatly combed behind his ears and his T-shirt tucked into his jeans. He walked slowly, talked slowly, and ate slowly, with the deliberate relish of someone who considered consumption an art form.

"It'll be fine," he said as he discarded. "German is wonderful. And art history is the most beautiful concentration, really."

Yaya frowned at the hand she'd been dealt, brushing absent-mindedly at her sleeve. She was wearing the faux-mink coat she'd had since fall. It was much shabbier now.

We were in Molina's music room, an incense-perfumed space furnished with brocade chairs, music history books, Chinese black lacquer screens, and a grand piano polished to a high gloss. Watercolor paintings of foxes and herons hung on the white damask wallpaper. Diego and Yaya had taken to retiring to the music room after dinner to drink and play cards. Sometimes, after a few bottles of wine, Diego would sit at the piano—his posture perfect, even drunk—and drawl out wandering, melancholy nocturnes while Yaya sang along, swaying like a flower. She made up the lyrics as she went. She wasn't a very good singer.

"Have you been to the gallery yet?" Yaya said to me, without looking up from her cards. "It's unreal. Totally gorgeous."

"Are you applying to art history, too?" I asked.

"Yaya's doing mathematics," Diego said. "She's brilliant."

She laid down her cards. "Gin."

"What?" Diego bent to look at her cards. "Oh dear."

"But I don't want to take German," I said.

"*Wie schade*," Diego mumbled. He glanced at me, and then said, "Oh, don't worry. You still have time to sign up for the introduction. It's not too bad."

The days distended as winter melted into spring. Snow dripped down the house's walls and mucked up the yard. Outside, the maples molded green. Inside, the rooms grew stuffy with a feverish humidity.

Following Yaya's suggestion, I visited the art gallery, a suite of three rooms in Ashley's basement used to display Catherine's collection. The first two rooms were filled with paintings—landscapes, portraits, abstract color fields—from floor to ceiling, like a Parisian salon. The third was larger and exhibited only a few artworks, each hung with a more modern sense of display.

My footsteps echoed as I walked through the third room, up to a painting of a ballroom.

The girls in the scene whirred in dance. Their cheeks and lips and frothing skirts were all the same shade of pretty pastel pink. On the table, a champagne coupe beaded sweat.

Somewhere out in the world, real girls were drinking real champagne. They were eating cherries and kissing each other with flushed, rosy lips. They were prancing on tables. They were laughing.

Soon after I left the gallery, I was lost. I turned a corner and realized I didn't know which direction I had come from.

I got lost in Catherine a lot. Usually I found made my way out to the yard and from there back to the entryway into Molina. This time, I kept going.

I went down one hallway, up another. I passed an empty sitting room with cornflower-blue wallpaper, then a closet full of brooms. Behind another door, a bathroom with the toilet removed.

Then the hallway twisted into one with burgundy wallpaper patterned with tiny gold figures. I looked closer. They were little umbrellas.

Was I still in Ashley?

There was a stairway at the end of the hallway. Before that, in the middle of the hall, was a door. The door had a keypad by the handle.

I tried the handle. It was locked.

"What are you doing?"

I turned.

A new materials concentrator, the girl with the long black braid, strode toward me with an irritated frown.

"I'm trying to open this door," I said.

"Well, don't," she said. "You're not *allowed* in here."

"Why not?"

"Because you're not."

She stepped in front of me. She pulled a card from her back pocket.

She turned when she realized I was still watching her. "Could you, like . . . stand *back*, please?"

I stood back.

She swiped, and the door clicked. She frowned at me one last time before slipping inside.

The door clicked shut behind her.

I walked down the umbrella hallway and back up onto the yard.

❧

Theo had been right; after our coming in, our class was allowed into weekly sessions. Our ushers gave no announcement about the change, nor did we receive any notice or letter from the administrators. But before our coming in, any first-year who tried to enter the great hall during session was turned away. Now we were in.

Session began at sunset. Beneath the weak glow of the chandeliers, the great hall felt like an in-between place, a room between here and nowhere. Our shadows shifted as we filed in. None of us sat at our usual tables; even the professors abandoned their dais to be among the students. Only Viktória kept herself apart. While we settled into our seats, she stood by the windows, arms folded.

Once we were quiet, white cakes and clay cups of wine were passed around, as they had been during our coming in. But there were no plasm pins. Apparently that part was over.

After we ate the cakes and drank our first sips of wine, Viktória straightened. Then any noise stopped.

She waited, eyes fluttering behind her closed eyelids. Then she began:

Your hands are on the table. The table in the hall, across the yard, in the house. The house is in the woods. In the woods, across the yard, in your hands, is the cup.

The cup is in your hands. Your hands are in the house.

Her voice echoed through the hall, as compelling as a hallucination. And we chorused in response:

The cup is in my hands. My hands are in the house.

The house is in the woods. The woods are in my hands.

At least, that's what everyone else did. I didn't chant. I didn't say anything. I thought some aide or professor would scold me for sitting stubbornly silent, but no one seemed to care. And I went to session only twice before I decided I hated it. I hated Viktória's voice and the droned response, the minutes slipping into hours as the crowd hummed on. Their chants made my brain buzz against my skull, so bored it felt like panic.

During my second session, I watched Baby as she chanted. She was sitting two tables away from me. Tears streamed down her face. Her lips were moving, but her voice was lost in the chorus. She squeezed her hands tight and raised them high.

Joyful. That's was she was. She was full up with joy.

The pins and the sessions, and our classes, and the house—somehow they were all part of the same experiment. I could tell. It made me nervous. But no one had said anything about sessions being mandatory, so I didn't go. Instead, I found the back entrance to the kitchen, where aides set cookies and pastries to cool after baking. They let me take some before laying them out for dessert service. I ate them alone in my room.

A bland night in March. The aides had mowed the yard that afternoon, and the whole house smelled green and harsh. I was walking back to my bedroom when I heard a quiet electric noise.

I stopped. I was in the boys' hall down the way from ours. It must have been long past midnight, because the hall was silent except for the faint melodic thrum.

I crept close to the wall. I leaned my ear against it.

Music.

I knocked on the door.

There was a long hesitation before I heard feet patter over. Theo opened the door, his eyes wide with surprise.

"Can I come in?" I said.

He stepped back to let me pass.

Theo had a single, like Yaya, and his bedroom was the neatest I'd seen at Catherine. The bed was made, the floor swept, the notebooks on his desk arranged in a meticulous stack. Even the baseboards looked scrubbed. The only signs of life were the Keds by his door and a plate of almond cakes on his desk.

I loved the messy rooms of the boys I slept with. Dirty teacups cluttered their desks and sweaty wads of T-shirts lurked under their beds. Their sheets always had a sour animal smell. I liked the smell. I liked how their rooms, like their bodies, felt so dumb, casual, and warm.

But Theo's room didn't feel warm. And his sneakers, lined up so tenderly by the door, made my heart hurt.

I picked up an almond cake. "I think they're serving these all week, you know," I said. "You don't have to hoard them."

Theo, watching me from the doorway, gave a little smile. "Habit, I guess," he said. "No one forgets being hungry."

I set down the cake. I could feel Theo's big Bambi eyes, so stupidly easy to read, staring at me with bright curiosity.

"What about thirsty?" I said. "Do you have any wine?"

He opened his closet, reached far into the back, past crisp T-shirts and jackets all hung and ordered, and pulled out a half-empty bottle. He passed it to me.

I took a swig as I sat on the edge of his bed. I wiped my mouth with the back of my hand before giving him the bottle. He took a swig, too.

He lounged on the floor. He may have kept his room ruthlessly neat, but every gesture of his body was easy and loose. He was watching me.

I said, "What were you listening to?"

Surprise flashed over his face. "Listening to? What do you mean?"

I took another swig from the bottle.

He opened his mouth, then closed it. He shook his head with a slight smile. "Look under the mattress."

I rooted around until I felt something plastic. I pulled it out.

It was a Discman. A set of tangled earphones, too. I turned the Discman over in my hands. Its weight, color—submarine-gray—and alien shape were familiar, though I hadn't held one in a long time. I ran my fingers against the buttons. There was a disc inside, paused. I could feel it. The Discman still hummed with energy.

The commissary would rent boom boxes and tapes to us for parties, but the Discman felt different somehow. It wasn't just any Discman; it was Theo's. His artifact from a different world.

"You okay?" Theo said.

"Yes," I said.

"Man, how did you know that I had it?" he said. "Did you hear me?"

I touched the wall behind me on the bed. "You were here, weren't you, leaning against the wall? I could hear it bleeding through. Your headphones aren't very good."

"Oh."

"What were you listening to?"

He held it out to me. "See for yourself."

I slipped on the headphones and pressed play.

A chorus of *sha la las* echoed over a menacing guitar. Then a sad, hysterical voice sang: *Life goes on here—day after day. I don't know if I'm living—or if I'm supposed to be . . .*

I pulled off the headphones.

"Like it?" he said.

I cradled the Discman to my lap. "Have you had this the whole time? You snuck it in?"

He nodded.

"Aren't you worried about getting caught?" I said. "You could go to the tower for this. Or worse."

He shrugged. "Music saved my life," he said. "More than once. I would give up a lot for Catherine. But not music."

I held out a hand for the wine. He passed it to me.

"I thought you were happy," I said after I drank. "You and Nick—you're always laughing. I thought you were so happy."

"What makes you think I'm not?" he said after a long time.

"This isn't a happy room."

His eyes drifted over the empty walls and floor before settling on the empty desk. He stared.

"I'm . . . not so good sometimes," he said. "But I'm working on it. Being happy. I'm trying really hard. We've been adjusting my prescriptions since my annual. The doctors here are really good. And I'm okay in the day. When I'm outside, with friends—and since the coming in. I've been better, since then."

His eyes flashed on me. It was the first time I had heard anyone mention the coming in.

"I'm still sad," he said. "But I think I'm going to be better."

"Do you really think so?"

"I'm trying."

I ran a finger around the lip of the wine bottle.

"Is that your only CD?" I said.

He hesitated.

"You're not going to rat me out?" he finally said.

"No."

He got up and reached behind me, under the bed. I watched as he lifted the sheet, dug his hand into a slit in the mattress, and pulled out a CD booklet.

I flipped through them one by one. Seventies prog rock, R&B, psychedelic jazz.

"What's this one?" I said, pointing to a burned CD with a heart drawn on it in permanent marker.

"Just a mix."

"Did a girl give it to you?"

He grinned.

I popped it into the Discman.

The first track was a sixties girl group song. I could see them: a trio of girls in matching black dresses singing with perfect, pretty charm. *How gentle is the rain that falls softly on the meadow!*

What was it like to be so sweet?

"Do you like it?" Theo said as the song finished.

"One second. I'm listening to it again."

I skipped back.

Afterward, I slipped the headphones off and said, "Do you think anyone in the world is really that nice?"

"What do you mean?"

"So sweet and happy. So in love."

"Maybe. I'm in love."

"With Andie?"

Andie was the second-year he was currently dating. She was a pale, pretty girl, taller than him, with big teeth and thick, horsey blond hair. They liked making out in the stairwell before dinner.

"Andie, yeah. And other girls. Everyone. It ain't good." He laughed. "Aren't you the same?"

"No. I don't fall in love."

He laughed again.

"What?"

"You fuck, like, everyone."

"That's not love."

He shook his head. "Shameless."

I hugged my knees.

"Don't you want it?" he said. "Love and butterflies, all that? Most girls do."

"I don't think so. No, not really."

"Then why do you do it?"

"Do what?"

"Fuck around."

I had never wondered that before.

"I don't know," I finally said. "It feels good. To be touched in such a . . . silly way. To be so close, surrounded by all that skin and squeaking. You can't see anything and can't hear anything . . . it's like the rest of the world is muffled. I don't know." I shrugged. "It's something to do."

I handed the Discman back to him. "Thanks."

"Sure thing."

"Can I come back and listen to it?"

"Sure. Whenever."

I took another glug from the wine.

"How about right now?" I said.

He passed me the Discman.

I lay back on his bed. I clapped the headphones over my ears.

After leaving Theo's, I returned to my room. I crept over to Baby's bed and pushed at her warm body. She shifted, then continued snoring. I let her sounds soothe me.

What do you want? M. Owens had asked during our meeting last semester.

I tried to imagine the crystal vases, the yellow buds and curling pink petals. I squeezed my eyes tight and tried to imagine full, beautiful things.

I mostly just felt tired.

We weren't supposed to remember anything of our past lives here at Catherine. But I remembered everything about that night and that room—the room where everything twisted. I remembered the girl's warm hands in mine as we jumped on the hotel bed, laughing and posing for the man's camera, *click-click-click*; I remembered his necklace, glinting in the greenish light, as he turned to close the curtains; I remembered her giggles as she begged, pretty please, for more. I remembered slumping down in the bed, staring at the room service tray. I remembered dirty napkins, half a tuna club sandwich, and three silver bowls of melting strawberry ice cream.

That was the last thing I remembered—those ice cream bowls. And when I woke up the next afternoon, he was gone, and she was there, staring into me. Vomit pooled beside her on the bed.

I'd touched her cheek. It wasn't warm anymore.

I curled up closer to Baby.

It wasn't your fault, I tried to tell myself. You barely even knew her name.

But why hadn't I called for help? Why hadn't I screamed? Why had I run away?

I didn't know. But I wished I had stayed. Maybe then I wouldn't see her face now, drifting behind my closed lids like a pale balloon. Her eyes, dead and staring. Her graying skin. Her whitish mouth.

I rubbed Baby's shoulder.

What do you want to do?

I'd already done everything I wanted to do. I'd swum naked at night in heated pools. I'd kissed the most beautiful boys. I'd lounged for hours in squeaky restaurant booths eating plate after plate of buttery spaghetti, laughing as men felt me up under the table. And it all turned me toward that face.

I closed my eyes and breathed in the smell of Baby's neck. Her hair cream smelled like almond blossoms.

❧

Beginner's German met on the top floor of the Ashley tower. The room was so high up that during class I watched the flat blue sky through the window and wondered if we had drifted away from the rest of the house.

I couldn't daydream too much, though; German was hard. Every day we had new vocabulary to memorize, essays to write, and skits to practice and perform. But I liked it more than my other classes that semester. The modern art history survey, Literature of War, Black Visual Culture, and Electricities, with its cryptic syllabus, were all impenetrable, whereas German could be translated. German had rules. And in the merry, cartoon-colored world of our textbook, everything was simple. There was a family with a mother, father, son, daughter, and cat. The family lived in a big house. The parents loved the children. The children loved the cat. The cat said *miau*.

Anna and Nick and I sat together at the back of the table, as far away from M. Amsel's glare as possible. Anna was the perfect student, sharp, energetic, and always on time. Nick and I were usually late and hungover. As we slouched into the room, M. Amsel would *tch tch tch*, slap the table, and cry out, *Nehmen Sie sich selbst ernst!* I didn't know what that meant. She never stayed mad at Nick, though; in his effortless, indolent way, he was acing the class. I was not.

One day Anna came in late. Nick and I were already practicing our dialogue—my name was Hilde, his was Günther, and we were looking to rent a student apartment in Berlin—when she opened the classroom door.

Anna handed a note to M. Amsel, who barely glanced at it before nodding and gesturing to our table.

"What was that?" Nick whispered as she sat down with us. "Can we just show up whenever we want now?"

"You already show up whenever you want." Anna slipped out of her jacket and leaned back in her chair. Her cheeks were flushed fresh apple red from the cold. "I had an evaluation."

"An evaluation?" I said. "For what?"

"For the new materials concentration."

I must have looked confused, because she went on: "Acceptance into the concentration isn't based only on your grades and test scores. You're also assessed for, like, general fitness for the discipline."

Nick wasn't listening anymore. He was drawing bigger boobs on one of the women in the textbook. He had an imperious way of quickly losing interest in a conversation.

"What's it like?" I said. "The evaluation? What are they looking for?"

Anna shrugged.

"What kind of questions do they ask?"

She pulled her hair up into an impatient ponytail without meeting my eye. "I don't know. It's like the stuff they asked on our Catherine interview, you know, the third one? Like that, but more, I don't know. Intense." She snapped on the hair tie. "Want to make sure you can handle the pressure, I guess."

My third Catherine interview had been nine hours long. Nine hours seated at a mahogany dining room table with five middle-aged strangers staring at me. I'd drunk glass after glass of orange juice as I tried to keep up with their endless questions, questions that seemed to have no pattern or significance. Did I bite my nails? When did I get my first period? What was my most embarrassing moment? Who was my third-grade teacher?

I didn't remember how I'd answered them all, or if I'd even answered honestly. I couldn't imagine what Anna meant by calling this evaluation "more intense."

Nick rested his golden head on his textbook. He closed his eyes.

"Can you?" I said.

"Can I what? Handle the pressure?" She shrugged. "I don't know. But I have to try."

"*Auf Deutsch, bitte!*" M. Amsel crowed.

Anna glanced at her before saying, "*Das plasm ist* . . . it's the whole reason I came here. If I don't get in, I don't know what I'll do. I guess concentrate in history or some shit."

Nick's lips parted in his sleep.

Anna's face was dark.

"What did they ask you about?" I said.

"I don't know. Friends, family. My brother."

"Why would they want to know about your brother?"

She turned to me. "I don't *know*. I have nothing to say about my brother."

I'd never seen such a sharp expression in her eyes. But before I could apologize or ask anything further, she'd already turned away and flipped open her textbook.

I wondered, not for the first time, how Anna had ended up at Catherine. Not that she wasn't smart. I saw her calm, satisfied expression whenever she received exam results. But she had the kind of simple, amenable intelligence that would have succeeded anywhere. I could easily imagine her at a real college, playing hacky sack on some quad or chugging cheap beer at a tailgate. She was fun. She was friendly. Compared to most of us, Anna was as tanned and open and easy as the sun.

But sometimes I sensed something else in her—a tension in

her fist as she took down notes, a hesitation before she laughed at an insult. Sometimes I felt she had only learned to be herself by pretending.

Anna's eyes roved as she read the assignment on the blackboard. She narrowed them in concentration.

Whoever Anna was before Catherine didn't matter. She was here now.

"*Herr Townsend!*" M. Amsel cried. She threw a piece of chalk at his head. It clattered off the table.

"I'm up," Nick said, lifting his head. "I'm up."

The pressure of applying for the new materials concentration was getting to Baby. Whenever I came home, no matter the time, Baby would be awake, muttering to herself as she hunched over one project or another. She was taking an advanced mathematics course this semester, one of the classes that broke many of the would-be concentrators. She spent hours staring at lines of intricate code before writing out page after page of solutions. I didn't know what any of it meant. I just brought her tea and snacks from the dinners she missed. She took the tea, but otherwise ignored me.

I was lying in bed chewing the remains of a cough drop when, in one great push, Baby shoved all of the notes off her desk. They swooshed to the floor.

Her face was clammy, her hair undone in a shocked mess. For a moment I thought she might burst into tears, but her eyes stayed stark wide.

She said, "I can't do this."

"Yes, you can."

"No, I can't," she said. "You don't understand. We had our midterm—and I was below the curve. We haven't gotten our grades back. But I know I was."

"I'm sure it's fine, Baby. Look at all this." I gestured toward the pages. "You're doing so much. I'm sure it's all better than you think. You're not going to fail."

"I need to relearn this second theorem—but I don't have time. I'm trying so hard, but I never have enough time." She leaned back in her chair. "I'm going to fail."

"You, sweet Baby? You're not going to fail."

"Stop *saying* that. I might. And if I do, I don't get into the concentration. Don't you understand?"

Her body heaved. She closed her eyes.

"Baby, dear."

I slipped off the bed and sat down at her knee. She didn't look at me. Her lips were twitching.

"You'll get into the concentration," I said. "I know you will. But even if you don't, it's fine. You can concentrate in something else. It'll be fine."

"What do you know? You don't even go to class."

"I go to class."

"Not really. Not lately."

She was right. I had been skipping more and more. Whatever drive I'd had at the beginning of the semester had puttered out. My classes were too broad, too crooked and abstruse, every lesson more incomprehensible than the last.

Either way, midterms were over, and finals too far away to worry about yet. It was a warm, soft night in April. A floral breeze passed through the window. A group of students were hanging out in the courtyard. Every once in a while they would burst into sudden crazy laughter.

"You don't get it," Baby said with a singsong tone. "You're someone—"

She suddenly grasped my hand.

"*You* are going to be okay," she said. "Do you understand?

You are. You're pretty, and you are—cool. You're going to have a good life. You'll meet new people and go new places. You will be glad sometimes and sad sometimes. You will be okay. Most people will be okay. But I'm not."

"Why do you think that?"

She looked down at the pages on the floor. I couldn't tell if she had heard me.

"When I was accepted here, to Catherine," she said, "at first I thought it was a mistake. I'm not special like everyone else. I'm not creative. Not very smart. I'm not good at anything, really. But then I realized. It's because of how badly I want it—plasm. It's the only thing I've ever cared about. The only thing I've ever loved."

"Baby," I said, "you haven't even worked with plasm yet, have you? How do you know you love it?"

"I don't know," she said. "But I do—love it. I always have." She raised her eyes to me. "I was rejected from every college I applied to—did you know that? Even my safety. Everywhere except Catherine."

I rubbed her arm.

"I couldn't have gone anywhere else but Catherine, either," I whispered. "I didn't come here for any good reason. I was running away."

"You say that," she said, "and maybe you think it's true. But look at you." She was almost sneering. "Of course there's something *special* about you, some reason you belong here. You could have run anywhere. But you came here."

I thought of Mr. González's face, his smile as he handed me a macadamia nut chocolate. He'd thought I belonged here, too.

"I have nothing else," Baby was saying. "Plasm is the only thing. The only thing for me."

"Baby." I rubbed her arm. "You're eighteen. And you really are smart. Much smarter than me. And you work so hard. How do you know what your life will be like? You can graduate and get a job, like as a chemist or a librarian or something. Live in a nice house, marry someone—maybe Jason. Isn't he nice?"

Jason was a mumbling boy with pink cheeks and long eyelashes who shuffled over to our room sometimes to ask Baby for help with a problem set. His crush on her was sweet. She never noticed him.

"You could marry Jason," I said, "and live with him in a nice, big yellow house. A yellow house full of babies."

Baby was idly examining the tip of her pencil.

"No, Ines." Her voice still had a singsong lilt to it. "This is it for me. This is as close to the world as I'm ever going to be."

"Catherine isn't the real world."

"*Plasm* is real. Plasm is the world." She put down the pencil. "Haven't you read the Shiner report? Plasm isn't just some new material. It's *every* material. It's everywhere, in everything. And I'm failing at it."

"The Shiner report was fake."

"No. It wasn't."

Was that true?

A moth batted against the window.

I thought of Baby's face during sessions, the apparent ecstasy as her mouth formed the words. *I am in the house. My hands are on the table.*

"You know what you need?" I said.

Baby sniffled. "What?"

"A cookie. A big, chewy cookie."

She sniffled again.

I brought her down to the kitchen, where they were baking butter cookies for breakfast tomorrow. We stole four of them before going back to the Molina parlor, where we cracked open a window and curled up on the sill. We ate the cookies and told each other jokes from old episodes of *The Simpsons*. It smelled heavy outside, like a dense spring rain.

Baby was brushing crumbs from her pajamas when she said, "Guess what?"

"What?" I mumbled. My mouth was full of cookie.

"My sister isn't dead."

I put down the cookie, slowly.

"There was no car accident," she said. "She's alive. She just went away to college—Brandeis. She's really smart. Then after college, she got a job as a radio announcer. So she went farther away, to Toronto. Do you know where that is?"

I nodded.

"So. She just left. She lives in a nice apartment and has a lot of new Canadian friends. And every morning the whole city wakes up and listens to her pretty voice. She's not dead. She could come back to me. But she won't."

Baby tugged at her pajama sleeves. Her voice was flat as ever, as if she were telling me what the hall was serving for dinner.

"But that's all right," Baby said. "People leave me. I know that now. That's why I have to do other things. Big, important things."

I tried to look her in the eye. But she was staring out at the clouds.

That was the night I realized: I didn't know Baby at all. I didn't know her then, and would never know her, not ever. Her brain was mapped in some corrupt, fantastic pattern. And she would make choices I could never understand.

I rubbed her leg. It was unshaven, like always. Most of us had given up shaving our legs after a few weeks at Catherine. I doubted Baby had ever shaved hers, though, even before. It didn't seem like something that would have occurred to her.

Lightning flashed outside, stark and strange. Raindrops pricked the sill. I closed the window.

Weeks later, a letter came for me on the morning tea tray. A powder-blue envelope addressed in looping handwriting.

"What's that?" Baby said as I ripped open the envelope. She sat cross-legged on her bed, picking Master Locks. She had stayed up all night working on a problem set that was due in an hour. The set was stacked neatly on her desk, ready to submit, but I could see that half the pages were blank. Her pick clicked against the lock.

I read from the note: "Your presence is requested at a private meeting in M. Viktória Varga's office at 12:15 today."

Baby stared at me, her face shiny with sweat. It was only May and already the house was stiflingly hot.

"What?" I said.

"A private meeting with Viktória?"

I dropped the note back on the tray. I poured myself a cup of tea.

"Ines," she said.

"What?"

"That is a big deal."

"I'm sure it's not. Everyone meets with Viktória at some point."

"Yes, but in our second and third years. Why do you think she wants to talk to you now?"

"I don't know."

Baby stared at me as if waiting for more. I sat beside her on the bed.

"How come you've never shown me how to pick?" I said.

She opened her mouth, and then closed it with a sigh. She handed me one of the locks.

Later, I was sitting on the bench in Viktória's reception office, squeezing my hands between my knees. Daphne, Viktória's assistant, sat typing at a desk cluttered with peel-off calendars, Peanuts figurines, and potted geraniums. An intercom sat by Daphne's elbow, next to a computer that looked much newer than the ones in our lab.

"Cleared right up, didn't it?" Daphne said, still typing with rapid focus. Her blue denim dress had a matching denim belt knotted over her thick waist.

"What?" I said.

"The rain. Didn't you hear it raining this morning? But it cleared right up, didn't it?"

"Yes."

"She'll see you now."

"What?"

Now Daphne looked up. "You may go in." She gestured to the office door.

I stood.

No noise came from behind the door.

"How did you know?" I said, turning to Daphne.

"How did I know what, sweetie?" There was a bite to her voice that hadn't been there before.

"That she was ready for me."

She pointed at the intercom. A green light had turned on.

"Should I knock?"

Daphne looked up, clearly exasperated now. "Yes."

I knocked, heard a silken, "Come in," and opened the door.

Viktória sat behind a vast glass desk with a bronze pen in her hand, head bent as if in prayer. A single piece of paper was laid in front of her.

"One moment, please," she said without looking up from the page. "You may take a seat."

I sat in one of the chairs in front of her desk. The chair was so deep that as I sank back, my feet lifted off the floor.

Viktória's office was unlike any other room in the house. It must have been built around the same time as Ashley—its walls had the familiar Victorian paneling and plaster molding around the ceiling—but the furnishings were spare and precise. The white leather office chair had been burnished spotless, the jade vase of peonies polished to a milky sheen. Every object had a magic, talismanic weight to it. The windows were veiled by gray gauze curtains so sheer they made the sky outside appear luminescent. Even the air in here was so sumptuously cool it seemed to hum. The room smelled like Viktória, like lilies and tobacco.

"My apologies," Viktória finally said, and set down the pen. "Ines."

She folded her hands.

Viktória's eyes were wide-set and very black. Her silvering hair was pulled into a low ponytail. It lay swished over her shoulder like a fur stole.

She said, "How are you feeling today?"

"Really great. How are you?"

She leaned back in the chair, slowly. She wasn't smiling.

My mind flashed to the other time our eyes had met, at the coming in. When she saw my pin was loose.

"I just returned from a conference in Oregon," she said. "Afterwards, an old friend and I went on a hike through the pine forests there. The most beautiful old forests—so green and dark, the needles are like jewels. Have you ever been?"

"No."

"You should, someday. But it is good to be back."

She tapped a fingernail against her glass desk.

"So," she said. "Why do you think you are here?"

"Here in your office?"

"Sure."

"I think I'm in trouble."

The humming, I suddenly realized, was an air conditioner.

I could see it installed in her window. I hadn't even considered that's what it might be. There were no other air conditioners in the house.

"Before the conference, I had a meeting with M. Owens and M. David," Viktória said. "We are concerned about your academic performance."

"I haven't failed a class since the fall," I said.

"That is true. You've managed to not quite fail anything. But this"—she put a hand on the paper in front of her—"is not the quality of work that we require here at Catherine. And it is not what you are capable of."

I tried to shift forward in the chair but sank back down.

Viktória glanced down at the page. "You plan on applying to the history of art concentration, is that correct?"

"Yes."

"Are you enjoying your classes this semester?"

"I don't know."

"You don't know?"

"I don't go to them very often."

Viktória crossed her legs. They shone lustrous and smooth.

"Some students," she said, "have already been asked to leave Catherine. They were not suited for this house. They never were. But this is not the case with you. I remember your application, Ines. I found it very interesting. You are not brilliant, but your interviews, your project submissions—those fantasy body interiors—they were fascinating, really. More fascinating than you knew. Your recommenders were right about you. Not every young girl is so . . . vibrant."

Her eyes flashed at the word.

"You remind me of myself," Viktória said with a small smile, "if I may be so bold. Myself, when I was young."

She was still tapping her finger.

"But youth and energy are not everything," she continued. "Catherine could craft your mind to be not merely energetic, but successful and creative in meaningful ways. You could accomplish great things here at Catherine, and beyond Catherine, if you took yourself seriously."

"I like my German class," I said. "I really do. I'm trying."

"You are not trying," she said. "You are not doing anything. You've been given chance after chance. You've been fed, clothed, sheltered, and given every opportunity to learn the most wonderful things—and still you refuse to do the most basic work. You are throwing it all away. You are lazy."

Tap, tap, tap.

"You are trying to run away, as you have always run. You have run from your mother, your friends, your lovers, and the law, and now you want to run from Catherine. But my dear—where are you going? You dream of beautiful adventures, of traveling across continents and overseas, as if you might find joy on some distant island. But you won't. Because you are miserable. You are a miserable girl, Ines."

My mind was blank. She spoke slowly, but I was still having trouble following along. I felt I had missed something crucial.

"I'm fine," I said.

"You are miserable," Viktória continued. "So, for you, Catherine is a prison. But if you weren't here, you could learn what a real prison is like. Isn't that right?"

I touched my head.

She folded her hands. She leaned forward.

"I know you have come here from a difficult time in your life," she whispered. "You have been in some dangerous, ugly situations. But you are not an ugly person. You can be beautiful. You can be good. Can't you see that, Ines? When you look around here"—she gestured vaguely toward the lush carpet, the gleaming glass desk, the crown moldings of plump cherries, grapes, and curling leaves—"don't you feel you could be good?"

The clock on her desk ticked.

"Am I being kicked out?" I said.

"Do you want to leave?"

"No."

Viktória stood. Her kitten heels made no sound as she walked across the rug and leaned on the front of her desk. She crossed her arms as she stared at me.

"You're going to spend a few days in the Restoration Center," she said.

I squeezed my hands tighter between my knees.

"This is not a punishment," she said. "It is time for you to learn how to really be here, at Catherine. And when you come out, we'll revisit your academic standing. All right?"

I looked up at her.

Leave me alone, I wanted to say. Please, just let me go.

But where would I go?

After a long pause, I nodded. I said, "All right."

Viktória squeezed my shoulder, suddenly, with kindness. My throat seized. I hadn't been touched that way, so gently, in a long time.

She twisted to press the intercom button on her desk. "Daphne, can you add Ines to the center schedule for next week?"

I whispered, "Thank you."

Viktória glanced at me, finger still on the button. She nodded.

❧

If you weren't here, you could learn what a real prison is like.

Viktória knew about the hotel room.

How had she heard about it? Did Mr. González tell her? He was the only one who knew about my wanderings that summer. I'd sometimes called him from whichever parking lot or abandoned house I was staying in at the time. But if he had told her—why was I accepted? Why had Viktória taken me in if she knew how poisonous I'd become, the evil things I'd done?

An aide came in the middle of the night to take me to the tower. I had napped all day, but now I was awake, alone, trying to write an essay for my Black Visual Cultures class. I was supposed to be analyzing an Igbo dance ritual. I had taken out three books from the library. I had a nice new notepad and three sharp pencils. But I was just staring at the notepad, tapping a pencil against the blank page and imagining the pretty trio of singing girls from Theo's song, when someone knocked on my door.

The aide was a flabby, red-faced boy I sometimes saw walking in from the far reaches of the yard. I now realized he must have been going back and forth from the tower. Tonight he wore a wax-coated canvas coat and chewed a boisterous wad of gum.

"Hi," I said.

"You ready to go?" He smacked the gum.

"I'm working on an essay. For class. Black Visual Cultures."

"Classwork is suspended until you're released from the tower."

"But look. I'm working so hard." I stepped back so he could see my desk. "I got books from the library."

He cracked his gum again. "Come on. We're already late."

I slipped my feet into my Keds, closed the book, and turned off my lamp.

He looked me up and down in the dim hallway light. "You don't want to take anything else? Playing cards? A book?"

"Can I?"

"No. But some kids try."

The aide led me down the stairs and through a back entrance, out into the murky, muggy night. The yard back there, in the southeast, was overgrown with weeds and restless with the noise of insects. The footpath snaked us through underbrush and mud patches and past an overgrown tennis court. But when the path turned back toward the house, we didn't follow it. We waded into the grass in total darkness. Dew dampened my ankles.

The tower appeared like a gray planet in the trees. One bare light bulb illuminated the door. In the light, I saw that it wasn't a tower at all, but a squat building with pale vinyl siding. I couldn't tell how deep it was, or whether there was a gate or porch.

The aide opened the door and stepped aside to let me in.

I blinked in the tower's sudden brightness. We were standing in a windowless, wood-paneled room crowded with an armoire, a rolltop desk, and a wall of shelves covered by blue latex curtains. Another aide sat reading a magazine with her feet up on the desk.

A door stood between the armoire and shelves. The door was painted yellow.

"Hey, Russ," the aide said as we walked in. Her oily black hair was braided into two long plaits down her back. She glanced over me. "She's coming in?"

"Yep. First time." He twirled a set of keys around his finger. "I'll be back to cover second shift?"

"See you." She winked at him.

When he was gone, the aide stood and came closer to me. Her limbs were long and spider-spindly, her eyes dark.

"All right," she said, so close now I could feel the heat of her breath on my cheek. "Strip down."

I pulled off my shirt, then my pants.

"Underwear, too."

"I'm on my period," I said. "I have a pad."

"We'll give you tampons."

I removed my underwear and pulled off the pad. As the aide put my clothes in the armoire, I wrapped the pad in a tissue and stuffed it in the trash.

The aide was pulling aside a latex curtain. The shelves were filled with towels, cartons of soap, and, yes, tampons.

She touched my shoulder as she handed them to me.

"It's going to be fine," she whispered.

She pulled a key from her pocket, unlocked the yellow door, and flicked on the lights inside.

The room was large, and too empty. A skinny bed with a gray quilt was pushed against one wall. A bookcase holding two books and an elephant figurine stood against the other. A small white tea table with a packet of playing cards sat in the corner. That was it.

The room had no clock.

I turned. The aide had already closed the door behind me.

I walked slowly into the middle of the room.

The other side of the room held a back door, one that looked like it hadn't been opened in years, and a curtain. I pulled the curtain aside to see a toilet and sink installed on a patch of tiles.

I set the tampons on the back of the toilet.

❧

At first I was fine. I sat on the bed and listened to myself breathe for a long time. There was nothing scary about the room. There was nothing unusual about the room at all. Nothing stirred. Nothing made any noise.

I curled up on the bed and took a nap with the lights on.

When I woke up, I didn't remember where I was. Then my eyes drifted to the elephant figurine on the bookshelf. Its little red trunk was raised in salute.

I was still here.

I played a game of solitaire. I won. I dealt the cards again but didn't play.

I got up.

I flipped through one of the books, a thriller called *The Second*

Lady. I got back in bed and tried to read a chapter but couldn't concentrate. My mind drifted without settling.

I put down the book. I folded my hands over my stomach.

What time was it?

Were they going to feed me?

I masturbated indifferently. It took a long time. Then I closed my eyes and curled up tight. My throat pulsed against my hand.

What was Baby doing right now? It was lunchtime, probably. Was she eating alone? I hoped she wasn't alone. Maybe Yaya was sitting with her. Maybe they were serving tomato soup, Baby's favorite, and she was feeling all right today. Maybe she was doing fine.

I uncurled myself. I stared at the ceiling.

I hadn't realized that the house made so much noise. Students shuffling down the halls and slamming doors, clicking silverware and rustling paper. Pipes whooshing in the walls, whispered conversations echoing through vents. The noise had reverberated through my days like memories of a dream. Here in the tower, there was only silence.

I pressed my hands to my temples.

I needed to move.

I sat up on the edge of the bed and took three breaths. I walked to one end of the room. I walked to the other. Then I did it again.

Something clicked. I turned.

A young, skinny, blue-haired new materials concentrator came through the door with a tray. "Oh my God, I'm so late," he mumbled as he set the tray on the tea table. "Sorry, it rained this morning, the yard's all muddy. Took me forever to get across." Then he looked at me with a grin. "Actually, I guess you don't know what time it is, do you?"

I wondered if I should try to cover up with the bedsheet, but he didn't seem to notice my nudity. So I just watched him.

His tray held my dinner: a peel-top plastic cup of apple juice, a slab of grayish chicken breast, carrots from a can, and a green cup filled with wine. But the tray also held a set of plasm pins. He was fiddling with the pins now, picking one up and testing it against the flat of his hand in a way I had never seen before. It beeped.

"All right," he said after a few minutes of this. "Take a seat. Right there on the bed is fine."

"No," I said.

He looked up.

"You're not going to put those on me," I said.

"They don't hurt," he said slowly, as if I were an idiot. "They're, well, kind of nice, actually."

"I don't want this," I said. "I don't want—I don't want to be experimented on. I don't want to be brainwashed. I'm fine."

His eyebrows knit in confusion. "The pins don't *brainwash* you," he said, as if he were offended. "They just give you a little . . . realignment. A mending."

He stared at me, waiting.

But I had already decided: I couldn't do this. I couldn't let those pins hunt through my brain. I had an idea what they might find.

"I don't want those," I said. "I don't want this."

He opened his mouth, then closed it again.

"Where do you think you're going to go?" he finally said. "What are you afraid of?"

"You can leave the food."

He stared at me for a long time, his lips pursed tight. But he said nothing more.

He slammed the door as he left.

The chicken and vegetables tasted fine. It had been a long time since I had eaten anything so plain. I licked my fingers clean of the meat's oil, then drank the wine while reading another chapter in the book.

❧

Over the past months, I had been trapped in Catherine's cycle of teas, breakfasts, lunches, and dinners, mornings and nights, classes and parties, hours, days, and weeks. But now, alone in the tower, I wasn't trapped. I was nowhere.

The wall next to the bed was discolored, the white paint darkened to yellow. I ran my hand over it.

The concentrator's words echoed through me: What was I afraid of?

I lowered my hand and lifted my chin. I didn't know what I was afraid of, but it certainly wasn't him.

I watched the door, as if willing him to come back and fight me. But the door stayed stubbornly closed.

I flopped down in the bed.

How many other students had lain here? Had other sweating backs curled into these sheets? Had other shitty, screwed-up kids been trapped here, hating their bodies and brains?

Did they really get better?

❧

I rubbed my eyes with the heels of my hands. It could be any time of day or night. I could be alive or dead.

The minutes slid by.

The same concentrator, the blue-haired boy, reappeared with the same tray. Sometimes it held a sandwich, other times tea, but always the pins. He never again asked to put them on me. He came, left the pins on the table, and took them with him when he went. Each time I saw them, my heart beat faster.

What was I afraid of?

I clutched my skull.

I couldn't be here anymore. I couldn't be in me.

But I couldn't be anywhere else, either. I had nowhere else to go.

I don't know what made me choose the moment I did. But then I was doing it, clearing my throat to say my first words in days, and touching the concentrator's arm as he set down the tray. His skin was warm and human beneath my fingers.

I said, "I'm not afraid."

His eyelashes fluttered as he glanced at me.

He could tell I was lying. It didn't matter. I was never going to be ready. But there was no other way out.

I watched as he sorted through the plasm pins on the tea table. They beeped and clicked against each other.

"How do they work?" I asked.

He stared at me for a while, as if sizing me up. But he must not have seen anything interesting, because he finally just shrugged.

"Well," he said, lifting one of the pins, "you've seen these used to mend objects, right?"

"In the Shiner videos," I said. "I guess . . . I thought that footage was fake."

He hesitated. "Just because M. Shiner—" He bit his lip, then started again. "He did . . . exaggerate a bit. Obviously. He got a little too excited, and said some things that were a little, um, bombastic. But who wouldn't? When he'd found something so incredible?"

"So it wasn't all a hoax?" I said. "Then what about those other labs, the ones that tried to re-create M. Shiner's experiments? Why couldn't they get plasm to work?"

He smiled slightly. "Those other labs aren't Catherine."

I watched the pin as he lifted it again.

"So," he said. "The pins haven't changed that much since M. Shiner's time. They're pretty basic, really. This end here"—he made the pin chirp—"is the reader. And here on the other end is what we call the 'exchange.' The exchange is kind of like, well, think of it as a kind of plasm magnet. So when used together, the sensors and the exchanges can realign the plasm in your body. I'm simplifying it, but that's the idea." He turned the pin to admire it from another angle. "The pins are simple, but they work. Usually." He was frowning now. "Mending objects like M. Shiner did is a strange science, you know, and a tricky one. Broken things don't talk. But humans do. So we've found that in some ways, it's actually easier to work on humans. The plasm in us isn't any different from the plasm in everything else."

I shivered.

"Anyway, don't worry," he said. "The pins are completely safe. Better than safe, really. The process should be like a kind of . . . guided meditation. You won't feel anything that isn't already there."

"What does that mean?" I said. "What will I feel?"

He shrugged. "Only you can tell us that."

His hands, as he fixed the pins to my body, were quick and sure. He didn't hesitate and didn't talk. The only sound in the room was me clearing my throat and the beeping of the pins. I could smell him, though. He smelled like peppermint.

After he attached the last pin, the one next to my belly button, I touched his arm again.

"Bye," I said.

He turned out the light as he left.

I touched my hair gingerly. I lay back on the pillow.

I waited.

I opened my eyes.

How had I thought the tower was quiet? It buzzed, loudly. The bed buzzed, the shelves buzzed, I buzzed. I was inside them all, the bed, the shelves, the walls, the woods. I was buzzing in them like a tooth in a jaw, a part in a machine.

I put my hands to my head. I could feel the pins sticking into my skull and belly. Was this a dream?

No. I was awake. But where was my body? I couldn't feel it.

Here I was. I was sitting on the bed. I was in the tower, in the house, in the woods, by the dark trees. My hands were on the bed. I was on the bed. I was in the walls, the house.

I was awake.

I turned. Something had made a noise.

The boy, the concentrator, was here. He'd come with someone else, too. They were adjusting the pins.

I didn't feel them. I didn't feel anything.

❧

I lifted my hands.

I was perfect.

❧

But the next time I opened my eyes, I felt sick.

I got up and walked to the other side of the room. I pulled aside the curtain.

I knelt on the bathroom tiles.

I stared at my hands there, splayed in front of the toilet.

I counted my fingers. One, two, three, four, five. One, two, three, four, five.

I counted the tiles. One, two, three, four. One. Two.

The numbers didn't make any sense. There was no difference between me and them.

I opened my mouth. I could taste it there, the poison, in the back of my throat. It tasted like every bad decision I had ever made, every stupid choice that had led our bodies, mine and hers, into that hotel room.

But I wasn't in that hotel room anymore. I had left those bodies behind. And now I was here—here, in the house.

I tried to count the tiles again. One, two—

Then I threw up. I threw up a lot. I let it all come out of me, all the poison, for a very long time. It hurt, but I didn't stop. I didn't stop until it was gone.

I was naked in the bed again. Viktória was standing in front of me, hugging her elbows. She wore a black linen dress.

"I," I said, trying to sit up.

Viktória sat beside me on the bed.

"You're here," Viktória said. "You're safe."

I lay back down. I was covered in sweat, and shivering. The pins had been removed. I could see them in their tray on the tea table.

Viktória tucked the quilt around my body.

"It's over," she said. "Your past life, the things you've done, everything. It's all over. You are never going to speak about it again. Not about your family, your friends, your teachers, your lovers, your enemies. You are never even going to think about them. Because none of it matters. Because it is over. Do you understand?"

I nodded.

"You are new," she said.

She brushed a cool hand over my forehead.

"You did beautifully," she said. "My beautiful girl."

Her wrist smelled like her perfume, like flowers in heat. I pulled it closer.

"How are you feeling?" Viktória said. "Good?"

"Yes," I breathed. "Yes."

❧

I slept in the tower a few hours longer. Then the aide unlocked the door.

After I got dressed, I walked across the yard alone. A pearly, fragrant dawn was breaking over the trees. The house stood huge and dark and solid as an animal, intricate and deep, beneath the translucent clouds. Shadows moved in its windows. Birds flew, singing, over its turrets.

My throat hurt.

Baby turned from her desk as I opened the door to our room.

"How was it?" she said.

I kicked off my sneakers. "Okay."

"Five days," she said. "That's a long time to be gone."

I nodded.

I sat on my bed, then stood up again. I gathered some papers from my desk without really seeing what they were.

"Where are you going?" Baby said. She was tapping her pencil against her lip.

"The library," I said. "I need to work on my Igbo essay."

"Can I come with you?"

I put my books in my bag. "Sure."

I waited patiently as she packed her things.

BABY

After I was released from the tower, I behaved myself. I took cold baths every morning, right after tea with Baby, and dressed in clean clothes. I combed my hair and brushed my teeth. I showed up to class with freshly sharpened pencils and sat at the front of the room. I took notes. I stayed awake. I went to the library and checked out books. I read them, mostly.

But at night, as I lay in bed listening to Baby snore, I was suddenly there again. In the tower. In the dark.

My brain seized. I clutched my stomach.

I lunged to turn on my lamp, then blinked fast at the sudden light. I tried to breathe.

Two moths had slipped through our open window. They quivered now around the lamp.

I waited for my breathing to slow.

The concentrator had told me the truth; I hadn't been brainwashed. I still felt like myself, whatever that meant. And I could still remember the hotel and my life before Catherine. But that life seemed much further away than before, like something that had happened a long time ago in some unimportant world. Yes, I had gotten into trouble. Enough trouble that I couldn't go home without having to answer some ugly questions. Yes, I hadn't been able to stop what happened to that girl. I had run away.

But where had I run to? Where was I now?

I clutched the bed.

I had failed one class last semester: Electricities, of course. I had passed all the others, though. I wasn't expelled, but I was still on academic probation. If I failed a single class this semester, I was out.

I couldn't let that happen. I had to keep going.

Delirious spring blurred into heady, verdant summer. The fig trees' leaves shrouded our bedroom windows. The grass on the yard turned electric-green and grew anxious with the noise of bees and mosquitoes. Clouds of gnats brooded over the weeds.

I spent hours that summer in the garden, behind the brick wall on the west side of the yard. The garden was a darling little fantasy of a place furnished with rows of vegetables and herbs, a stone fountain, tangling rosebushes, and a hill of bluebells. That hill was where graduations were held. The garden reminded me of the illustration from my old book. When the roses bloomed in June, their humid, ancient perfume flustered me. It made me feel like I was going insane.

I used to think of Catherine as a dead place. In those first months, as I passed through gray libraries, parlors, and ballrooms, followed brown hallways into brown courtyards, and fell asleep, drunk and cold, in claw-foot tubs, I felt like a ghost wandering through a dream. But in the velvety summer nights, the house felt vital, like something alive. More than alive; it was mutating.

At first it was strange to take classes in the summer, but the three-year curriculum demanded it. I was taking a class called American Photography that semester. My favorite spread in the textbook was a series of snapshots taken at parties in New York apartments during the 1980s. I spent hours one Friday studying each photo in turn. Slutty, glittery men and women, their eyes glassy with drugs and sex, laughed as they kissed each other. Lipstick smeared across their faces. They danced until they blurred.

I was so lost in the photos that I was late to that night's session.

When I arrived, the chanting had already begun. Viktória stood by the windows in a white dress. The great hall reverberated with her voice and the echoed response.

I slipped into a chair next to a tiny freckled girl. I folded my hands.

I am in the house, I said. *My hands are on the table. The house is in the woods.*

My brain slumped, drunk. Machine noise, steel drilling against steel, reverberated through my teeth. The noise stopped, then started again. I pulled the pillow over my head. I dreamed that a mad scientist was boring into my skull.

When I woke up, it was midmorning and I wasn't home. I was in Ashley, in some girl's room. I could hear her moaning in the bathroom. She'd invited me over to study for our Japanese Prints midterm. She'd brought the flash cards and I'd brought the wine.

"Are you okay?" I called to her.

She burped.

I crawled over to the window, the blanket still pulled over my head.

We were in the Ashley tower, looking over the yard. I hadn't dreamed the noise; a Ferris wheel had been constructed on the grass. It loomed, inhuman and sinister as a spaceship, over a neon-blue high striker, cornhole game, and tug-of-war rope. A bouncy castle swayed in the breeze. On the far side of the yard, aides were setting up grills and picnic blankets. The trees' trunks were wrapped in blue and yellow ribbons.

The Founders' Festival. I'd almost forgotten.

I got dressed and slipped downstairs.

Out on the yard, I stared up at the Ferris wheel. It was huge and silent, blinking slow in the dense, muggy atmosphere.

"Baby," I called. I could see her in the distance, hugging her elbows as she watched the cotton candy machine churn.

"Hello, dear," I said as I approached her. "Did your midterms go okay?"

"Yes," she said.

"Did you want cotton candy?"

The machine whirred like an engine. An aide twisted a pile of the pink stuff onto a paper cone. Baby eyed the cone without expression. "No," she said.

I laced my arm through hers.

"I'm happy to see you," I said.

She let me hold her arm.

A five-man brass band was arranging itself on a makeshift stage, unfolding chairs and pulling horns out of cases. As I watched them, I felt myself move closer, as if drawn by some thrilling perfume. They weren't Catherine students. They wore suits and ties and whispered to one another as they eyed us. Sweat dampened their armpits.

Yaya and Anna stood watching them, too, giggling.

"Aren't they dreamy?" Yaya said as we came near. "Guess Viktória decided we should get some real entertainment for our precious founders. Whoever they were."

"Do you think the band will be let inside?" I said. "In the house?"

"Ha," Yaya said. "I'd like to see one of them try. Viktória will have them peeing in the bushes." She peered at Baby over the top of her peppermint-pink plastic sunglasses. "Girl, what's wrong?"

"Nothing," Baby said.

"Your eyes are red."

"I'm tired."

The tuba player, all skinny arms and wiry dreadlocks, glanced around with nervous energy as he adjusted the instrument over his shoulder. His eyes flickered over the yard, the house, and us, the goggling kids shifting around him. He wouldn't meet any of our eyes. When some second-year playing cornhole gave a triumphant shriek, he jumped, startled by the sound.

What did we look like to him? Scrawny, shaggy-haired, furry-legged beasts? Lunatics in matching outfits?

The tuba player wasn't a lunatic. He was perfectly normal. He probably lived in a condo in Scranton, maybe, or Allentown, one with wall-to-wall carpeting and vertical blinds. He bought his toothpaste and dish soap at a drugstore. He had a pet dog, a mutt, and a girlfriend, maybe. He took her to breakfast at Denny's. She ordered a Belgian waffle with bacon. He got the Grand Slam.

Tomorrow morning, at Denny's, he would tell his girlfriend about the famous Catherine House. He would say it didn't seem so haunted, really. Or maybe he would bend in and whisper that it was just as strange as the stories said.

"The Ferris wheel's starting," Yaya said. "Wanna go?"

"No," I said.

"Come with me."

"I'm not going up there."

"Are you afraid of heights?"

"Look at that thing. Who installed it? It could fall to pieces right when we're at the top. You don't know. It's not safe."

"Oh my God, this is adorable," Yaya said. "I thought you were fearless."

We went into the bouncy castle instead. Baby disappeared back into the house while Yaya, Anna, and I crawled one by one into the orange dream. Nick appeared with cups of wine and we tried to drink, woozy and wobbling, but kept falling down.

"This is delicious," Anna said, licking her lips as she crouched in one of the corners. She was wearing her new Pearl Jam tour T-shirt, the only commissary clothing I'd ever seen her excited about. She'd spent all her points on it. "Wine is amazing. I almost forgot."

"Cheers," Yaya said, "to you finally escaping that awful concentration."

"You're not applying for plasm anymore?" I said.

"Nope. It was going to kill me." Anna said it with indifference. "Theo's still applying, though. Baby is, too, right?"

"Yes," I said.

Nick stood up. He bounced. We all rebounded. Yaya's sunglasses went flying off her nose.

"Do you know . . ." I said. "The new materials concentrators—when do they get passes to the umbrella room?"

"The what?" Anna handed Yaya's sunglasses back to her.

"The room in the hallway with the umbrella wallpaper. Not the regular plasm lab, the one downstairs in the Ashley basement, I think. It's locked with a keypad."

"Oh, that's M. Neptune's lab. Only M. Neptune's students get to work in there. Even if you're in the concentration, you have to be working with him specially to get in."

Nick flopped on the floor. We all bounced again. "This is amazing," he declared. "I'm going to live here."

"Does that make you a bouncy king?" Yaya said.

"Yes," he said. "Bouncy king of the bouncy castle."

"What kind of work does he do?" I said. "M. Neptune?"

"Some kind of specialized plasm research, I guess. Who knows?" Anna swirled her cup of wine with a shrug. "None of *us* are ever going to find out."

There was a testy edge to her voice now. Her cheeks were flushed.

Yaya straddled Nick. She kissed him on the mouth.

The day our midterm grades were posted, I stayed out late with a boy. By the time I stopped by the registrar's office, it was four in the morning.

I found my envelope in the bin outside the office and pulled out my grade sheet. I scanned the numbers.

Most of my classes were fine. Not great, but fine. Except for Japanese Prints. Japanese Prints I might fail.

I closed the sheet. I'd memorized the difference between the Katsukawa school and Kaigetsud school and that was pretty much it. I had to do better.

I walked back to my room, my hands in my pockets. As I made my way through the house, I listened for the construction workers pounding at the baths in the Harrington basement. I'd heard rumors about the baths for months; apparently Catherine's founders had built an expansive, luxurious complex of underground pools under the house when the school was first established. The baths had been closed for years, but over the past few weeks workers had been coming every morning and leaving every night. Though I heard the workers, I never saw them. I don't think they ever saw us, either.

I opened the door to our room expecting Baby to be asleep. She was still up, sitting straight-backed at her desk.

"Hello, Ines," she said without turning.

She was fully dressed, with shoes on and hair pulled into a tight French braid. The room smelled like soap bubbles. She had just taken a bath.

I shoved my grades in my pocket as I walked over to her desk. She was folding a piece of paper, running her fingers along the fold to tighten the crease.

"What's that?" I said.

"A horse."

"Origami?"

She nodded, flipping the paper over. "I used to do it more. I don't know why I stopped."

I sat on my bed. Both of our desk lamps were on. The night outside was shapeless with the dark and our translucent shadows on the window.

Baby flipped the paper and made another crease.

"Do you want a banana?" she said. She gestured to the bunch on her desk. "I took them from tea. I don't know why I thought I could eat them all. They'll go bad soon. I don't want them—to go bad."

"Sure."

She broke one off. I opened my hands, gesturing for her to toss it over, but she only stared. I got up and took it from her hands.

She watched blankly as I peeled the banana.

"I'm going to the tower," she said.

I swallowed my bite of banana.

"Are you surprised?" She wasn't meeting my eye.

"A little."

"I cheated on my chemistry test."

I put the banana down. I moved to sit on her bed.

"I knew I was going to fail," she said. "I didn't have time to study after biology—and I was supposed to take biology last semester, you know. If I had taken more advanced classes in high school, I wouldn't have had to take Biology III and Chemistry III at the same time, and my midterms wouldn't have coincided like this. Anyway. I was in M. Tran's office asking for clarification about one of the labs. I knew he was administering the chemistry midterm, too. And when he went down the hall to get his notes, I thought he might have copies of the test right there in his drawer. And he did. So I took one."

She placed the origami horse on the desk.

"When M. Tran told me to stay after class today, I wasn't even surprised. I knew I was going to get caught. And you know what? I'm glad. I'm glad they caught me." She wiped her nose, though she didn't seem to be crying. "I've been doing those interviews for the concentration, you know? And the professors ask more and more questions, watch me closer and closer, and—I have no idea what they're looking for. But whatever it is, I don't have it. I'm not smart enough. I'm not strong enough. I don't have anything special, and I don't want anything. I don't even want to die."

"Lie down with me," I said.

Baby didn't look up as she crawled into bed with me. I wrapped my arms around her.

"It's going to be okay," I said.

"Yes. It is. I'm not even so upset, really. Viktória . . ." Baby cleared her throat, her voice stronger at the mention of Viktória's name. "Viktória and I, we're going to have a nice long talk before I go into the tower. Can you believe that? Just me and her. You're not the only one she cares about, you know. She—sees me, too."

I ran my hand over her shoulder.

"I have this dream," Baby whispered. "It's not that I'm a different person or that I'm gone, exactly. I'm still here. But I'm not myself. I'm full of light, only light, shining forever. I don't feel any more pain. All I am is beautiful."

I wished I could see her eyes, but she lay facing the wall.

"I thought plasm was that light. I believed in it. But I'm not sure anymore." Baby shifted in the bed. "I'm messed up," she said. "I told you. So they're sending me to the tower to fix me."

"When are you going?" I said.

"Tomorrow morning. Well, today now. Seven o'clock."

"For how long?"

"Two weeks."

My throat clenched. I held her tighter. Two weeks, fourteen days and fourteen nights, in that blank, empty room.

"It's not so bad," I said. "It's a little vacation, really. And you'll feel so much better when you get out. You'll feel brand-new."

"Yes," she said. "I think so. I wish I weren't missing forums. But I think this is the right thing."

"I'll miss you."

"No, you won't. You'll have the bathroom to yourself." She shifted in the bed. "You'll love it."

I ran a hand over her forehead. I closed my eyes.

"You should," Baby whispered. "You should believe in it."

"Believe in what?"

But she didn't answer. She was falling asleep. So was I.

When I opened my eyes, the sun was shining across our floorboards. I was still in Baby's bed, but Baby was gone.

I sat up, rubbed my face. My mouth was mucked up with sleep.

❧

Baby went into the tower in the beginning of July, the first day of forums. Forums were a series of presentations from the second-years that were supposed to synthesize their previous years of study and outline their plans for third-year tutorials, our final projects. The presentations were directed toward their professors and advisors, but the larger Catherine community was invited to attend as our schedules permitted.

I sometimes skipped classes to go to forums. They were held in the Harrington auditorium, one of the coolest rooms in the house during the summer months, and snacks were usually provided. I would sit in the back of the room so I was closest to the platters of melon balls and mint iced tea. The tea tasted lavishly sweet and cool.

The presentations varied. Some were creative, like preparatory outlines for scripts or stories, or analyses of Latin texts, or dissections of particular critical approaches to early twentieth century American literature. Others were more research-based, presenting new histories of various mathematical proofs or color theorems. But no matter the topic, the questions from the professors were ferocious. A student would barely begin to speak before the interrogators set in. *This approach has already been challenged in recent years. How do you plan to differentiate your work from what has already been done? How can we extend this model in a meaningful way? Are you taking this work seriously?* Students would step down from the stage red-faced and shaking. One girl, after discussing her work on Vodon folk myths, sobbed with pleasure when her advisor only commented that her ideas seemed "adequate enough."

Viktória usually arrived late. Her heels would click over the parquet floor as she slid into the seat beside M. Neptune. Then she watched in perfect stillness, face impassive and chin in her hand, saying nothing. At the end of each presentation, she jotted a note on her pad of paper, her tiny gold wristwatch glinting.

"But you've *misunderstood*," a professor said. It was the final day of forums. The presenter, a chubby redheaded girl with huge watery eyes, had spent the past twenty minutes on Alexander Rodchenko's design for a Soviet workers' club, and something she said seemed to have offended her advisor. "It is not just a *propaganda* machine. His space, this club—it is a *utopia*. A new world, beautiful. Do you not see?"

The girl nodded. Her chin trembled.

"Painful," Yaya whispered as she laid down a card. We were in the back of the auditorium, playing Go Fish. "Just let the poor girl go home and cry."

A new materials concentrator went next. I recognized him as the same acne-faced boy who had tried to pin me during our coming in ceremony.

As he introduced himself to the auditorium—his name was Burt—two aides wheeled a wooden stand and cart onto the stage.

I couldn't see what was on the cart, but rafts of heavy fabric hung from the stand's posts. It took a moment for me to recognize the fabric as the remains of a ripped and faded tapestry.

Burt turned his back to us and faced the cart. I heard the clink of metal instruments. Plasm pins.

Yaya poked me. "Any queens?"

"No," I said. "Go fish."

"You are such a fucking liar."

"Shh." A third-year turned to glare at us.

"Over these past semesters," Burt was saying, "my new materials classes have focused on plasm theory, research, and analysis using data from the, um, the *valid* past experiments, with the assumption that this data is still relevant." He cleared his voice and spoke louder. "But this is not necessarily the case. Some of these experiments were performed twenty years ago. The experiments did produce fantastic results in object, body, and psychosexual healing—or *mending*, to use the proper term." He inclined his head. "But we must move forward with the assumption that today's even more rigorous methodologies, more . . . more careful science can produce results that are just as fantastic. If we recreate some of these original plasm experiments, if we attempt to once again understand plasm directly, not through theory but through its use, through observed results—"

"Burt, my friend," M. Neptune said. He was tapping his pen against the armrest he shared with Viktória. "Come on. You're telling us things we already know, and being way too vague besides. Say what you really mean, and be precise. What are the parameters of your tutorial, specifically?"

Burt flushed. "I want to . . . I will reperform one of M. Shiner's early experiments, the mending of the tapestry. I will mend three of the early tapestries in Catherine's collection using plasm manipulation. I've already been working on this one." He gestured to the fabric hanging from the stand. "M. Donna says I would need to complete two more and do a write-up to meet the project requirements."

"Great," M. Neptune said. He jotted down a note. "But really, when you submit your proposal, remember to be specific. You're one of the few new materials concentrators submitting an experimental research project. You're going to have to be totally clear about the limitations here. I don't need to explain why that's important."

For a moment Burt looked like he was about to retort. But he just pressed his lips together and nodded.

An aide turned off the lights, and the auditorium filled with gray shadow.

Burt stepped in front of the tapestry. He seemed to be pressing the pins onto the fabric one by one along the rip, as if he were sewing. The tapestry lifted and dropped.

Then he stepped away. And the tapestry kept going, lifting along the rip, sewing itself together.

Burt spoke as he worked, applying more pins and adjusting them on the fabric—something about pattern sensing and temperature corrections. But I couldn't hear him. I was watching the tapestry come together.

"Hey," Yaya was whispering. "Ines. Any kings?"

So far I could only see the top of the image. It was the hand of a Roman god, lifting a silver cup.

"Ines." Yaya snapped her fingers in front of my nose.

I looked back down at my cards. I had three kings.

"No," I said. "Go fish."

I did miss Baby while she was in the tower. Those July nights were cloyingly hot, and I didn't sleep well without her. I would sprawl across my bedcovers breathing out of my mouth and staring at her desk, wishing she were there. I missed her noises and smells: her sniffles and pencil scratchings, her cinnamon toothpaste and almond hair cream. I just missed her. I hated being alone.

I hoped the tower would be good for her, though. If the plasm pins could sew the tapestry back together, maybe they could do the same for Baby's heart and brain—fix them so she felt better. I didn't understand what the tower had done to me. But whatever it was, I hoped it would help Baby.

The days were even hotter than the nights. The house wasn't well ventilated. By late afternoon, the classrooms were so humid and fetid they made me feel drunk. I watched sweat gleam on the back of students' necks as their drowsy heads bobbed. The parlors, with their heavy curtains drawn to keep out the sun, grew colorless and dim. The halls smelled like sweat, sunscreen, and like Catherine, a woody, dead-rose perfume that stifled my nose and mouth.

When I wasn't in class or hunched over a computer in the lab, I was out on the yard. I brought my books, as if I were studying, and lay dead on the grass. I pulled my T-shirt up over my stomach. I closed my eyes.

We spent evenings after dinner out on the yard, too, drinking iced tea mixed with moonshine. We did our homework and gossiped. As the nights grew later, we whispered about the outside world.

"I hope the Bulls are having a good season," Henry said. "I miss them, the Bulls. Isn't that stupid?"

"Do you know what I miss?" I said. "Sour Patch Kids. I could eat a whole bag of Sour Patch Kids right now."

Henry turned to me. "I never thought of you as someone who'd like candy."

"I like candy."

"I miss my brother," Anna said.

I took a sip of my moonshine tea.

She blinked drunkenly. I brushed her hair from her face.

One endless Thursday afternoon, I wandered into Theo's room alone. I didn't know what made me do it except that his door was the only one open in the hushed hallway; everyone was in class, like I should have been, and tea was still hours away.

I pressed his door open farther. No, he wasn't home. His room was silent and tidy as ever, his bed crisply made and books neatly arranged. Today he had a plate of shortbread cookies on his desk. He always seemed to have some snack there.

I walked to his window and peered down at the Molina courtyard. I liked viewing the courtyard from different angles. It made me feel like I was someone completely different, seeing things in a completely different way. Theo's window was obscured by the leaves of a fig tree. I could barely make out the benches, painted tiles, and stone fountain.

As I turned from the window, a flash of color caught my eye. Something slipped behind the radiator. I fished it out.

It was a photograph. A stiff, older black woman sitting on a pink couch, her shoulders strained in a way that made me think she was in pain. The coffee table in front of her was cluttered with tea candles, Minnie Mouse figurines, a wobbling stack of cassettes, a dirty cereal bowl and spoon. Her face was tough, her eyes wide and frank in a way I instantly recognized. She must have been related to Theo. His grandmother, probably.

And there he was, in the background, in graying socks, frying something up on a creaky old stove. He was sticking out his tongue and winking at the camera. His legs were knob-kneed and skinny.

I stared at the photograph for a long time before slipping it back behind the radiator.

The summer drawled on.

There was a hole in my bedroom window screen. Every night I was startled awake by a sudden horrible mosquito drone by my skull. By morning, everything itched. I scratched until I was red and puffy all over.

I did catch a mosquito, once. I was alone, lying awake in the pale morning light, and saw it land on the wall by my bed. It stood, legs arched, so silent and still, waiting. I smacked it dead.

Baby died on the hottest day of the summer, a day so hot the third-years upstairs decided they couldn't take it anymore; they were going to break into the baths. Yaya overheard their plan: The rooms, down in the Harrington basement, were still roped off, but apparently the pools had been filled and chlorinated days ago. The administration was waiting for some final inspection, but the construction workers were gone. No one was watching.

After dinner, Yaya and I crept together through the halls. We went down the stairs, through a snaking shadowed hall, slipped beneath a construction rope, and opened the door to the baths.

I felt I had crept into a mountain, into some dank palace grotto built by gnomes. The low ceilings were ribbed with hundreds of tiles that arched over a grand green expanse of pool and, on the other side of the room, a steam bath. Naked students splashed in the water, laughing and kissing and drifting around one another with wine bottles held aloft. The air was heavy with humidity and the overwhelming smell of chlorine.

I peeled off my T-shirt and jeans and slipped into the pool. At first the water shocked my bare skin. But soon it felt luxuriously smooth and cool.

I leaned back and closed my eyes. I floated.

Someone tapped my shoulder. I opened my eyes. Yaya gestured her bottle of wine to me.

Hours later, I walked alone back to Molina, my brain dully buzzing. Through the fog, I heard voices echo from down the hall.

I turned into the parlor.

Our grade dean, M. David, stood there with Anna and one of our few international students, a tiny strawberry-curled girl named Paola. A lamp was on, its yellow glow weak in the dawning daylight. Anna and Paola must have been up all night studying. Their Modern Philosophy books and notes were strewn across the table, the notes now forgotten. Paola was holding her hand pressed against her mouth. M. David, dressed in a full suit, stood with his arms folded tight to his chest.

The three of them turned to me as I came in.

M. David glanced at his watch. "It's four-thirty in the morning," he said. "You should go back to sleep."

"I wasn't asleep," I said.

Anna said, "You have to tell her."

M. David shot Anna a glare. She didn't flinch. Her eyes were shining and her hair was frizzed up at the crown. She looked too tired and sad to be intimidated.

"She was her roommate," Anna whispered.

"What happened," I said, "to Baby?"

M. David sighed.

"We planned to talk to you all in the morning," he finally said. "I didn't mean to run into . . . I didn't want any of you to find out like this."

He dropped his arms.

"Barbara has passed away," he said. "Her—she was found in the tower yesterday."

Birds were chittering in the fig trees outside.

"I don't understand," Paola gasped. Her face was wet with tears. "She was in the tower. She should have been safe, no?"

"When someone chooses to go," M. David said slowly, "nothing can be done to stop them."

"She *murdered* herself." Paola hiccupped a sob.

"He's not going to tell us," Anna said. She wasn't crying. Her voice was steady and low. "He's not going to tell us anything." She looked at M. David. "You fucked up."

"Miss Montgomery," M. David snapped. "The circumstances of Barbara's death are a private matter—"

"This isn't private, this is a *school*—" Anna began, but M. David continued, louder:

"I do wish the news hadn't come out like this, but now that it has, I hope you will respect Barbara's family's wishes during this difficult time and refrain from such prurient speculation."

Anna's cheeks were still flushed, but she didn't look angry. She looked hurt.

"Ines," M. David said, turning to me. "We will want to meet with you tomorrow." He blinked three times. "I can only imagine this will be quite disruptive for the Molina community, for you especially. I imagine . . . you must have been quite close."

He blinked again.

"Yes," I said.

M. David kept talking. He said something about counseling sessions, a memorial, gathering her things. I didn't hear most of it. I just watched his face as I waited for him to finish.

When he did, I went to the bathroom. I peed. Then I went back to the room I had shared with Baby.

Her bed was made, its pale coverlet stark in the now-brilliant dawn. Her papers were still there, arranged in neat piles. Her shoes were lined up by the door. Her closet was closed. The only thing out of place was her brush, out on her desk. A tangle of dark, intimate hair was still there, caught in its plastic bristles.

One of the images we had to memorize for my American Photography course was a print of a young boy astride a stallion in a desert landscape. The boy's mouth was set in a determined frown, his arm tense with power as it grasped the rein. The sunset behind him was wild and courageous. A simple portrait of the heroic American West.

But as I'd stared at the portrait, I'd noticed something: The boy's other hand, the one not holding the rein, rested on his thigh. It seemed he hadn't known what to do with it. He was picking at his cuticle. He was just a boy.

Cameras were forbidden at Catherine. At first I thought this was to maintain the house's privacy and isolation; the administration wouldn't have wanted the *New York Times* style section running some silly snapshot of our great hall or auditorium. Now I saw it was more than that. Photographs, in their honesty, would have captured the house's specifics—the peeling wallpaper and dirty wineglasses—but missed the smell of the garden in June. Photographs would flatten it all into real, dull detail, and Catherine didn't want detail. Catherine wanted glamour.

I wished I had a picture of Baby, though, the way Theo had one of his grandmother. Maybe one of her examining Billie Jean, peering at him in that shrewd way of hers, poking at his tentacle. Or her studying in bed, feet propped up on the headboard. I didn't care what she was doing as long as there was something that was real about it, something I didn't quite expect. Maybe the shape of her nose had been different than I thought, or she had flexed her toes in a way I didn't remember.

Because Baby had been bigger than me. She wasn't mine. She wasn't anyone's.

Days passed and people said nice things about her. She was such a good student and friend; what a pity it was that her life ended so tragically, so soon. And I, too, crafted my own story of her short life and death, the sad plot points that led to this somehow self-evident end.

But that wasn't right. Her life wasn't a story, and it didn't have to end this way. She was a girl. She was real. It was true.

Baby's memorial was held on Friday in the Molina parlor. All of the Molina first-years were there, leaning against walls and squeezing four to a sofa. A few of her professors came, too, and students from other halls, some upperclassmen. Some of them I didn't even recognize.

Why were they here? They hadn't known Baby. No one knew Baby.

I didn't sit with anyone. I stood by the door, hugging my stomach.

Lukewarm cups of tea and plates of cookies drifted around the room. Porcelain clinked.

Paola was sitting on the floor, leaning forward with an eager tilt. She wiped her face with a crumpled tissue. Her mouth was buckled in a silent sob. Her eyes roved the room before squeezing out a few more tears.

A plate of pastries arrived in front of me. I picked an empire biscuit with a glacé cherry.

The vase on the mantel held a bouquet of long-stemmed lilies. The bruised blooms drooped with the heat. Their extravagant fragrance intoxicated me.

Viktória sat in one of the armchairs, legs crossed, hair brushed behind her ears. Her face, so exposed, looked frank and drawn. Something was different about her eyes today. Whatever it was, she seemed younger.

She had been staring down at a slip of paper on her lap, idly turning her ring around her finger. Now she laid the paper on the side table and looked up. The parlor quieted.

"We're here today," Viktória said, "to honor the memory of Barbara Pearce—Baby—our dear child."

Viktória wasn't wearing mascara. That's what was different. Her eyes looked tired, naked.

Paola sniffled theatrically.

Someone tried to pass me a teacup, except I was still holding the biscuit. I hadn't eaten any of it. I set it down to take the teacup. "Thank you," I said.

"Baby represented the best of Catherine," Viktória said. "She was creative, diligent, and rapaciously intelligent. She was a beloved classmate and friend. Her professors, two of whom will speak today, were endlessly impressed by her thoughtful scholarship and dedication to her work. She had big dreams. She aspired to devote her life to the study of new materials, of plasm. She wanted to stand on the frontier of our future world, to pioneer new ways of relating to our bodies, our minds, and our environments. There is no doubt in my mind that she could have done it. I truly believe she had the heart and the intellect to change the course of history. But every girl, every boy, every woman and man, everyone has a private struggle that is sometimes too much to bear. Baby hurt. And so now . . . we hurt."

Viktória touched her heart. Her nails were unpolished.

"We hurt," she said, "because we miss her. This is understandable, of course. But it is not necessary. Because Baby doesn't hurt anymore. She is home now, truly home. Yes, in some ways she is gone. But she is also everywhere. She is in our windows and trees and walls. She is with us in the library, and in the dining halls as we eat our desserts. She is everywhere in this house, in everything. I believe that. I do."

Viktória's fingers clutched at her heart, eyes lowered.

"I can feel her," she whispered. "Here." She opened her eyes. "Can't you?"

I looked down at the cup. The tea had been over-steeped. It was so dark it looked almost like blood.

❧

I spent the last stunningly hot days before finals alone in the library. I wrote long lists of artists, stared at textbook images of photographs, and memorized dates. *Lewis Hine, 1910. Frederick Sommer, 1943.* I wiped sweat off my neck. I rewrote my class notes for Japanese Prints and German again and again. When I couldn't keep my eyes open anymore, I napped on the library floor, underneath a desk. Then I crawled right back out and opened my books again. I studied until I was stupid.

After lurching through finals, I returned to what had once been our shared bedroom for the first time in days.

Baby's bed was stripped bare, her desk emptied. Her dresser had been cleaned out. Everything of hers was gone.

I sat on my bed.

How could Viktória feel Baby here?

None of us at Catherine had seen her body before it was taken away. Did her parents get to see her one last time? Did they arrange for an open casket? Her family must have organized a funeral. One in a nice church, with a sermon and singing and a reception in the basement serving fruit punch, pound cake, and macaroni and cheese. All of her family and friends and old teachers would be there, remembering what she was like when she was a cheery little girl. They would touch her hand as they bent over the casket to say goodbye.

At lunch and dinner, I heard students whispering, wondering what had really happened to Baby. If she killed herself in the tower, how had she done it? Did she hang herself with a bedsheet? Someone's cousin knew a boy who had hanged himself with a bedsheet. It could be done.

I didn't care. I knew that however it happened, it was Baby's choice. That was all that mattered. Baby had given everything to Catherine. She believed in Catherine. When I remembered the joy in her eyes as she chanted during sessions, I couldn't help but think that in the end—the very end—she was happy and full of light.

I picked up my grades from the registrar's office on a bright blue August day. I found my envelope in the bin, slid out the sheet, and unfolded the letter. I scanned the page.

A B+ in American Photography, two Cs, and a D. The D was in Japanese Prints, of course. And below that, an official confirmation of my acceptance into the concentration in history of art.

I'd passed. I was no longer on academic probation. I was officially here at Catherine for two more years.

The envelope included a list of everyone in our class along with their concentration. Yaya had been accepted into mathematics. Diego was in history of art with me, and Anna in chemistry. Theo was the only one of us accepted to the new materials concentration.

Baby wasn't listed at all.

I folded up the sheet.

I didn't take my usual walk to the great hall that day. Instead, I turned to pass by the parlor where the black girls held their salon.

The door was closed, but when I bent close I could smell their honey-rose hair creams, hear their secret laughter.

I stared at the door for a while, and then kept going.

In the great hall, at lunch, I saw my friends gathered in our usual corner of the Molina table. Anna waved to me. She was wearing her Pearl Jam T-shirt. I felt a surge of affection for her right then, but didn't feel like talking to anyone. I pretended I didn't see her. I grabbed two big handfuls of blueberries from the dessert service before leaving.

I ate the blueberries as I walked to the parlor. Their juice stained the tips of my fingers.

Two more years.

I sat in the window seat. I leaned against the glass.

Today was graduation day for the third-years. The ceremony was private but I knew it took place in the garden, in the bluebell field. The third-years would wear the yellow and blue sashes I had seen hanging in the laundry. Daisy garlands would circle their heads. After the ceremony, they would dance all night.

Over the past semesters, I had watched the house as if through glass. I was never really here. I wasn't anywhere. But Baby, my mean, precious Baby—Baby had been here. According to Viktória, she was here still.

Don't worry, I whispered to Baby. I'm here too. I'm staying with you.

I sucked on a blueberry and fell asleep slumped by the window. When I woke up, it was time for dinner.

Year Two

FUTURISM

M. David glared down at us from the auditorium stage. He had spent the past half hour trying to confirm that we were ready for the new semester—that we'd finalized our class schedules and refilled our supplies, submitted our grades and picked up our laundry. But none of us were listening. His sign-up sheets drifted down rows and crammed themselves between seats. He kept clearing his throat with a snippy raise of his eyebrows. I might have been the only one who noticed.

It wasn't our fault we couldn't pay attention. It was dozy late afternoon, and we were full on a rich lunch of the last summer produce: peas in butter, mushrooms with braised lettuce, and for dessert, pineapples filled with berries, almonds, and vanilla ice cream. We didn't care about the fall semester. We just wanted to nap.

Yaya leaned her head against my shoulder. "Wake me up when I've graduated," she mumbled.

One year ago, I had sat in this same auditorium for Catherine orientation. I had been up in the balcony, far from the introductory video with its long shots of then-unfamiliar rooms and explanations of rules I had no intention of following. Back then, every aspect of the auditorium—the nap of the navy velvet seats, the bronzed ceiling's greasy sheen, the water-damaged walls—had seemed softened and blurred by distance. Now I sat down in the front with Yaya, Theo, Nick, and Anna—kids who were my friends, actual friends—watching M. David pace the stage in his sharp, familiar way, and I could hardly remember this room ever feeling new. What had the auditorium smelled like then? Did it smell like this, like clover? Had I been able to hear the lawn mower outside, droning like a lazy bee? Had the sun shone in this lemony way? And the students who lounged around me, faces so recognizable as they flickered with whispers and giggles—had they all been here, too, back then?

The door banged open. M. David scowled at the students trooping in late, but they didn't seem to notice him. They were too busy whistling and waving at their friends in the back. M. David rubbed his eyes with the heels of his hands.

"Name three cars," Anna said. She and Nick were playing MASH.

Nick idly twisted a blond curl around his finger. "Dodge Viper. Aston Martin DB5. A Mustang, let's say . . . 1967. Oh, or a Porsche, the 911 Turbo. My uncle got one last year. He's going through the most fabulous midlife crisis."

"Well, that's all very nice, but I said name three cars, not every car."

"Can I do a motorcycle?"

"No, and you're taking too long, so I'm deciding for you. You're getting a Dodge, a Mustang, or a Ford Probe." She scribbled on her paper. "Now, three girls."

"Wait," Nick said. "Come on. Put in the Porsche."

"For those only just arriving, please seat yourselves quietly, if you can *possibly* manage that," M. David called toward the back of the room. A peal of distracted laughter rang out from up in the balcony.

"How many kids do you think you might have?" Anna asked Nick. "Three? Four?"

"Zero? Babies are foul."

"Let's say five to eight." She scribbled again.

Theo gave Nick a thoughtful look, chin on his fist. "I could see you with babies. Eight fat babies."

"If you have not already discussed your semester plan with your advisor, I would advise you to set up a meeting to do so at your *earliest* convenience," M. David said, louder now. "This is your second year. That means the work will become harder, not easier. We aren't going to hold your hand anymore. Your studies are your responsibility. And— Where are you going?"

A girl was hopping by the door. "I have to pee," she said.

"*Please* be seated."

She sat down right where she was, cross-legged, on the rug.

"You're going to marry Claudia Schiffer," Anna said, "and drive a Mustang, and have seven babies, and live in a shack. Congratulations."

"Please also keep in mind," M. David was saying, "this summer, in just a few short months, you will find yourselves on this very stage, at forums, presenting your work to your peers and to this community of scholars."

Somehow, the auditorium had quieted.

"Your studies of the past year, and those of the coming semesters, all converge into this one presentation, and that will lead into your tutorial. While you do not need to have already finalized your topic, each of you should be planning with your advisors. Make sure you're taking the requisite classes. Get yourselves on track. I know that right now it seems like you have all the time in the world, but these semesters go quickly. Before you know it, the year will be gone, and you will be here."

M. David gestured toward the stage.

"Now is the time," he said, "when you must decide what you are doing here at Catherine. And you must be sure."

He cleared his throat. He seemed uncertain what to do with our attention now that he had it.

"That is all for now," he finally said. "Please pass the sign-up sheets to me."

"My advisor has no idea what she's doing," Nick said as we slunk through the hallways. "I think she's been trying to seduce me. It's wonderful."

"Mine's terrible, too," Anna said. "And she's still disappointed because I decided against new materials. Speaking of . . ." She tugged Theo's sleeve. "Congratulations on getting into the concentration. Aren't you excited?"

"I'm kinda nervous, to be honest," Theo said, though he didn't look it. He was focused on peeling an orange. "Lab starts next week."

"Don't be nervous," she said. "They don't accept anyone who couldn't do it. But this is probably going to be the last time we ever see you. That course load is no joke."

"Goodbye, kid," Nick said. "Claudia and I are going to miss you."

Theo threw an orange slice at him.

❧

So Catherine swung into the new year. The dining rooms served dishes I remembered from my first few months here: squash soup, zucchini salad, cold rainbow trout arranged on glittering beds of ice. Our shorts and sandals were taken away and our closets restocked with the familiar jeans, sneakers, and sweaters, sized to fit our new bodies. Somehow, despite all the rich food, we were all skinnier.

One night I was reading one of my old Betty and Veronica comics in bed when I suddenly shivered. A cool, mossy breeze had slipped through my open window.

I got up, stood in front of the cracked window, and closed my eyes. The breeze smelled like fall and decay and the woods—like my first days at Catherine.

M. David's words rang in my head: *You must decide what you are doing here.*

Did anyone really know what they were doing here? Was anyone sure?

Baby had known. Baby had been sure. She'd hurt, yes, but she knew what she was doing.

I closed the window.

Much was the same as that first fall at Catherine, but not everything. The third-years were gone. Baby was gone. And I was older.

A new class of students arrived. I spent their move-in day hiding in the Molina library, but even there I could hear the noise of their invasion. Suitcases clunked on stairs and sneakers squeaked down the halls as they ran back and forth to the commissary. They yelled to their ushers, pleading for more soap, refilled prescriptions, and phone credits. They were idiots. I napped with a pillow over my head.

By the next day, the halls were filled with their unfamiliar faces, smells, and hair they seemed to shed like dogs. They hovered together outside bathrooms and below stairways, trying not to seem as lost as they were. They referred to their professors as *Mister* and *Miz* and spent hours arguing with the pharmacists about their prescriptions. And they never knew where to sit in the great hall. They just lingered around the dessert service.

But they were nice enough, and they were new. They were suntanned. Their hair was shiny and cut into deliberate styles. When we asked, they gave us hints as to what was happening outside. America's president had been reelected and a new Nintendo system released. They spoke in unfamiliar voices with unfamiliar accents. They had unfamiliar bodies. They came to our parties, and we watched them, and they felt us watching them.

"They think they're such hot shit," Anna said, eyeing the girls on the other side of the morning room.

"They *are* hot shit," Theo said through a mouthful of banana.

"Just because they're, like, the new kids on the block," Anna said. The girls were sharing a plate of pear slices, giggling as their eyes darted around the room. "Like their shit doesn't stink."

"I just feel bad for them. They don't know how stupid they are." Yaya stirred at her yogurt. "Anyway. Growing up is fabulous. I plan on getting better with age."

"I can see that," Theo said. "You're going to be a very sexy grandma."

Yaya licked yogurt from the corner of her mouth. "I'm looking forward to it."

Some days, when I was avoiding everyone and everything, I holed up in the reference room, a dim, humid alcove wedged in the back of the Harrington library that housed Catherine's collection of dictionaries and encyclopedias. In addition to rows and rows of dusty leather-bound volumes, the shelves held old Catherine ephemera. It was easy to forget that this place had existed before we arrived, and that there were hundreds of men and women out in the world who had lived at Catherine before us. But here was the evidence in graduate circulars and annual reports, old Blue Books and director's office scrapbooks, taped-together newsletters and boxes of microfilmed press clippings. According to the microfilm canisters, the clippings dated all the way back to Catherine's founding in 1851, when the house was first officially chartered as a school. But I couldn't get the reader to work to see for myself.

Instead, I flipped through the scrapbooks. The linen pages were filled with memos, mission statements, and celebratory dinner menus. There wasn't much information about plasm, except for one memo dated thirty years ago announcing the new concentration: *A concentration in the revolutionary, transdisciplinary science of new materials.* M. Shiner, as the concentration's first head, was described as a well-respected chemist with a background in cancer research. The accompanying photo depicted a goggling, white-haired man, hunched and shy.

I didn't recognize the names of any of the previous Catherine directors until Viktória's arrival about twenty years ago. Her hiring was announced with an article and press portrait. She stood at the top of a glass stairway in a serious black dress, arms folded and legs crossed. "Art World Phenom Viktória Varga Tapped for Catherine Director."

I ran my finger over her unlined face. She looked young, maybe in her twenties. Not that many years older than I was now.

M. Neptune was named head of the new materials concentration about ten years ago. There were no clippings about M. Shiner's departure. M. Neptune must have been some kind of boy wonder; he'd gone directly from graduation to head of the department.

The scrapbooks also held letters from the directors to the Catherine community at large. I didn't know when the house had stopped doing those. The letters from the old directors were perfunctory and dull, but Viktória's first few were sweet, with long, eager descriptions of new programs, schedule arrangements, and fund-raising efforts for exciting renovations, classrooms, and labs. They didn't sound much like her. The letters became more reserved over the years. One from six years ago sounded like her voice as I knew it. It referred to the recent death of a student. *We hurt*, Viktória wrote, *because we miss him*.

That was what she had said about Baby.

The letter included a small school portrait of the boy who had died. The photo was hard to make out, reprinted in blurry black-and-white, but he looked friendly. I ran my finger over his face. I wished the image was clearer. The only details I could see were his dark curls, his crooked smile, and a mole by his lip. It was hard to believe he'd once been a real boy.

Baby's little hairs had been swept from the bathroom sink. Her bed didn't smell like her lotion anymore, her drawers were emptied, her shoes taken away. But the new students, the first-years, didn't even know she was missing. They had never met her. For them, she was never anyone at all.

M. Rogers, the professor of my Russian and Italian Futurisms class, was a giant woman who loomed over even the tallest boys. She wore her iron-gray hair combed up into a robust beehive and had the biggest hands I'd ever seen, and her voice was coarse and loud. The class was mostly reading. As we hunched over the texts, M. Rogers would pace the room, her voice resounding with a godlike boom as she read manifestos about the death of old, gray art and the birth of speed, technology, youth, and violence; drunken, rambling stories of burning down museums and building brass future machines; experiments in breaking down language into its component parts and building it up again to recreate the chaotic whoops and blares of a city street. M. Rogers spoke faster and faster as the class went along, punctuating her words by slapping the chalkboard until the dust rose.

We spent the first few weeks with only the grayscale reproductions in our text packets for reference. ("These fuckers won't even give me *slides*," M. Rogers would thunder, "while the labs put in orders for whatever shit they want. I swear to God, you want to see *fascism*? The politics of the place, I swear!") It wasn't until midterms that she finally received the slides she'd ordered and found a projector to rent. The day before our test, we sat in gray shadow as she clicked through painting after painting, a fusillade of commentary following each flashing image. "Here we go, *zang tumb tumb*, the city rises!"—a carnival of color, figures storming to work—"and Balla, lovely, lovely, a master of movement"—there, an image of a dachshund on a leash, its legs a scurrying blur.

The boy beside me snorted.

M. Rogers swiveled in her seat. "And just what is so funny, hot stuff?"

The boy hesitated, as if deciding how much of a debate he wanted to get into right now. Finally he said, "It's just . . . how can they think these paintings are revolutionary? We've spent weeks reading these treatises about blood and violence, revolutions in technology and culture, and this is what it comes down to? A painting of a puppy with blurry legs to show that it's running?" He lifted his chin. "It's not even a new idea to depict motion like this. Muybridge published *Animal Locomotion* in, what, 1886, '87? So, twenty-five years before this. The futurists write like they're conquering the world, and then they make these paintings that are just . . . silly."

"Hah!" M. Rogers said, slapping the table. "Yes. They are very silly paintings."

The boy looked at me, as if for defense.

"But don't you see where this is going?" M. Rogers said. "Remember Boccioni?"

She bounded up as she clicked forward to a slide of a Boccioni sculpture. *Unique Forms of Continuity in Space.*

We had seen the sculpture in black-and-white, but it was different now to see it in color, in bronze. Here was a man running, his body warped by its own velocity, his arms and legs mangled into motion. He wasn't just human; he was a speed machine. He was action itself.

"You're right," M. Rogers said. "These paintings are pretty shitty. That's obvious." She ran a hand along the screen. "But look at *this*. This is all right. Remember Boccioni's manifesto of Futurist sculpture? What did he say?" She slapped the screen for emphasis. "Futurist sculpture creates ideal new forms by using *motion* to break down the barrier between an object and its surroundings. To join the object's *exterior plastic infinity* to its *interior plastic infinity.*"

She let her hand drop. She shook her head.

"Interior plastic infinity," she said. "It's like they almost knew what they were talking about."

She clicked forward to an image of another sculpture. This one wasn't a person or an animal or any recognizable object. It was a bronze ovoid, abstract and nowhere, polished to a mirror shine.

"Brancusi," she said, "*The Beginning of the World.* Not that Brancusi was a futurist. Brancusi wasn't anything. But look at this. Look at this—this plastic infinity."

She touched the screen again.

"What is it?" she said. "An egg, maybe. A baby's head. A womb. The instant when one cell splits into two. It is the moment of life, the generation of a world, all in one object, one surface, reflecting this. An exterior and interior plastic infinity. Here. Can't you see it?"

She turned back to the boy, still pointing to the screen.

"Here," she said, "is your futurism."

❧

Plastic infinity. Was that what Baby had been looking for?

At session, I sat by the windows and folded my hands. These sharp fall days, the sun set earlier and earlier, turning the light in the great hall a deep gold. Viktória was standing far from me, by the windows, her body shadowed against the sunset. I couldn't see her face.

I closed my eyes.

I am in the house, we chanted. *The house is in the woods. My hands are on the table. The table is in the woods.*

I opened my eyes.

M. Neptune's students were sitting toward the back of the hall. I'd noticed that even among the new materials concentrators, his students stuck together. I watched as the seven of them chanted, *The door is in the hall, the hall is in the house*, eyes fluttering in beatitude. Their voices disappeared into the collective sound.

I closed my eyes again. I squeezed my hands tighter.

When session was over, everyone else drifted out of the hall, but M. Neptune's students still sat smiling in dazed bliss. They didn't move.

One of the students, a girl with long princess-blond hair and mean blue eyes, was cradling something in her lap. I craned to get a better look.

It was a rabbit. A real rabbit, white, with silky ears and sleepy eyes.

No one else seemed to notice the girl's pet, and none of the professors reacted to it, either. The other concentrators lounged near their table, waiting for everyone else to file from the room. The girl stroked the rabbit's little head.

Finally, the concentrators all stood and left together, the girl still holding the rabbit.

I followed them.

I walked slowly at first, quietly, a few paces behind. I don't know why I bothered to be so careful; they were too engrossed in their conversation to notice me. They wandered down the hall, past a basement passage, up a stairway, and around a corner. They took turns holding the rabbit as they argued about an episode of *The Twilight Zone*.

I crept behind them. Up more stairs, this staircase illuminated by a bright skylight, and down a long yellow hall. I thought maybe they were going to the umbrella room. Instead, they walked toward the main plasm lab in Harrington.

They went into the lab and closed the door behind them.

I stared at the door for a while before turning back. I was a long way from Molina.

❧

Someone knocked on my door with a high-spirited rap, then opened it without waiting for an answer. It was Yaya in her new favorite fur-collared wool coat and electric-pink lipstick.

"So, I've discovered the trick," she said, with no preamble. "From a very enterprising first-year whom I completely *detest*, and I'll tell you why on the way there."

"On the way where?"

"To—" She looked me over. "Are you coming dressed like that?"

It was late afternoon, and I was lying on my bed in my pajamas, eating toast with tangy lime marmalade. I hadn't realized I'd be following her on any adventures today.

I climbed out of bed. I held the toast in my mouth as I pulled on a jacket.

"It's muddy out." Yaya plucked the toast from my mouth and took a bite.

I slipped my feet into boots. The pajama pants bunched at the ankles.

She slipped her arm through mine. "Excellent, dear friend. Open."

I opened my mouth. She put the toast back in.

As Yaya led me down the stairs and out into the cool October twilight, she outlined her plan. "Okay, so you know how the commissary gets new items on Wednesday? Well, everything comes in through the loading dock on Monday, and it's processed out there. And the manager used to be a total hard-ass, but now he's about to retire and kind of stopped giving a shit. He's become much more lax about letting kids in during processing. So, this first-year—oh, and I hate her because she's used half, fucking *half*, of that nice honey-lavender lotion I'd been saving in the bathroom, which we apparently now share, but after a little discussion she knows to keep her hands off my shit. Anyway, she imparted this *delightful* little intel to me in the spirit of restitution. I hope some good stuff's come in. I've been dying for something new to play with."

Out on the yard, raw purple dusk had fallen. We huddled close together as we walked over the twisting footpath, past the tennis court, and through the grass, the same way I had gone to the tower. Crickets chirruped in the pines. Like the tower, the storage silos and loading dock were far to the house's southeast, where the shipping truck came in from the back road. It was easy to forget about the back road and that, even here, so far from the house, we were locked inside, everywhere, by the gate.

"This way," Yaya said, leading me around the loading dock, a squat cement building with fluorescent white windows. We walked up three steps, knocked on a metal door, waited a minute with no answer, and then entered.

The door opened into a wide, bright room as cluttered as a thrift store. The walls were lined with cardboard boxes stacked haphazardly against each other and metal shelves filled with books, toys, and toiletries. Commissary goods, still untagged. Some of the cardboard boxes were labeled—CANS X, XL, CARROTS, BEDSHEETS (TWIN XL)—and others not.

A side door was open to the back of a truck. A man stood in the truck taking notes on a yellow legal pad.

"Bunny?" Yaya said.

The man turned around. He was short and white, with thin gray hair, pudgy around his face and belly. He glanced from one to the other of us with slow, shy eyes.

"I'm Yaya," Yaya said, extending her hand. "Sarah Beth King said we could come by? And this is Ines."

Bunny shook her hand, then mine. His hand was soft as a girl's. He looked at us each in turn again.

"So," Yaya said, "can we look around?"

"Yes," Bunny said. He had a lisp. "I don't think—don't think there's much that you girls would like, though. You should come earlier."

"We will. Next time. But for now . . ."

Yaya wove her way expertly to one of the shelves. Something had already caught her eye.

I ran my fingers over the shelf nearest me. It was stacked with old faded coloring books and packets of crayons. Silly things like that came through the commissary sometimes. Catherine graduates donated back to the school without really considering what we might want or need. They probably couldn't remember what life was really like here. I couldn't blame them; even being here now, the days blurred.

I flipped through a *Sesame Street* coloring book. Ernie giggled back at me. He was getting ready for a bath. He had a nice towel and scrub brush.

"Do you like it?" Bunny said. "The book?"

I turned to see that he had been staring at me. I couldn't read his expression.

He handed me another coloring book, on top of the one I had, then gave me a packet of crayons, too.

"They're nice books," he said.

"Thank you," I said.

Through the window, in the last shadows of daylight, I could just make out something there, in the trees across the lawn: the white wall of a building. I blinked, thinking I must be imagining things.

No, of course; that was the tower. I hadn't realized it was this close.

"Ines," Yaya said. "Come look."

She had found a string of fake pearls at the bottom of a Tupperware full of toys. I helped her unknot the pearls and do the clasp. They shone plasticky-white as she wound them around her neck.

She turned to me, touching them.

"Aren't they everything?" she said. "Aren't they just divine?"

"Yes," I said. "Divine."

She turned to look at her reflection in the dock's darkening window.

"I've always loved beautiful things," she whispered. "It's stupid, I know. I've gotten into the worst messes for stupid, beautiful things."

She smiled at her reflection. She stroked the pearls.

❧

I had been keeping up with my Shakespeare readings, more or less, but the midterm was going to be brutal. Half of the terms listed in the study packet read like a foreign language. Anna and Diego were in the class, too, so I asked if I could study with them. It seemed like a friendly thing to do.

The three of us holed up in the Molina library with books and blankets and pots of tea. We took turns quizzing one another, editing our review answers, and napping. Later in the evening, silly and stupid, we gave up on studying and helped Anna write a love letter to the first-year she liked. *Dear Robert*, it began, *Thee art the man of my dreams, the prince of my soul, the architect of my joy everlasting.*

"Tell him you want to fuck him in the parlor," I said. "The one on the second floor of Ashley. They fixed the leaking there, it's nice again."

Anna laughed, shaking her head. "You are something else."

I sipped my tea. It felt nice, pretending to be normal.

After I took the midterm, I slept, though not for long, and woke late that night. I blinked until the gray bedroom settled into shapes. I patted my belly. I stared at the ceiling for a long time.

I slipped out of my bedroom.

I walked downstairs, past the baths in the Harrington basements, then farther, winding my way through the moonlit halls until I was in Ashley. My head felt two sizes too big. I hummed to myself, a French lullaby I hadn't realized I remembered.

Somehow, I ended up in the hallway with the umbrella wallpaper. The hallway with the door to M. Neptune's lab.

I found myself in that hallway a lot. I didn't know why; nothing ever happened there. I hadn't even seen anyone go in or out of the door since that one student many months ago.

I continued on, passing through a crooked burgundy hall that held a painting of an owl. The hallway led to a humid green glass-paneled conservatory that opened, suddenly, onto a balcony.

The broad stone balcony was rimmed with a balustrade and decorated with a profusion of potted plants: impatiens, zinnias, and funny little lemon trees. The plants' leaves were gray and crabbed, their blooms theatrically drooped. Abundant ivy tangled over the stone.

I walked to the balustrade. It was an unseasonably warm night for late October. The air smelled rich with damp earth and dying leaves. The sky was high, vaulted, and starlit, the clouds sublime purple and white.

"Ines."

I turned.

Theo stood in the cold moonlight at the other end of the balcony. He was holding a sheet of paper, big as a road map. A mess of fabric and string was bundled at his feet. Nick down there, too, sprawled on his stomach, openmouthed. For one uncanny moment I thought, *Nick's dead, Theo killed him*, but then Nick snorted.

Theo flashed one of his loose smiles. "Man, we're never really alone here, huh?" he said, slurring. "Even at four in the morning on a secret balcony, you might run into some ghost."

"What are you doing?" I said.

"Making a kite." He flipped over the paper. It was covered with instructions and diagrams. "We got this kit in the commissary. Nick was supposed to be helping me, but he's drunk as shit. We finished our Ethics test, then we were playing cards, and then we were gonna make the kite, but Nick's out."

"You're a little drunk, too."

He was smiling. "Yeah."

I went over to read the instructions. The kite was supposed to look like a sailboat.

A dream ship floating through the ocean-sky. Something about the image made my nose hurt, as if I might cry.

I sat on the cold stone and hugged my legs. Nick honked again but didn't wake up.

Theo sat down, too. He was watching me. His stare, even drunk, was intensely direct.

"Do you remember?" I said. "A few months ago, I came to your room and you played music for me. You played that pretty girls' song."

"Of course," he said. "When was that—March, April? Feels like, I don't know, longer. I think." He rearranged his legs on the stone.

"You're different now," I said.

"Am I?" He patted his hair. "I don't know."

"Yes. You fit in here more." I rested my chin on my knees. "You didn't feel well then."

"No," he said.

"Do you feel better now?"

He nodded slowly. "I'm getting there," he whispered. "I'm getting better. The doctor here . . . she's good. I take three pills now. One in the morning, two at night. They've been helping. A lot. I never thought I would feel better. But here I am. Feeling better."

I thought of the photograph I'd found in Theo's room, the one of him with his grandmother. Her fragile body in its flannel housecoat, the casual way Theo had slouched beside the stove. I assumed they lived together, that they loved and took care of each other. There had been a sweet comfort between them. Maybe I recognized it so sharply because it'd always been missing for me.

But could his love for his grandma really have been so simple? Weren't there nights when his friends were off having fun—drinking on rooftops or kissing on fire escapes—and he was alone, watching his grandma fall asleep in front of the TV, her hands twitching as they reached for something he couldn't see? On those nights, had he felt his love for her turning into a sick, shameful hate? Had he sometimes gone to bed in the dark and thought, What if I never get out of here?

Theo looked up at me.

"What about you?" he said.

"I'm the same," I said. "I never change."

He laughed. "We're supposed to be getting smarter, anyway."

"I guess."

He leaned back on his hands. "You're doing all right. I see you. You're working. You're studying."

"I have to, now. I was going to fail out."

"Shit."

"Yes. What about you? You're dating Sophie now."

"Mmm." His lip quirked into a smile.

"You like her."

"Yeah. You should hear her—she has this laugh. It cracks me up, just hearing her laugh at any stupid shit."

Theo was running a hand over the concrete, still staring at me. I thought, *He always likes to be touching something.*

"What?" he said.

"You see," I said, "such wonderful things. You look around, and all the world is wonderful."

He smiled a little. "Not all the world. But all of Catherine? Yeah, maybe. I mean, don't you realize how lucky we are? Sleeping in these nice rooms, eating these ridiculous meals, reading and drinking and playing with friends? How can you see this any other way but wonderful?"

"I don't know," I said. "I never see anything right. My eyes are backwards. Everything I see is upside down."

Theo picked up one of the dowels. He rolled it between his fingers.

I reached for the instructions. "So," I said, "how is this supposed to come together?"

We tried joining the ribs of the kite with the string, but they kept coming loose. It was a long time before we realized that Theo, in his drunkenness, had left part of the kit in his room. I pushed him. He couldn't stop laughing. The moon lowered and the sky paled.

We shook Nick awake. As we dragged him back to his room, he leaned all his weight against Theo, mumbling about ethics and love. After we finally got Nick into bed, pulled off his shoes, and tucked him in, Theo sang him a Boyz II Men song as a lullaby.

Theo and I went to the morning room. We filled two bowls with oatmeal and took them to the parlor. We ate them cross-legged on the parlor rug.

"You know," Theo said, stirring at the mush, "everyone thinks you're cool, but I know you're not."

"I am," I said. "I'm very cool."

"Nah. You're, like, gorgeous and mysterious and act like you don't give a shit about anything. But I bet there's something you give a shit about."

"I don't think there is."

He raised his eyebrows.

I took a bite of oatmeal.

"What's your favorite animal?" he said.

"Snails."

"Okay. You like snails. What about places?"

"I want to go to Egypt one day," I said. "I want to be buried in a pyramid."

"Me, too. Let's go together." He set down the bowl. "What about movies? Do you go to the movies?"

"Everyone goes to the movies."

"What's your favorite kind?" He didn't blink as he watched me. "Horror? Action?"

"I like musicals."

"Really?" He cocked his head. "Huh."

"Yes," I said. "I like dancing. And big happy endings."

"Sure," he said. "Who doesn't like happy endings?"

He stuffed his mouth with a huge bite of oatmeal.

I said, "I wish I cared more. Gave more of a shit. The way you do, and the way Baby did. How you care about your studies, and about plasm. I wish I loved anything like that."

Theo put down his bowl. He yawned.

"What is it?" I said.

"What's what?" he said.

"What is plasm?"

He glanced at me, then down.

"Everything," he said tonelessly. "It's just . . . everything."

I stirred at the oatmeal. Suddenly I was angry. Just tell me the fucking truth, I wanted to say. Use actual words.

Theo lifted his bowl, then set it down again. He stood up.

"I'm going to fall asleep if we keep sitting here," he said. "Let's go explore."

We crept out of the parlor and up the pink marble stairs, ending on Molina's fourth floor, in a room with mauve brocade-covered walls and heavy rosewood furniture: a dresser, an armoire, a bed frame with no mattress. The dresser held only a packet of bobby pins and, in the bottom drawer, a box full of faux-ivory elephant statuettes.

We clattered the little elephants to the floor. We staged a tiny war between them on the rug.

When Theo fell asleep by the bed frame in the midmorning, I kept playing. I danced a little elephant over his arm and onto his neck.

In my first days and weeks at Catherine, everything happened for the first time. I attended my first class, failed my first quiz, and ate my first butter cake. I lost my first game of bid whist, then won my second. I took my first nap in the library sun.

But first times became many times. The house, in the architecture of its rooms, schedules, and surfaces, had a pattern, and I patterned into it. This was the way I twisted the bathroom door handle to get it to turn; this was how my face looked in the mirror over the sink; this was the way condensation beaded on the wallpaper over the tub. This was how I walked to the morning room, class, great hall, and parlor, and this is how I walked back to my room. Small sensations—tea trays clinking down at our bedroom doors, pink mornings glowing on the yard, cold bowls of egg salad for lunch—repeated and fluxed. Breakfasts, tests, and teas, essays, festivals, and baths. Days cycled into weeks, weeks into months. And now here we were, in November again.

On bad days, I could feel the whole year swinging underneath me like a dead thing. But there were good days, too. Days when I didn't think about Baby, and Yaya made me laugh, and the hall served maple ice cream for dessert. Days when I felt okay.

When I first came to Catherine, the house's repetitions made it feel dull and small. Now, somehow, the house felt bigger. Catherine didn't twist in on itself; it recurred infinitely. Pencils and T-shirts and slices of melon flashed against one another like mirrors against mirrors, continuously unfolding into smaller and smaller details: the swan pattern on a parlor's wallpaper, a broken tile in the courtyard, and the humid smell of wet stone and moss, in one vague moment of a rainy afternoon.

❧

Catherine's annual fall festival was held the day after our finals. My first year, I hadn't watched the parade, though Baby and I could hear the noise from our room. We heard the drunk third-years march through the courtyard with whoops and stomps, the underclassmen cheer as wine and vomit splashed against stone. But inside, I was painting Baby's toenails. I used a bottle of sparkly blue polish I'd found abandoned in the Ashley music room. Baby stared at my hands as I worked and flinched from my touch. "You can relax," I said, but she didn't.

I did watch the parade this year, though. From my window, I could see the mummers, the third-years costumed as homemade ghosts, monsters, and aliens with plaster heads and fuzzy ears. They screeched, banged on drums, laughed, and danced as they paraded across the courtyard and back into the hall. My Molina classmates gathered by the trees or leaned out of windows to watch. They cheered as they tossed streamers, candies, and noisemakers to the crowd below.

I curled up on my windowsill. I hugged my legs.

Could I ever stop thinking of Baby? Would she ever stop haunting me?

Theo and Nick stood among the crowd in the courtyard. I saw them slouching against a fig tree, watching as the parade passed. Every few minutes, Theo clapped his hands above his head in stupid pleasure. The two of them looked very drunk and very glad.

What did it feel like? To be so glad?

Theo and Nick were eyeing a first-year girl now. She was dancing with her friends. Every time she laughed, she turned to make sure the boys were still watching. Theo looped his arm over Nick's shoulders and whispered something in his ear. I wondered what he said. The girl was pretty, but I was more beautiful than she was.

Viktória had said my past life was over. That felt true. I was new, here at Catherine. But I would never be a good student or a good person, like Baby. Not really. There was no point.

But I had other ways of learning things. I had done it before, outside, and I could do it again. I could pretend to be normal. I could have friends. I could kiss boys nicely and whisper in their ears, and get them to whisper in mine. Because Catherine was my home now, the whole house, all of it—its bright places and dark ones, its conspiracies and secrets—and I wanted it all. I wanted everything in me.

Someone banged on my door.

"Ines, are you in there?" Anna called. Her voice was loose and drunk. I could hear Diego laughing behind her. "What are you doing? Come down!"

"Yes," I said brightly and prettily. "Yes. I'm coming."

OMENS

The house's heating had been malfunctioning all week. Mornings had turned black cold and harsh as wind whistled against the windows and through the cracks in our doors. It was hard enough getting out of bed; a long night in the chasmal great hall sounded unbearable. So we decided to bring our beds to dinner. Yaya, Anna, Diego, Nick, Theo, and me, we all bundled up our blankets and pillows and dragged them down the stairs. Our table became a sleepover nest. We snuggled in.

"What's the difference between leopards and panthers?" Anna said. She struggled to butter the slice of white lemon bread in her hand, wrestling with the blanket draped over her shoulders.

"Panthers are black," Diego said.

"*Black* panthers are black," Nick said. "What about other panthers?"

"All panthers are black," Diego said. "Panthers are black leopards."

Anna said, "That doesn't seem right."

"What about jaguars?" Nick said.

"What *about* jaguars?" Diego said.

"Aren't jaguars something else?"

"Everything else is everything else," Yaya said. "Oh my God."

I put my head down on the table. Yaya petted my hair.

"I thought mountain lions were bobcats," Anna said through a mouthful of lemon bread.

"Ugh," Diego said. "Look at them."

A group of Molina first-years was sitting down the table from us. One of them, a tanned, golden-eyed girl with a compact gymnast body, had the most obvious crush on Nick. She always tried to sit near him at breakfast and laughed too hard at whatever dumb shit he said. Now she was staring at him with her chin lifted, her lips painted glossy red.

"That lip stuff cost her a fortune in points," Yaya said. "I saw it in the commissary last week. Oh, Nick, take pity on the girl." She shook our empty platter. "Go get us more bread. She'll be right behind you."

"She does not need any pity," Anna muttered. "I know that kind of girl. Looks cute, but watch out."

"How awful." Nick winked at Anna. He slunk out of his blanket.

The girl followed Nick as he loped over to the dessert service, smoothing her hair into place before scurrying up to him. In that moment, in one quick flash, I saw Nick as the first-years did: one of the house's happy golden princes, tall and rich and laughing and bright.

I wondered if I would remember this feeling after Catherine. The feeling of seeing a friend—someone I knew and who knew me, too, someone who cared about me—walking in through a door or waving from across a hall or bending to whisper in another friend's ear. Of being inside, so inside, such an intimacy, and at the same time seeing it from outside. A feeling of being seen, beautiful and young, seated at a mythic table.

It was a nice feeling.

I took a bite of the white lemon bread. It tasted sweet, with a tart bite. The wine warming my insides was good, too. I had to study later tonight, but I wasn't thinking about that. I wasn't thinking about anything. I was being a good friend. I was doing okay.

I touched Theo's arm. "Want to make milkshakes?" I said.

The milkshake machine was this semester's new addition to the dessert service. Most people stuck to basic chocolate and vanilla, but we'd become more inventive with our creations. That night, Theo wanted to try mixing brandy applesauce with peanut butter and vanilla ice cream. I helped him spoon in the applesauce as he held the mixer. The applesauce fell off the spoon in slurping gloops.

"Oh no," I said, watching as the machine stirred it all up into brownish sludge.

Theo took a sip. He made a face.

"Is it good?" I said. "Or are you going to throw up?"

He covered his mouth.

"Let me try," I said.

Someone bumped into me as I did. One of M. Neptune's students, the short one with grayish skin and dark curls.

I swallowed the milkshake. "Sorry," I said.

The boy was grasping the arm of another student of M. Neptune's, the girl who wore her hair in a black braid. She loomed over him, even though she wasn't very tall, as she piled mini-cheesecakes onto a dish. The boy didn't help. He just stared up at the ceiling. I followed his eyes upward. I couldn't tell what he was looking at.

I had never seen a face quite like his before. His eyelashes were so long I almost couldn't see his eyes. He had a slack mouth with a little mole near his lip.

"Hi," I said.

The boy lowered his gaze. His eyes were slow to focus on me.

"Hello," he said.

The girl glanced at me and tugged his arm. "Come on, Sandy, let's go," she said, pulling him away.

"It needs more applesauce," Theo said, eyes narrowed at the milkshake. "That's the problem. I think."

I lifted the porcelain lid off the applesauce tureen.

By the time we returned to our table, most of our friends were gone. Only Nick was still there, chatting with the girl at the other end, their heads close together. Everyone else had probably gone to study. Everyone always needed to study.

I snuggled back in my blanket.

Theo sat across from me. He sipped the milkshake. His face puckered.

"Stop drinking it," I said.

"It grows on you."

"It does not."

He took another gulp before handing it to me. I sipped. It did taste a little better.

That night, I slept with a Harrington girl I'd met in Intermediate German. I liked watching her mouth work around those harsh syllables. Now, in her room, I bit her neck and pushed her onto the bed.

In the dark, after she had fallen asleep, I stared out her window at the murky clouds and thought about M. Neptune's student, the one at the dessert service. His eyes had been so white, so imprecise. Even when they'd focused on me, his stare had still been off somehow. Like he hadn't really found my eyes but was looking slightly lower. At my mouth, maybe.

Did that happen to all of M. Neptune's students eventually? Did they lose themselves in the insane studying, the numbing grind, the endless hours in the lab? Would they all become phantom shadows of the boys and girls they once had been?

Would it happen to Theo?

I couldn't imagine it. Theo with his warm skin and bright eyes—Theo was so human.

I turned to the girl again. I stroked her shoulder.

Wind shuddered through the house's windows and wheezed over the yard. We huddled around radiators, rubbing each other's hands warm. The air was so dry and brittle it made our noses itch.

The first snowflakes fell as I was working in the Molina library. I was curled up on my couch with a pad of paper on my lap, drinking hot water with moonshine and drafting an essay on Bosch's *Haywain Triptych*. I closed my eyes to take a sip, and when I opened them again, there was the snow: white, all white.

By the time I finished my essay, dawn was rising and snow covered the yard. I went to sleep and dreamed of being weightless. I didn't have a body at all.

When I woke up, I looked out the window. The snow was already trampled by the tracks of students going back and forth to class and, judging by the mess, having snowball fights. But the rooftops were a dreamy, dazzling white.

I stuck my head out of the window. The air smelled like a cold fantasy wonderland. I breathed.

I pulled on my boots and went downstairs.

I was on my way to the Ashley tower when, in the back of Molina's courtyard, I found what at first looked like a giant snowbank. As I came closer, I realized it was far more thoughtfully constructed. It was an igloo.

I paced around it. The igloo was big, human-sized, about as tall as I was. A couple of milk crates lay abandoned by the courtyard bench. From the pattern on the igloo's hump, I supposed its engineer had used the crates to form snow bricks, then packed them into shape.

"Ines," someone called from inside, "are those your feet?"

I peeked inside the entrance.

Anna and Nick were crouched in the dim interior among a

mess of blankets, tea trays, chemistry notes, and flash cards. Theo was there, too, sleeping in the back, cradling his head against a pillow.

"Crazy, isn't it?" Anna said as I crawled in. "We helped, but really it was all Diego. He has that engineering presentation tomorrow, remember? I think this was his way of dealing. Look at these bricks." She patted the igloo wall. "Totally solid."

Theo let out a sudden snore. He was puffed up in a fluorescent-pink-and-yellow ski jacket, one of his recent treasures. His soft mouth fell open.

"That doesn't even look comfortable," Nick said, glancing at Theo's sleeping form. He poured himself more tea.

I snuggled up next to Anna. She pulled a blanket over our legs.

"Who's studying chemistry?" I said.

"Me," Nick said. "With M. Olsen. Who's amazing, but a bit of a bitch."

"Want me to quiz you?" I said.

"Weren't you going somewhere?"

"It's okay."

He handed me the flash cards.

The igloo was surprisingly warm inside. It was late afternoon now, the snow shadowed ghostly blue. I quizzed Nick. He got a lot of the answers wrong, but didn't seem to mind. He barely noticed when I finished. He'd leaned in to Anna and was braiding her hair, eyes half closed in sleepy disinterest.

I set down the cards and snuggled closer to Anna, too. She smelled like toothpaste and soap.

Theo still lay asleep on the igloo floor with his mouth open, gently snoring.

"He's so exhausted," Anna said.

"We're all exhausted," Nick said, though there was a lazy drawl to his voice as he said it.

"Well, him especially."

"Young Theo Williams does not need your pity." Nick combed through Anna's hair to redo the braid. The first one had been terrible. "He knew what he was getting into when he applied for the concentration. Other kids work just as hard and don't get nearly as much glory."

"We work hard, yeah," Anna said, bending toward Nick's hands. "But not as hard as new materials concentrators do. Haven't you noticed? He's gone for hours at a time. He keeps missing sessions and feasts—he barely eats and drinks. He's fucking miserable. And he's just getting started."

I sat up.

"Please," Nick said. "He's not miserable. He loves it." He patted Anna's head. The new braid didn't look any better than the first. "Don't be jealous. I know you were rejected from the concentration."

Anna shrugged. She didn't look bothered. "I'm not jealous, and I wasn't rejected," she said. "I dropped out." She poured herself more tea. "And when I dropped out, I thought I didn't have it in me—that I wouldn't be able to keep up. But that's not true. I have new materials concentrators in my chemistry classes, and I get better grades than them. I'm smart enough. I've always been smart enough. But there's more to the concentration than ability."

"What else is there?" I said.

Anna glanced at me. She waited, considering, before she said, "The concentration—the professors, the structure of the curriculum, everything—it asks more of its students than I could give. It asks for them to be brave. Brave in ways that I'm not."

Last week, I had watched Anna eat two earthworms on a dare. She'd popped them both into her mouth at the same time. She hadn't even seemed grossed out as she chewed, just bored. What was she not brave enough to do?

"Are you kidding?" Nick said. "Sure, it's an intense department, but it hasn't done anything interesting since M. Shiner was laughed out of town. Those kids are just running numbers and mending broken tennis rackets over and over again. Reproducing the same experiments because they can. It's all theory. Honestly, the house probably doesn't have the funding for anything else."

"Do you really think we need funding?" Anna said. "Have you been in this house?"

"Yes, I have," Nick said. "A windowpane fell out of the Harrington music room last week. Literally fell out of the wall."

"Okay, there are some upkeep issues," Anna said. "But we're not paying room and board. Listen, Catherine is structured differently from other schools. Our endowment, our graduate network, and our plasm—and plasm really is *ours*, in a way, for whatever reason. We're totally self-sufficient." She hugged her legs, shivering. "The department's only gotten more radical, not less, since the Shiner scandal. Because now they know we have something extraordinary here, and they're going to protect it. Plus, with M. Neptune running things, instead of an actual chemist? They're not just pinning tennis rackets, they're pinning animals and people. They're pinning *us*. You've been to the nurse. And . . . you remember. You know what they did to us."

Nick narrowed his eyes. "The coming in was important," he said, in a low, serious voice. "And it was a long time ago."

"Sure, it was a long time ago," Anna said. "But we have sessions every week. Maybe they don't use pins in sessions, but it's all part of the same experiment—the experiment of us, in this school. And I don't think the coming in was the last time they're going to pin us. I heard, after forums . . . I heard they try something else."

I slunk down in the pillows.

Nick scratched at his jaw. His eyes were still hard.

"You could be right," Anna finally said. "Maybe the concentration is just numbers and figures and critical theory now. But when I think about when I was applying, all those interviews and tests . . ."

Anna chewed at her lip.

"They wanted more from me," she finally said. "They wanted devotion. And I wasn't ready to give that." She shrugged again. "And that was just for the regular concentration. The ones who work in M. Neptune's lab? I can't even imagine."

"What about Theo?" I said.

Anna turned to me again. "What about him?"

"Do you think he would give it?" I said. "His devotion?"

Anna stared at his sleeping figure. His cheeks were flushed a strange, feverish pink, like a marionette's.

A gust of wind blew past the entrance of the igloo. For a moment I thought I heard, in the wind, someone shouting my name.

❧

As second-years, we were finally allowed to have jobs—or "trades," as the Blue Book called them—to earn extra points. With trade points, we could afford better things from the commissary, things like running sneakers, romance novels, cake mix, and barrettes. Before, such toys had been the economy of upperclassmen and those who slept with them, as Yaya did. Now we were the upperclassmen, and we were the beautiful people with the beautiful things.

Yaya had come to love Bunny so much she applied to trade on the loading dock. Anna was one of the many second-years assigned to the great hall; we whooped and slapped our table in glee whenever it was her turn to serve us. Nick's trade was in the main library, where he spent most of his time lounging, gossiping, and making out with whoever else was at the desk.

Somehow I was accepted to work for the art gallery, the one

in the Ashley basement, one of the more coveted trades at Catherine. I wasn't even going to apply for the position, but M. Owens wouldn't sign my class schedule until I promised I would. I shouldn't have won the spot. I doubt they were impressed by my application essays or transcript. M. Owens must have put in a good word for me, though, because soon I was spending my Tuesday and Thursday afternoons in the gallery office, a tiny gabled room on the third floor of Harrington. I reorganized the library, updated object cards, and sorted through donor files until it was time for dinner. I liked the work. I liked rubbing my finger across the names on the donor cards. *Gift of Stephen Charleston, Gift of Mr. and Mrs. David Kingsley.* I could imagine them, the powdery-pale, wildly rich fairy people dressed in lace and silk, hosting their many diamond parties in penthouses, estates, and mansions whole worlds away from here.

Those winter nights I slept in Yaya's bed. Her neck and shoulder were warm beneath my hand, and the rosy smell of her hair cream made me feel drowsy and calm. We shared scary stories, gossiped, and farted on each other. We made each other laugh until we cried. When we fell asleep, I felt like we were babies, wrapped up after a bath.

I still didn't like being in my own room, alone in the night. I heard Baby there. Baby turning in her bed, Baby humming as she rifled through her closet, Baby padding to the door. I heard the click of the pipes as she turned on the faucet in the bathroom. I heard her slip into the bath. I heard her sigh.

On Mondays Yaya wasn't in bed but at the dock helping unload the truck. When I couldn't sleep on those nights, I'd bundle myself up and tramp alone across the yard. The dark felt as cold and tremendous as black outer space. At the dock, Bunny ran a space heater and played music on his tape deck. I wasn't sure if he was supposed to have music, but when I asked, he just stared at me.

He did what he wanted, whether it was playing cassettes or letting Yaya filch all the good clothes for herself. So while Bunny and Yaya inventoried the goods, I sorted through Bunny's tapes and chose new songs to play. He had a good collection of disco mixes.

I stood by the open dock and watched the road. It must have been around five in the morning, so early that the truck hadn't arrived yet. The road stretched out wide before me, and the grass glowed alien-gray with the coming dawn. I was drinking cream soda from a glass bottle. I was so tired my whole body felt heavy. I rubbed my face.

"Just go to sleep," Yaya said as she reached to pile some books higher on a shelf. "I don't know why you're still up."

"I had to finish my Environmental Geometry project."

"Which one? The leaf patterns? God, I hated that class."

"Yes. And now I'm waiting for breakfast." I shivered. My voice was coming out in white puffs. "And if I fall asleep, I might die."

Yaya sat beside me. She was dressed up in a long woolen skirt, tights, and white pearl earrings. She wasn't wearing any makeup. Her eyes looked tired. She took the cream soda from me.

"Tell me a story," I said.

She wiped the side of her mouth. "Once upon a time there were two lovely princesses. Named Ines and Yaya."

"What nice names."

"Yes. Princess Ines and Princess Yaya were the prettiest, kindest princesses in all the land. But they were trapped in an evil castle under an evil spell. The palace was full of trials and dangers and traps and terrible mysteries. But the princesses were smart. And best friends."

"And sisters."

"And sisters."

Yaya took a sip of the soda.

"Well?" I said.

"Well, what?"

"Do the princesses escape the castle?"

"Oh. I don't know. I guess we'll see."

I grabbed the soda.

Yaya leaned back on her hands. She was smiling.

"Yaya?" I said.

"Mmm."

"Do you know what plasm is?"

"What do you mean? Plasm, the new material?"

"Yes. Plasm. I mean, do you really understand what it is—exactly? Do you really get it?"

Yaya narrowed her eyes.

The truck beeped as it backed into the dock. Yaya smoothed her skirt over her knees.

"I don't think anyone *really* gets it," she said. "Except new materials scholars, I guess."

I wiped my nose. I might have been getting a cold.

I said, "That's why I'm going to seduce Theo."

Yaya almost choked on the soda. "What?"

"I want to understand plasm," I said. "Really get it. But I'm not cut out for the concentration the way Theo is. But maybe . . . you know. I can get him to spill some secrets to me."

Yaya laughed without sound. "I mean, girl, he'd definitely sleep with you. And he's not so, like, pretentious, like the other concentrators. But he's not going to spill any secrets. Not to you, anyway."

"Why not?" I gestured for the soda.

She passed it to me. "He'll fuck anything, obviously. But he's into, like, little *darling* girls. You know? The nice ones. Remember Andrea? And Marina, that girl who never stopped giggling?" She shook her head. "He's not gonna crush on you because you'd never even let him. To do that, you'd have to be open and real. Be nice to him and let him be nice to you. And that's not going to happen."

I put my chin in my hand.

Yaya yawned.

"I can pretend," I said. "I can be nice. I have friends now. Haven't you seen? We study together."

"Ines, child," she said, "why do you even care? Don't fuck with Theo, and don't fuck with plasm. Don't let this house eat you up. If you keep messing with shit you don't understand, you're going to get stuck. Just let it go."

I picked at the label on the soda bottle.

Of course Yaya would say I should let it go. She didn't care about plasm because she cared about other things—her family, her beauty, her friends. She had a life outside of Catherine. But what did I have?

What if I wanted to get stuck?

Bunny was tramping up the steps. "Truck's here," he called to Yaya.

Out back, the truck was already opened and a stout little woman bent over the boxes, ticking off numbers from a bag of papers. Her skin was wrinkled and dark, her wiry gray hair twisted up with a pencil.

"Hey, Glo," Yaya called to her as we climbed into the truck.

"You've got to help me here," the woman mumbled without looking up. "I think I lost my glasses."

I stepped farther into the truck as Yaya went to help find Glo's glasses. It was damp and warmer in here than out on the dock. Like the inside of a bear's winter den. I ran my hand along the wall.

A memory flashed: Green lights on the windshield as I drove past a gas station like I was blasting through the cosmos. Mucus clogging my throat. Fast-food wrappers crumpled on the dashboard. The smell of grease and sweat.

It had been such a long time since I was on the road.

"There are definitely too many combs," Glo was saying.

"No," Yaya said. "These are good. We use them at the salon."

"Let me go back to my list." Glo tramped into the room with an exhausted limp, clipboard in hand.

I walked farther into the truck. Through the window in the back, I could see the driver's cabin and the windshield.

"Weird, isn't it?" Yaya said.

She stood behind me, tapping a pencil against the truck wall. But she wasn't looking at me. She was staring ahead.

"If we went straight down that road," she said, "for a long time—we could be somewhere real. Like Philadelphia. Or New York."

Glo grunted as she tried to lift a box. Yaya ran to help her.

"I don't know how you girls stay here," Glo said as Yaya took the box from her. "Three years without TV? Without my little magazines?" She rubbed at the knee that seemed to be the source of her limp. "I'd go crazy, I really would."

"We are," Yaya said, grunting.

"Are what?" Glo said.

Yaya set down the box. "Going crazy."

That winter, I was taking a seminar on landscapes. It was one of those classic Catherine surveys that whirled back and forth, up and down, through centuries, objects, and personalities with no concept of narrative. The class met Thursday evenings in the basement of the Ashley tower, in a narrow windowless room with an overactive radiator. There, cramped together in the clammy dark, we watched the projector click through vision after vision of faraway dreamlands: mountain crags whitened by sea foam and wind; cities limned by red and blue grid lines;

hellscapes so bloody and grimy and crowded with sex they made my heart beat faster.

Watteau's garden fêtes were my favorite. His bouquets of women shimmered in pink taffeta and lace as they romped over flowering meadows and gazed over rosy white skies. Their giggling faces were as pretty as cupcakes.

We visited the Ashley gallery in January. The professor shuffled us from panel to panel as he delivered anxious, rambling lectures on how space approached and receded from the picture plane, the order and disorder of the subjects in space. When he finished, he shooed us away to take notes for our essays.

Most of the other students hung around the main galleries, but I went alone to the third room. My footsteps echoed as I entered through the doorway and sat. The room was almost empty except for my painting, the one I had chosen for my essay. It was a good enough landscape. A nice calm view of verdant fields, pale windmills, and blue skies.

I tapped my pencil against my notepad. I had nothing to say about it.

"You're not looking very closely, are you?"

I turned. Viktória was standing by the door. Viktória, wearing a green satin dress and three silver bracelets.

"Sorry," I breathed.

She took two steps closer, bracelets tinkling and heels clicking against the floor. She gestured to the painting. "Look closer," she said. "Pay attention."

I tried to turn away from her.

"It's not just a simple pastoral scene, is it?" she said. "See the field workers in the background? Look how their forms mirror the forms of the windmills, and how the windmills mirror those of the clouds. It's not just a landscape. It is a story, a story of man working in harmony with nature. Humanity in rhythm with grass and soil and atmosphere. Every particular in concert, in control. How strange. Don't you think?"

She sat down next to me on the bench.

"I should come here more often," she murmured, so low it could have been to herself. "I always feel better when I do."

For a moment I felt as if I were intruding in one of Viktória's private spaces. The thought made my stomach flutter.

I heard myself say, "But what about the sparrow?"

Viktória blinked, as if coming out of a reverie. "The sparrow?"

I pointed at the bird in the foreground. There, a little brown sparrow splashed in a puddle, wings blurred with movement.

"You say everything is in harmony, in control," I said. "But the sparrow isn't in control. It just . . . flew here, in smears of paint. It's wild."

Viktória stared at the sparrow for a while.

"Yes," she finally said. "The precious bird with its smears of paint." She was smiling a little. "Weissenbruch couldn't capture its fluttering by design, could he? Not like the workers and the windmill and the farm. The bird, so alive—it escapes painting's architecture. It escapes design and description and discipline. Weissenbruch could only capture it as a moment, here, on the real painting surface." She reached out a hand as if to touch it, that place where the sparrow's oil paint encrusted the canvas. "Because, like the painting, the bird is present. It is real. And the only real thing is matter."

She opened her mouth, then closed it again. If I hadn't known better, I would have thought she was about to cry.

"So real and alive," she said, "so beautifully alive, forever."

She turned to me.

"I know these past months have been hard for you," she whispered. "But I see you. You're doing so much better than you were, Ines. You're working hard. And you're doing well. You really are."

She touched my shoulder.

"Keep going," she said.

Where was I going?

The nights darkened and twisted.

I was woken up by a knock at my door.

I wriggled in bed. I wasn't alone; a first-year was splayed naked on my floor, his back glowing like sharkskin in the moonlight. I didn't remember bringing him home. I didn't remember a lot of things from the night. The room lurched.

The knock sounded again. The boy on the floor didn't move. I stepped over him as I went to crack open the door.

Theo's eye peered back at me. "Ines," he said. "Sorry, I know it's late—" He looked me up and down. "Are you naked?"

"Why," I whispered, voice rasping, "are you awake?"

He met my eye again. "Man, you've gotta see what I've found," he said. "I was, I don't know, wandering around—I went down to the second basement—wait, let me just show you." He shifted from one excited foot to the other. "Come on. It'll be a nice walk. You're gonna love it."

I rubbed my face. "Give me a second," I mumbled.

I pulled on jeans and a T-shirt, then dragged the blanket from Baby's bed and draped it over the boy on the floor. He didn't move.

The house, as Theo and I wandered through it, was quiet and still, like it had slumped into a drunken languor. Theo didn't talk much, but his pace was excited. As we walked by the windows that looked out onto the black yard, our reflections drifted like spirits over the glass.

We went down into a basement hallway lined with yellow wallpaper that led to a slim white door. Theo pushed it open.

The room was tiny, and crammed full with a wreckage of cardboard boxes, office chairs, rolltop desks, and squashy vinyl couches. I could barely see to the opposite wall. The overhead light buzzed with electricity.

I reached into an open cardboard box. It was filled with leather albums. I flipped open the first one to see a photo of a blond woman and two grinning kids on a snowy mountain, the kids clutching skis in their eager, mittened hands. In the next one, the same woman lay on a bed, curled beside a black poodle. She was pretending to be asleep, but her mouth was quirked into a smile. She knew the photographer was watching her, and she liked him watching her.

"I think it's all stuff left over from when they moved the professors' offices," Theo said, voice muffled. He had moved deeper into the maze of boxes and furniture. "Storage that they never sent out. Isn't it amazing?"

I closed the album.

The next box was filled with old physics syllabi typed on a word processor. The next, hand-thrown pottery—misshapen bowls and ugly vases—cushioned by yellowing newspapers. I unwrapped the newspaper to read one of the headlines: "Hurricane Hugo's Path of Devastation."

"You still haven't noticed the best part," Theo said.

He was watching me now, grinning as he tossed a red yo-yo back and forth between his hands.

He looked pointedly in the corner.

There, propped up on a crooked stack of Yellow Pages, was a television.

I walked over to it. The TV was covered in a fine layer of dust. It looked like it might still work. A tangle of cords ran from it to the wall and a VCR.

I ran a hand over the TV's plastic body. I pressed *power.*

The TV popped to life. Its screen crackled with static electricity.

"It works," Theo said. His face was near mine, illuminated by the TV's blue light. "Doesn't get any channels, of course. But look." He kicked a milk crate beside the TV stand.

The crate was filled with videotapes. I recognized some of the titles—*Back to the Future, The Thing*, four tapes of *M.A.S.H.*—and others I didn't. Placed on top were *The Sound of Music*, *Bye Bye Birdie,* and *Hello, Dolly!*

"You said you liked musicals," Theo said.

I picked up *The Sound of Music*. The case showed Julie Andrews twirling, arms open wide as the sky.

"Are you happy?" Theo said. "You don't seem happy."

I set down the tape.

"Which one should we watch first?" I said.

We decided on *Bye Bye Birdie.* We pushed one of the vinyl couches in front of the TV and popped in the tape. We turned off the lights.

I had never seen *Bye Bye Birdie* before. It was a wonderful movie, colorful and big. I hadn't realized how much I missed being entertained without working, without having to read or write or talk. It felt good to watch giddy teenagers cheer and sing and dance with cotton-candy-colored Princess phones and swoon into each other's loving arms. Theo hadn't seen the movie before, either, but that didn't stop him from singing along. He made up lyrics as he went, belting so loudly the room echoed.

"You have a beautiful voice," I said. We were lying lengthwise on the couch, legs entwined.

"Do you really think so?" he said.

"Oh, yes," I said. "So beautiful. Really, really nice."

He was laughing. "You're such a fucking bitch."

I kicked him. He kicked me back.

"Do you know," I said, "you're the only one who thinks I'm funny?"

"You are funny."

"I know. But no one else thinks I am. Everyone else takes me so seriously."

Theo rubbed at his hair. He was concentrating on the movie again. He looked at everything with such focus.

I shifted closer to him on the couch. I touched his neck.

He turned to me. His mouth was still relaxed from laughing. He looked me up and down and smiled. But he didn't move any closer.

"What?" I said. There was a laugh in my throat, too.

"You don't remember, do you?" he said.

"Don't remember what?"

"We've already, um, slept together."

"No, we haven't."

"Sure did."

"Really? When?"

"Our first night at Catherine. After the party."

I tried to think back to that first night. I remembered lying in the bathtub, meeting Baby and Billie Jean, and being sick. Before that—yes, I had left the party with a boy. It could have been Theo, I guessed. It could have been anyone.

I sat back. "I didn't realize that was you."

Ann-Margret was singing her last song against the blue screen. The credits rolled.

I crawled over to the VCR to hit *stop*, then *rewind*. The tape whirred.

"Man, I wish we had some Twizzlers," he mumbled. "Or, what are those little things called . . . Raisinets. What do you want?"

"What?"

"What's your candy? You know, in a theater?"

"Oh," I said.

I sat up.

"I don't know," I said.

Theo ran a hand over my shoulder.

"Did you like the movie?" he said. "Do you want to watch another one?"

His voice was kind and sweet.

I got up.

"What's wrong?" he said.

"I just," I said, "I don't know. I need to go."

As soon as I left the room, I realized I didn't know how to get back to Molina. It didn't matter. I just started walking.

GERALD

Jeopardy! or *Wheel of Fortune*?" I said.

M. Owens stirred his tea. "Must we keep at this game?"

"What else are we going to do?"

He sank in the armchair, placing his teacup on the side table. "Well," he finally said. "*Jeopardy!* then, of course. *Wheel of Fortune* is imbecilic." He tapped his lip. "We used to watch *Jeopardy!* every Thursday at my in-laws' after dinner. Cheesecake, coffee, and Alex Trebek."

He sipped his tea. His eyes, watching the morning light shift over the bookcases, were rheumy and pink.

Our advisors had been invited to the Molina music room for our spring orientation, a supposedly casual get-together that did not feel casual at all. Most of the advisors roved the room with self-satisfied smiles, wandering up to unsuspecting students to quiz them on planned study courses or reading schedules, tutorial designs or project proposals. Some students rambled on for anyone who would listen. Others huddled by the tea service and tried not to meet their advisor's eyes as they shoved biscotti into their pockets.

For the first time in my academic career, I was actually ahead of schedule. I had decided to write my tutorial on the paintings of Agnes Martin. One of her works had been hanging in the gallery for a few weeks now. It was a simple painting of almost nothing: a square of white and off-white stripes. It made me feel calm.

When I had met with M. Owens earlier to confirm the topic, he didn't ask any follow-up questions. He simply nodded and ran through the requirements, which included two classes on mid-century abstract expressionism and minimalism, along with regular meetings before I even started writing the actual tutorial. That would be next fall and winter. Then he handed me the updated course catalogue and waited for me to leave his office.

Now we were here, and he was staring darkly at his tea.

I'm sorry you miss your family, I wanted to say. I wished I could help him. Professors at Catherine lived close to us students, but their lives felt so distant.

M. Owens looked up. He said, "Liszt or Chopin?"

I scratched my nose. "I think I like Chopin."

"Yes," he said. "I always found Liszt's compositions quite fussy. But Chopin . . ." He touched his heart.

"I like his Nocturnes," I said.

He pulled a handkerchief from his pocket.

Theo and his advisor were standing by the piano. His advisor, a hard, rod-thin woman named M. Donna, was hugging her elbows and pressing her lips together as she listened to Theo ramble on. She didn't look pleased.

"I'm going to get us more sandwiches," I said.

M. Owens nodded as he blew his nose into his handkerchief.

At the tea service, I picked up a salmon sandwich, only to set it down again. I drifted over to the curtains where I might overhear Theo.

"But the ideas do make sense, right?" he whispered urgently. "You reviewed my labs last semester, and the write-ups. The results were solid. They were great. So why couldn't I just—"

"Hey," M. Neptune said, "what's going on here?"

At first I thought he was talking to me. But he strode right past, toward Theo and M. Donna, without seeming to notice I was there.

Theo looked from one of the professors to the other. Then he lifted his chin.

"I know what I want to do for my tutorial," Theo said. "I want to study the manipulation of plasm as a network between objects, rather than as a discrete system. And I want to do some lab work as part of my project. But M. Donna has been saying she won't let me do it—not with lab work, anyway. But—"

"Theo, I agree with M. Donna," M. Neptune said.

Theo's face fell.

"Wait," Theo tried again, "did you see my lab with M. Lee last semester? The one where I used four exchanges per sensor instead of two? It went even better than we thought. All of our experiments have been engaging with plasm in isolate, in these arbitrary little object compartments, when that's not how plasm *works*. Right?"

"Theo." M. Neptune clasped his hand on Theo's shoulder. "This road has been traveled before."

"Of course," Theo snapped. "But—"

"Vague experiments lead to vague conclusions," M. Neptune said. "Vague, dangerous conclusions. This department is not going to repeat past mistakes. Object-based methods of plasm research are radical enough, and they are not arbitrary. They're disciplined. You know this, Theo. We've discussed it before."

"M. Shiner didn't have half the research we have now," Theo mumbled. He looked up. "*Did* you see my lab? The one I did with M. Lee?"

M. Neptune smiled sadly.

"You're a bright kid," he said. "I'm excited to see what you'll do for your tutorial. But it's not going to be this."

Theo's mouth set in a hard line.

"Jesus," Anna whispered. I hadn't realized she had been standing behind me. She took a bite of her salmon sandwich and mumbled, "That was brutal. Thank God my advisor doesn't give a shit about me."

I said, "Are there any more sandwiches left?"

She nodded toward the tea service.

❧

I couldn't focus on my reading. The page blurred as my thoughts circled, again and again, back to M. Neptune's words. *Vague, dangerous conclusions.*

I closed the book and leaned back in my chair. The rain pattered against the parlor windows, reminding me of a song, one I hadn't heard in a long time. I tried to think of the lyrics, but they drifted somewhere beyond my memory.

I closed my eyes. I could smell, outside, the soil dampening into spring softness. A warm breeze stirred the budding trees. An animal scuffled in the shrubs.

I opened my eyes to see Yaya standing in front of me, arms crossed. She wore a pink denim jacket, a pink denim skirt, and her costume pearl necklace. Her hair was long again, twisted into a million tiny braids that fell heavy as beads down to her waist.

"Ines," she said. "What's up?"

"I'm studying."

She glanced down at the books piled in front of me. They were all closed.

"I am," I said.

"Well, if you can *manage* to take a break," she said, "how about a little adventure? Remember you said you'd go to that attic with me?"

Yaya had spent all of dinner yesterday rambling about the attic. She'd found it that morning as she was wandering back from class, somewhere on the other side of the Ashley tower. She'd had only enough time to peek in and could already tell she'd need my help sorting through everything.

I followed Yaya into Ashley's shadowed halls. While we walked, Yaya rambled on about what she might find in the attic's depths. "I didn't get a good look, but I think maybe it's storage from when Catherine used to have a better theater department—you know, costumes and things. I think I saw some coats. What if there are furs? Real fur? Oh, but they would've sold those, if they were any good."

The dark stairs twisted up onto a landing, which led to a ladder. I followed Yaya up the ladder, hand over hand, to the attic door. She pushed it open and crawled through.

Up here, the noise of the rain on the low roof was as loud and overwhelming as a hallucination. I felt like I was in the bridge of a ship, looking out onto some colorless alien landscape.

Yaya flipped a switch and a ceiling light flickered on. Beneath its glow I saw that the attic was filled with dusty boxes, leather chests, piles of clutter, and racks upon racks of clothes.

Yaya strode over to one of the clothes racks. She plucked up a purple felted cloche and placed it on her head. She turned to me.

"Don't you just die?" she said.

I could see why she wanted my help going through everything. The boxes were crammed full of every kind of junk, from handkerchiefs to plastic swords, chess pieces to crusty bottles of shower gel. Yaya was probably right, that they were props left over from when Catherine used to stage productions. That was years ago, I'd heard. But now here it was: the profuse and random materials of those object-specific daydreams.

Yaya found a green velvet dress, a lace veil, some summer hats, and four sets of plastic animal masks that she decided she absolutely must keep. The only thing I wanted right away was one of the chess pieces. I chose a white rook, the castle. I liked the weight of it in my hand.

At the bottom of one box, I found a fake leather jacket. It had a tacky neon Chinese dragon embroidered on its back.

"I wonder if this would fit Theo," I said.

"What?" Yaya mumbled. She was buried in a clothes rack crammed with wool and velvet coats. "Why?"

"I don't know," I said. I turned the jacket over in my hand. The cuffs were a little frayed. Otherwise it was in good condition. "He'd probably love it. You know how he is."

"Yeah, I know how he is," Yaya said. "Falls in love quick and then quickly falls out."

I ran my fingers over the dragon's lurid body. It twisted and coiled as if in ecstatic agony.

I put the jacket back in its box.

In a chest of drawers, we found two dolls with long blond hair. We named them Yaya and Ines. In another drawer were eight packets of blank typewriter paper. Yaya wrinkled her nose.

"Wait, what's this?" Yaya said, reaching behind the chest of drawers. She wrenched at something with a clang, then pulled out a bicycle.

Even through a layer of dust, the bike's metallic blue sheen was almost supernatural. SCHWINN was written across the frame in graphic type.

"God," Yaya said. "I haven't ridden a bike in so long. My mama taught me how to ride. She'd take me out to the end of the street and make me practice over and over." Yaya ran a hand along the seat. "There were men there, at the end of the street. While my mama watched me, the men watched her. I hated it, the way they watched her. But she just let them stare."

Yaya touched her throat. She'd found a scarf in a pile by the window and wore it now clasped together with a frog-shaped brooch.

"I don't know how to ride a bike," I said.

"You don't? How can you not know how to ride a bike?"

I shrugged.

Yaya kicked at the wheel, testing its firmness. I couldn't read her expression. "My mama taught me everything," she said. "Everything I know."

Yaya and I slid the bike back behind the dresser. Then we gathered the dresses, piled hats on our heads, wedged the dolls under our arms, and shuffled our way back down the ladder.

❧

That spring, Diego and I were taking Introduction to Astronomy together. We both needed a science credit, and Diego thought studying the stars sounded more romantic than some dull environmental biology or organic chemistry course. It wasn't. The professor, a tough German man with a grim accent, would stand with his back to the class as he scribbled incomprehensible equations on the board and droned on about parsecs, black matter, and radiation theories, and I would be so bored I thought I was dying. Even Diego, who was usually an angel of a student, had trouble staying awake through the class.

But with Diego, even our suffering took on a kind of extravagance. We sat in the back of the room in our pajamas drinking glasses full of hot ginger tea. We composed songs to help memorize equations and sang them to our friends over dinner. And every Wednesday night we did our problem sets together in the Molina library. The sets shouldn't have taken us more than a couple of hours to finish, but with all our gossiping and drinking and sneaking off to the kitchen, our study sessions usually became all-night affairs.

"Why don't you just fuck Raphael?" I said.

Diego's lips twitched into a smile. It was two in the morning, and we'd just realized that we'd misread half the problem set. It would take us hours to recalculate everything.

"*Must* you be so vulgar?" Diego said.

"He's nice."

Diego took a careful, leisurely bite of an almond biscuit. "He's not very good-looking, is he?" he said after he swallowed.

"He has pretty hair." That was true. It was black and silky, strong as a horse's mane.

Diego shrugged. "He's just a silly kid. It's not worth it."

"Not worth what?"

"I don't know," he said. "The whole thing can be quite exhausting."

"It's easier when you don't have a heart."

"You have a heart."

"I don't," I said. "I used to, but not anymore. I cut it out years ago and hid it in a box and buried it in my backyard."

Diego yawned, stretching. He bowed his head to the table.

Our textbook was open to a black-and-white illustration of a galaxy. It whirled like the sea.

"Diego," I said, staring at the galaxy.

"Mmm."

"Do you know if Theo's decided what he's doing for his tutorial?"

"No," Diego mumbled into his arm. "Why would I?"

"I don't know," I said. "He . . . told me that he had almost settled on a project, but then his advisors wouldn't let him do it. That he should do something less . . . risky."

Diego blinked his eyes open.

"Don't you think that's weird?" I said.

Diego licked his finger.

"Don't hint at what you mean," he said, dabbing at the biscuit crumbs in that neat way of his. "Just say it."

I straightened in my chair.

"What if the new materials department isn't as innovative as it seems?" I said. "Anna thinks it is. Especially with M. Neptune in control. She thinks they're doing wild experiments again, testing on animals and everything. That they're even planning to do another experiment on us, sometime after forums. But if the department were really innovative, wouldn't they give Theo's ideas a chance?"

Diego licked his finger again.

"Everyone here believes in Catherine's research," I said. "Especially the new materials concentrators. Those kids applied here because despite everything—despite Catherine's scandals and defamations, despite all logic and evidence against us—they applied because they believed that this school had found something amazing. I don't know why they believed, but they did. Now they're in, and they see that they're right to trust in Catherine. But just because plasm is real doesn't mean we understand it. What does the department actually know about new materials? We can reproduce M. Shiner's results, sure, but can we do anything else? I mean, when was the last time you heard of us publishing new research?"

Diego didn't meet my eye as he dabbed at the crumbs.

"Just because the department hasn't been publishing does not mean it hasn't been working," he finally said. He spoke slowly and carefully. "Of course Theo couldn't do some risky experimental project for his tutorial. Tutorials are public projects. But nothing the department *really* does is public, not after M. Shiner. We learned our lesson there—we can be as radical as we like in this house, but out there we have to be conservative. We're not going to share any more of our research before it's ready. So, who knows what Theo's actually going to work on? What do any of those kids really do?"

"But M. Neptune himself told Theo his idea was impossible. 'Vague and dangerous'—that's what M. Neptune called the project. I heard him."

"Exactly," Diego said. "You heard him. Which means M. Neptune was talking where you could listen. Which means he probably wasn't telling the truth."

I chewed at my tongue. According to the scrapbooks in the library, M. Neptune's whole world was plasm. He'd come to Catherine for plasm research, studied nothing but plasm for three years, and now spent his days, weeks, and years testing and analyzing and theorizing plasm. When I saw him wandering through the house's halls or laughing chummily with professors and students, he seemed like a completely normal man. But really, he was like Baby; plasm was his life. So if his lab's work was so groundbreaking, wouldn't he want to share it with the world?

Diego was dabbing at the biscuit crumbs again.

"You agree with Anna, then," I said. "You think they're still doing big experiments. Testing on animals and everything."

"Do you really think they're not?" Diego gestured around the library. "Ines, look around. This house, it doesn't make sense. It's not playing by any real rules. Have you ever seen a health inspector here? Do you think we pay the kind of taxes we should?" He shook his head. "M. Neptune is going to do whatever he can get away with. More, even. Viktória knows that—that's why she hired him. We know it, too. Who cares?"

He dropped his hand.

"I didn't come to Catherine to be practical or to play by the rules," he said. "You didn't, either. We came here to be something else."

"What?" I said. "What did we come here to be?"

"Oh. I don't know. Just . . . something else. Something better."

I was getting a headache. I closed the textbook.

He rubbed my back. "Ines," he said.

"Yes?"

"Can we go get more almond biscuits?"

I sighed. I nodded.

Nick lived on the other side of the Molina courtyard from me and Theo, in a suite of four. His roommates were three rich, tall, athletic boys who all took the same classes, played the same games, and slept with the same girls. Their parlor was always loud and sticky and dank with sweat. Whenever Theo and I stopped by, one of them would be in the bathroom peeing, shitting, or brushing his teeth with the door open, and the others would be splayed over the sofas, boasting and laughing, loud as kings. They wrestled and farted in each other's faces. They spat into teacups that they then lined up on the windowsill like trophies. I didn't ask why.

If a nice girl visited their suite—an usher, maybe, or a pretty first-year asking to borrow a book—the boys performed with perfect grace. They offered her tea, warmed her slippers by the radiator, and told elegant jokes about the weather. I never received such genteel behavior.

"Come on!" the boys were shouting. "To Ashley!"

Theo laughed, hugging his belly. It was the day after midterms, and the two of us were hanging out in Nick's suite. I was delirious with sleep deprivation after staying up all night to study for my Monuments and Memorials test. The boys were making me feel human again. They taught me a game involving sipping wine, clapping and stomping, and hooting and screeching like various jungle animals. It was a good game. I couldn't keep track of the rules, but I knew I was losing. The boys laughed with me. Their mouths were stained wine-black.

Then they were shouting and gathering up their things. There were some girls in Ashley they were hoping to get to know better. Theo couldn't go. His stomach hurt. He didn't want to move. So the boys disappeared to the party, and I stayed with Theo.

I shuffled the cards. I dealt for gin rummy.

Theo's eyes swam over the cards. He tried to sit up straight.

"Fuck," I said as he laid down a run of clubs.

"Four points," he counted. "Five points. Plus three—that's twenty-four. Oh my God. I'm already winning. I feel amazing. How do you feel?"

"Amazing," I said. "I feel amazing."

Theo gathered his cards and shuffled them together. Each of his fingers had a little bit of hair below the knuckle. Sometimes I forgot he was fully grown—that he was a man, not a boy.

"It's going to be so wonderful when I win," I said. "It's going to be the comeback of the century."

"You're never going to win. At gin. Win at gin." His face was flushed.

"I can win other things."

"What can you win?"

"Cooking. I make good scrambled eggs."

"I don't believe you."

"I really do."

"Man, my eggs are better. Cream, that's the trick. Add a little cream. I bet you don't do that."

"I guess we'll never know."

"No, I do know. My eggs are better. The only thing you win at is *watching*."

I laughed. "What?"

"Your eyes." He gestured toward his own, though he wasn't looking at me. "You stare. You don't blink. I bet you'd win, like. Any staring contest. Even in, like. A carnival."

"*You* stare. You're the one who stares." I rocked back on my heels. "Look at me."

He looked up.

"Wait," I said, "let me get my eyes moist."

I closed my eyes, then opened them again.

I could do this. I could win.

But he was already laughing and shaking his head. He reached for the bottle of wine.

"God," I said lightly. "I'm already stressed about my tutorial project. My advisor wants an outline of my prospective reading by next week." I crossed my legs. "How's yours going?"

He shrugged.

"What are you doing it on?"

He hesitated. "I have a topic," he said finally. "A good one. But the department doesn't want me to do it."

"Why not?"

He shrugged again.

"What's the topic?"

"It's—come on, it's not interesting. I promise."

I said, "I'm interested."

He swirled the wine in his teacup.

"All right," he said. "Well, it's hard to explain if you don't have a real understanding of plasm, which most people don't. But think of it this way." He shifted on his heels. "Most new material experimentation and mending has been done discretely, on one particular object or one particular animal or person. Even when we're mending across holes or whatever other distances, it's about uniting disparate parts of a single item. Or what we're thinking as of a single item. But the truth is, plasm doesn't really work like that. It's material, yes, the *prima materia*—the substance of creation—but more importantly, it's a network connecting all things, everywhere. Everything real, anyway. And that conception of plasm as a network is what's really exciting. The network is what makes mending possible in the first place. So I want to experiment with not just mending one object or another, but mending across objects, in a system. Get it?"

"No," I said.

Theo downed his cup of tea.

I placed my hand over his.

"Show me," I whispered.

He looked into my eyes. He wiped his lips with the back of his hand.

"In the new materials lab," I said. "I've never been. I want to see. If your stomach feels better."

He stood up.

"It feels—" He tripped over his feet as he reached for shoes. "Never better."

The new materials lab was in Harrington, where I had followed the concentrators after session so many weeks ago. Now here I was following Theo past the same chlorine-scented halls and up the same stairway. The walls shifted with moon shadows. He grabbed my hand to steer me along the long yellow hallway. My heart thumped.

Theo opened the door and flicked on the lights.

It was a narrow, ugly room in the stark fluorescence. Students from outside the concentration weren't necessarily forbidden from entering, but the space still had a hush of privacy about it. Long lab tables covered with various messes of flasks and books and random things—embroidery kits, broken pocket mirrors—receded into the depths of the room. Plasm pin kits lay open, forgotten, on stools and across pages of scribbled reports. The blackboard was filled with notes and equations I didn't understand.

I paced the room, running my hand along one lab table's sleek laminate surface. The stainless-steel fixtures flashed.

So this was where Catherine's funding went.

I wrinkled my nose. The room had a warm animal smell. When I turned, I saw that a series of cages lined one of the walls.

I bent to look in. Most of the cages were empty, but one had a nest of shavings with a little family of white mice. And farther, deep in the shadows of another, sat a white rabbit. Its eyes were closed.

Theo strode toward the back of one of the lab tables. "So," he said, "you understand plasm as the *prima materia*."

"Kind of," I said, unbending from the cage. "Material as the origin of material."

"Right. So that when we manipulate plasm in an object—or an animal—we're manipulating . . . well, think of it like manipulating the object's soul. If souls were real. Right?"

"Yes," I said.

"Man, I bet you've never even seen—wait. Let me show you."

Theo pulled out a cage and set it on the lab table. A mouse was sniffing around inside.

He glanced at me. "You won't tell anyone, right?" Then he smiled. "Of course you won't. You never say anything."

He reached into the cage and deftly grabbed the mouse by the tail, as if he had done it many times before. At the same time, he pulled a knife out of a drawer.

He nicked the mouse's belly. For a moment, nothing happened. Then blood began beading on the mouse's fragile skin.

Theo placed the mouse on the lab table. He grabbed two plasm pins that had been sitting nearby.

"I know they don't look it, but these are pretty powerful," he said as he stroked them along the mouse's wound, then wrapped them along its body. His voice was low with concentration. "Pretty big procedure for a cute little guy like this. Look."

The mouse sat frozen under the touch of the plasm pins. Its

nose twitched in wild panic. But the blood had stopped beading. It had stopped flowing at all.

I shouldn't have been surprised to see the plasm pins mend a live wound. I imagined the Catherine doctor used the pins in her cabinet for cuts and injuries. And, of course, I knew how powerful the pins were; I had felt them myself. But for some reason, watching the mouse's cut close up, I felt queasy.

I blinked. "Right," I said.

"So," Theo said as he placed the mouse back in its cage, "it looks impressive, but it's really not that different from the psychosexual mending we've been doing. It's easy, surface-level stuff. We're just manipulating . . ." I could see his brain working, trying to figure out how to explain it to me. "We're just manipulating what's already there," he finally said. "All the changes are very local. And in terms of plasm, animals and objects are basically the same. That's what people don't get." He glanced at the mouse. "Anyway, this shit looks way more impressive than it actually is. We could do much more now. Like, what if instead of manipulating the plasm *within* each object, we manipulated it *between* objects?"

I followed Theo to the end of the lab table, over to a cardboard box. The box was filled with shavings and another little mouse, sniffing contentedly. There was also a cheap plastic mirror, the kind that hung in barbershops. It leaned against one side of the box, and a teddy bear slumped against the other. A fluffy, curly-haired, black-eyed teddy bear with a red ribbon tied around its neck.

Plasm pins snaked through the shavings, connecting the mirror to the teddy bear, and the teddy bear to the mouse.

"This is Gerald," Theo said, tapping against the cardboard. "Say hi, Gerald."

I bent toward the box. The mouse's eyes darted to me, but the pin stopped him from moving. "Hi, Gerald," I said.

"Gerald's been my buddy for a while now. But look—"

He reached inside, undid the pins, and grabbed Gerald. His little mouse legs squirmed as Theo turned him over.

Gerald's belly was nicked, just like the other mouse's. He was bleeding.

"You hurt him," I said.

"No," he said, "he's not hurt. Not really. I cut him there a month ago. The cut hasn't healed, but it hasn't changed, either."

I opened my hand. Theo slid Gerald into my palm. The mouse moved sluggishly, as if emerging from a deep dream. I brushed his tiny skull. I could feel his heart beating.

"Don't you get it?" he said. "I've used the pins to connect him to the plasm in the mirror and the plasm in the teddy bear. To a network. He's pinned to them. And you see, I can even remove him from the pins for a while, and the effect stays the same. It's like . . . he's knitted to them."

"You've joined them. Joined their exterior plastic infinities to their interior plastic infinities."

"What?"

I rubbed Gerald's nose. "It's from Boccioni's manifesto of Futurist sculpture."

"If you say so."

"You're not just mending one object," I said. "You're mending a circuit. Generating plasm off one thing and into another. Like a series of batteries."

Theo nodded. "Right," he said. "Exactly. Which only works because plasm really does operate as a system, not just as random individual clusters that make up one object, animal, or person. Nothing and no one is really alone. We have to stop thinking that way. We're all infinitely connected, all part of the same structure. And once we understand that, look what happens." He touched Gerald's head. "We get past the framework of deterioration versus recovery, age versus youth . . . And we find whole new modes of life. Life in suspended animation."

I slipped Gerald back in the cage. My hand was dotted with mouse blood.

"So," I said. "You guys really are testing on animals. Obviously."

Theo shrugged as he pinned Gerald back in the box. "I mean, yeah. And Viktória and M. Neptune test on us, of course. But even the coming in and stuff isn't anything new. That's still discrete mending, just . . . well, what's known as 'psychosexual' mending rather than corporeal. Souped-up Freud shit, basically. But this"—he gestured toward Gerald's box—"mending across multiple objects, using lifeless objects to sustain living beings—this is the future of plasm. It's gotta be. And that's the direction M. Shiner was kind of going in, but . . ." He shifted on his feet, then said, "I mean, we all know M. Shiner's methods were shitty and he was a bit, um, hyperbolic about his results. But he wasn't as insane as people think. It's just that people were afraid of his big questions. About life and death. So they never took him seriously. But what's the point of doing anything if you're not trying to answer the big questions?"

Gerald sniffed at his teddy bear.

For some reason I thought of the Weissenbruch painting in the gallery. The little sparrow, "so beautifully alive, forever," fluttering through its rigid landscape.

"Anyway," Theo said, "I'm just playing around. It hasn't come to anything yet."

Gerald settled into his shavings.

"Do you think you'll ever go into the umbrella room?" I said.

"The umbrella room?"

"The lab in the back of Ashley, in the hallway with the umbrella wallpaper," I said. "The room with the keypad."

"Oh, M. Neptune's lab." Theo smiled sadly. "Man, I wish. No.

I don't, uh, I don't do so good in M. Neptune's class. He says I'm a sloppy scholar, that my research is all over the place. And apparently, I can't write. *Cogently*, I can't write *cogently*. I get the worst grades from him. It's messed up."

He scratched his head.

"To be honest—I'm not doing so great right now," he said, lower. "None of my professors like what I'm doing. They're more into, like, philosophy and critical theory, which I'm pretty bad at. I can *show* what I mean, but I'm not good at explaining how it works. If it were fifteen years ago, maybe it'd be different, but the department's been pretty strict about who can experiment after everything with M. Shiner. I'm not getting into that lab. I might not even graduate in the concentration."

He picked up a pencil and passed it idly from one hand to another.

"M. Neptune wants to meet with me next week," he said. "To talk about my time here. My 'academic path,' he called it. You know what that means."

I looked up, but Theo wouldn't meet my eye. Would they really throw out someone as smart as him?

"I want to keep going," he whispered. "I can't change my topic. I just can't. I'm not going to write up some stupid critical research essay about, like, plasm in blood proteins or something. I'm not going to give up my project. This is what I came here to do."

Gerald had fallen asleep again.

"Maybe I can get the key to M. Neptune's lab," I said, "and tell you what's there. If it's even wilder than this."

Theo laughed. "What, without even being in the concentration? What are you going to do, seduce someone into letting you in?"

"Sure," I said. "I was going to seduce you, but if M. Neptune hates you, I guess I need another plan."

"Well. If you do get in, let me know. I bet they have some great shit in there."

"You, too," I said, "for me. If you get in, tell me. What's inside."

"Sure."

"Promise?"

"Promise," he said.

"Pinkie-swear."

We pinkie-swore. Then we spat on our hands and shook.

Spring warmed and swelled. Sweet grass perfumed the yard and petals blanketed the pathways. Down in the garden, the lilacs and honeysuckles bloomed and bees hummed over the fountain. On the balcony, in the afternoon, ants swarmed over our abandoned tea things, the honey and the creamer.

We ate light breakfasts of cantaloupe and yogurt and lingered in the morning room playing cards. In class, we passed each other notes and made paper airplanes. We lazed on the yard after dinner, drinking warm wine. We played Capture the Flag and Ghost in the Graveyard. I ran until my lungs hurt, then collapsed to the ground. The grass and soil felt so cool beneath my neck, the stars so high and whirling.

As I hurried between classes, my back damp with sweat, I saw everything with electric specificity. I saw a first-year girl's T-shirt ride up as she waved to her roommate across a courtyard. I saw the roommate wave back and giggle. I saw sun glint off her necklace. I saw my professor's hand twitch as it closed the classroom door and turned off the light. As the days heated up, everything smelled closer and hotter. I walked by a boy on a bench, smelled his sour sweat, and thought, *After class, he's going to fuck his girlfriend.* When I turned to look back at him, I was jostled by a girl jogging past me, and I smelled her, too. She was late to class.

Fantasy twilights softened into night. At session, the words flowed so easily I felt as if someone else's spirit were speaking through my mouth: *I am down the hall. The hall is in the house.* We ate dinners of salmon, melon salad, and peach shortcakes with cream. We did our homework on the yard. We drank more wine. We felt so good.

Anna and I stayed up late in the parlor putting together a jigsaw puzzle. The picture was of a kitten playing with a ball of yarn. "What do you think it feels like to be a man?" Anna said as we worked. "To have a penis and, like—just fuck over the whole world?"

"Incredible," I said. "So amazing."

The night grew longer, and Anna fell asleep on the puzzle. I picked off the pieces stuck to her face. Her skin felt cool and soft.

"Oh my God," Nick said as his croquet ball rolled into the bushes. "You are too mean."

"You can hit me back," I said.

He gave me the finger and darted after his ball.

"I love you," I said.

I hitched up my pajama pants, bent to get a better view, and aimed for my next move. I was going to ruin Nick's life.

We had set up the croquet game near the sunflower field. We assigned the mallet colors by personality—I was black, "because you're such a depressive mean-ass bitch"—and Yaya had brought the hats we'd found in the attic, because what was a garden party without sun hats? Nick's straw boater kept flying off in the breeze; Anna laughed every time he scampered after it. Diego had mixed up glasses of moonshine mint juleps for us. The ice cubes chimed like bells as we roamed over the grass, the glasses sweating against our palms.

I pushed down the brim of my hat and idly swung my mallet. The yard smelled cheery today, like strawberries and clover.

Theo and Yaya were striding over to us from the Molina courtyard.

Nick swung at my ball. He missed. He cursed.

"Ines," Yaya called to me, "come here. We have a surprise for you."

"What kind of surprise?"

"An important surprise," Theo said. "A life-changing surprise."

"I don't have time for life-changing surprises." I strolled over to my ball. "I'm about to murder Nick."

Nick slurped at his mint julep.

Theo leaned against a tree and tapped his arm. He was smiling at me.

"Be patient," I said. I lined up my shot.

After I won the game, I followed Theo and Yaya out of the garden, past the fountain in the bluebell field, and into the yard. There, leaning against an oak tree, stood the bicycle.

I walked over and pulled it upright. It looked different here in the daylight, out from the attic's gloom. The metal gleamed silvery rocket-blue, like some futuristic wonder machine.

"Theo helped me bring it down," Yaya said. "We decided it's time for you to learn how to ride."

I ran a hand along its leather seat.

First Yaya showed me how to brake. "I know it's not your style, but it really is a most important skill," she said with teacherly priss. I leaned against her arm as she placed my feet on the pedals. It was easy enough. But when I pushed off, my stomach dropped with the panic of falling, and I grabbed at Theo.

"Wait," he said against my neck, "you need *momentum*—"

I toppled against him. My pajamas pants were covered with grass stains.

They piled me back onto the bike and pushed me forward. After some shaky starts, I was really up, and my feet cycled faster. Theo was shouting, "Go! Go! Go!"

I was going. I was bicycling across the yard, toward the trees. I was flying. I screamed.

Then my legs scrambled, the sky tilted, and I was down again.

"Are you okay?" Theo yelled as they ran after me.

I couldn't answer, though. I was out of breath, and laughing.

Theo collapsed beside me. He was panting, too. His eyes were shining.

I turned to him. I touched his hand.

"Let's do it again," I breathed.

We took turns on the bike. Yaya cycled in beautiful lazy circles, her chin held high. Theo kept falling on his ass as he tried to do a wheelie. But I didn't want to do tricks. I only wanted to go farther and farther.

Soon Yaya and Theo were chasing me as I biked across the yard, over the path, into the west, into the shadowed trees—skipping over roots and stones—to the gate.

I stopped, gasping. I climbed off the bike. It had been a long time since I had been this close to the gate.

I reached a hand out to touch it. The iron was cool.

I squinted past it, into the trees on the other side. We were near Catherine's main entrance; I could just make out the yellow of the front road, where we had all come in as first-years. It was empty now.

"Hey," someone said.

I turned. A paunchy man had appeared behind me. He wore a gray suit and sunglasses.

Who was he? Did I recognize him from that first day, when we first checked into the house? I didn't remember. I didn't remember anything from that day.

His arms were folded.

"Hi," he said sweetly. "What are you doing so far from the house?"

"I'm just," I said, panting, "looking."

"That's a nice bike," he said.

A cloud moved, and light flashed over his sunglasses.

"I think you should go back," he said. "And leave the bike here."

"It's mine," I said.

"No," he said, "it's not."

I glanced back out through the gate.

A breeze passed through the dark woods. The trees shivered.

Theo touched my shoulder. I hadn't realized that he and Yaya had caught up to me.

"Hey," he whispered, closer now, his eyes on the guard. "Let's go. I think dinner's soon."

Yaya took the bike from me, glaring at the guard. She lifted her chin as if daring him to grab it from her. But he only smiled.

We were silent as we made our way across the yard. I didn't get back on the bike. I didn't feel like riding anymore.

THE KEY

Forums were scheduled for August, which should have been enough time to pull together a study plan and presentation. But the classes I was taking in preparation for my Agnes Martin tutorial—Philosophy of Postwar Abstract Expressionism, Semiotic Critical Theory—were lunatic. The text packets were full of oblique essays about haptic forces and hagiography, theoretical movements and progressive impulses. Too often, I would reach the end of an article only to forget which artist we were even discussing. In seminar, the professor would click on an image and ask me to analyze it within the framework of a particular historian's critical method and I couldn't even pretend to understand the question.

We had reading response papers due every other day. But how could I respond to those incomprehensible essays? I sat in the library staring at my blank notebook page and felt nothing, not even panic. I took naps and woke up without remembering who I was or what I was doing. I tried to do push-ups. I could do only two.

I wandered through the library looking for someone to distract me. When I found no one, I went to the reference room and paged through the old scrapbooks again. I studied the photo of the boy, the one who had died six years ago, and wished I were dead. Dead people didn't have to do homework.

I met with the gallery curator, my boss, to ask if she could lower my hours for the rest of the semester. I needed more time to study. But before I could even ask the question, I was staring into her soft eyes and crying.

"Sorry," I mumbled, wiping my face. "Fuck."

She placed her hand over mine. "It's difficult, I know," she said softly. "Catherine is a difficult school. This, what you're feeling, this is why we have such a reputation for excellence. It's not easy to become excellent."

I blew my nose.

I was also taking a class on late medieval art that semester. June afternoons, Diego and I wandered through the gallery examining triptychs and altarpieces with saints praying in craggy blue mountains, Jesus suffering in the garden. Their misery was flamboyant and gorgeous.

"There was an altarpiece in my church," Diego said, staring at an egg tempera of saints lamenting the dead Christ. "When I was little. Mary enthroned with little angels around her, flying with silver wings. Every Sunday I sat with the other altar boys and listened to the priest talk, but I couldn't really hear him. I just stared at her—Mary. She was so beautiful. Surrounded by gold."

Diego's voice was soft.

"I think it was the first beautiful thing I ever loved," he said. "All that gold."

He cleared his throat. He put his hands in his neatly creased pockets. He started to move on to the next work.

"But where is she?" I said.

He blinked, turning back to me. "What? Where's who?"

"Mary—enthroned, surrounded by gold. All that gold. What did M. Engels call it? 'The sublime surface.' Here." I gestured toward the saints, their flat faces and flat gilded world. "Where are they? Where is this setting? Where is Mary?"

Diego said, "Heaven."

That was right, of course. That's what they thought gold was:

the stuff of heaven, matter more magical than life. The birth of the world.

I felt I had asked the wrong question. There was something I didn't understand, there on the surface of the painting. But I wasn't sure what it was.

❧

The year before, I hadn't realized how unhappy and crazy the second-years were during the Founders' Festival. This year Anna and I spent the night before the festival drunk and dizzy, sleeping on the library floor. I wasn't sure of the time when Theo finally shook us awake. He lured us down to the yard with the promise of funnel cakes.

Going to the festival felt like returning to a dream. There was the bouncy castle, the Ferris wheel, and the high striker. There were the grills and picnic blankets and the brass band, though I didn't recognize any of the boys in it. There were the blue and yellow ribbons wrapped around the oak trees. Here I was, again.

"Look at them," Anna mumbled. She was watching a group of noisy first-years waiting in line for the bouncy castle. "Were we ever so young and free?"

"I don't know what you're complaining about," Yaya said. She stood with her arm slipped through Diego's. They both wore big purple sunglasses. "You're acing everything. You know your shit."

"Yeah," Anna said. "I do know my shit. I just wish I didn't have to keep proving it over and over again."

"I have an idea," I said.

They all turned to me.

"Let's pretend," I said, "for today. Let's pretend that our minds are empty, and we're kids, and we have nothing else to do."

So that's what we did. It was easy, because it was almost true. We ate hot dogs and cotton candy. We danced to the brass band.

We placed bets on who could hit the striker highest; then we bounced in the castle until we were dizzy. We drank lemonade and peach brandy moonshine. We collapsed on the dewy grass beneath the trees.

I lay with my head against Theo's thigh. He ran his fingers through my hair. Sweet summer sunshine warmed my legs and neck. Even though my brain hurt, I felt nice. The whole day felt nice.

Maybe all the work and the stress were a good thing. Maybe my boss was right. The essays, the images, the hours of talking with my professors—maybe this was what it felt like to become good.

Theo's hand crept down my arm.

A perfumed breeze drifted over the grass. It smelled like the house, rosy and mystic. Early fireflies winked in the pines.

How could I have ever thought Catherine was a bad house?

"Do you want more cotton candy?" Theo said, his voice close to my ear.

I nodded.

He rubbed my arm again, then slid out from under me.

"God," Yaya said as she watched Theo bound over to meet Nick in the cotton candy line.

"What?"

"Child, you're in trouble."

I shifted to look at her face. There was an almost-angry lift to her chin as she tugged at the string of pearls around her neck.

"What?" I said.

"You're sinking," she said. Her eyes were following Theo. "And you don't even realize it."

I didn't ask what she meant.

She plucked a clover. She pulled off its leaves one by one.

I sat up. The bouncy castle had made me so dizzy.

Nick and Theo were walking back now with big puffs of blue and yellow cotton candy. When Theo sat down, I could smell him—his shampoo, his sweat, the nape of his neck—and I felt, down in my stomach, a surge of something huge and indistinct. Something I didn't recognize.

What was I doing?

"What's wrong?" Theo said.

"Nothing," I said. "I'm hot."

I picked up the cotton candy, then put it down again.

A cloud of gnats swarmed over the grass.

"I'm sick," I said.

❧

I lay in bed later that night in the dark, tangled in my bedsheets, drunk and hot. I put a hand to my head. I had been dreaming. No, it was real. The memories of the day doubled and refracted like shadow visions: Yaya and me crawling into the bouncy castle with bottles of wine. Running across the yard and throwing up by a tree. Having sex with someone—yes, a third-year from my Critical Theory seminar—somewhere in the bushes, in the early evening.

I curled up tighter and hugged my stomach. We hadn't used a condom.

Maybe I was pregnant. I could be pregnant right now. I could feel some toothed little creature taking hold inside me, growing bigger and bigger.

There was no air in my room. I was going to die in here.

I turned on my lamp. I breathed.

Yaya was right; I was in trouble. Something was getting out of control. I had thought that going deeper into the house, filling myself with its dark places, would feel good. But something was wrong. I couldn't keep track of what was pretend and what was true. When I tried to remember anything real, all I could think of was Theo's sun-warmed hand against my arm.

Theo. What was I doing?

Theo never felt confused like this. He was so sure of himself, so confident that his work was good and important. I hadn't been able to coax him into telling me any more about his project, not since that night with the mice, but I could tell he was still working on it. He spent all his time in the plasm lab. He skipped lunches and dinners, even sessions. And I could tell from his shadowed eyes that he wasn't getting enough sleep. Who cared about sleep? This was why he came to Catherine. To create something vital and important.

But what if Theo didn't know what he was doing? His research could be wrong. After all, he was wrong about me; he thought I was nice. And M. Neptune thought Theo was a sloppy scholar, that his project was completely misguided. He didn't even consider Theo advanced enough to have on his team. What if Theo didn't know what he was doing?

What was he doing? And what was I doing?

I pressed the heels of my hands against my eyes.

I'm in the house, I whispered to myself. I'm in my room. I'm here.

My doorknob turned. It was Yaya, wrapped in a blanket, her braids knotted on top of her head. She waved a lazy hand at me before sliding into my desk chair.

"How are you feeling?" she said. "Any better?"

"No."

"Me neither," she said, though her voice was cheerful. "I think I'm dying." She stuck out a long bare leg and flexed her foot to examine her toenails. They were painted silver. "Hungover at midnight. How divine."

"I'm glad you're here," I said.

"You, too. Who was that?"

"Who?

"That guy you ran off with."

"I don't know. He's in my Critical Theory class."

She wrapped the blanket tighter around herself. "Girl, good for you."

She fiddled with one of the Master Locks lying on my desk. I'd taken to picking the locks with Baby's kit. I didn't have a reason. It didn't really calm me down.

I rubbed my stomach. "I need to eat something."

"The hall's closed."

"We can get cookies from the kitchen."

"Ooh." Yaya sat up, then back down again. "Oh, that's too far."

"I can get them for us."

"Would you really?" She crossed her hands over her heart. "My hero."

I padded through the hallways in my pajama shirt, bare-legged. The festival had spawned smaller parties in the house's bedrooms and parlors. Laughter echoed through a vent and a door slammed from the end of a hall. My footsteps echoed past the large windows.

As I approached the sitting room by the great hall, I heard a thudding noise that I couldn't place. I peeked through the door.

It was two of M. Neptune's new materials concentrators: Burt and Sandy, the short, strange boy with the dark curls and vague eyes. They were playing catch with a blue rubber ball. Burt tossed the ball to Sandy. The ball flew through the air in a perfect, high arc. Sandy dove for it, arms reaching, but missed. He tripped over his feet and stumbled with puppet-like gawkiness. The ball bounced under a chair.

Burt's sharp eyes followed Sandy as he crawled after the ball and brought it back. Neither of them said anything. Burt let him stand in place; then he threw the ball again, and Sandy missed it again.

I stood there, watching them play, for a long time.

❧

In the end, my forum presentation went fine. After all those days I spent writing essays and reports, nights spent sleeping on the library floor, the presentation itself was a blur. I stood onstage with a smear of faces staring back and was hit with the shock that I actually knew what I was talking about. The professors' questions were savage, but I answered them. Then the presentation was over, my plan approved, and I was done.

Yaya and Diego presented the day after mine. I brought them a breakfast of strawberries and yogurt and helped them get ready in the Molina parlor. Diego had asked me to quiz him with flash cards, then retreated to the bathroom as soon as I appeared. Every once in a while, a moan passed through the bathroom door.

I didn't feel good, either. I was hungover. My mouth tasted like sand and the parlor's morning brilliance pierced my brain. It hurt to think.

Yaya was trying to decide if she should wear her white pleather heels or wooden clogs. She sucked on a strawberry as she stepped into one shoe, then the other. Her dress flashed with dripping turquoise beads.

"The white ones," I said.

She stepped into the heel. "Really? Not too high?"

"Just high enough."

She bent to strap them on.

Theo was scheduled to present today, too. I would have thought he would be anxious, but some change had come over him in the past week. He was calmer, more awake. He didn't spend as much time in the plasm lab. He came to breakfast whistling, hung around the parlor after tea, even played charades with us in the evening. And last night, while Yaya and Diego practiced their presentations for me, I looked out the window and saw him crossing the courtyard. He was actually going to bed early.

He wasn't nervous. He wasn't worried at all. Which meant his project had come to some kind of conclusion.

And he was going to do it. He was going to show us everything.

The bathroom door clicked open. Diego emerged, wiping his mouth with a tidy handkerchief.

Yaya stood up in her shoes and put her hands on her hips. "Listen, child, are you going to be okay?"

Diego sat on the edge of the settee. "I do *not* like public speaking," he murmured.

"We're not in public," Yaya said.

Diego picked up a strawberry, then put it down.

Yaya sat beside Diego to rub his back. "Precious baby," she said.

He rested his head in her lap. "Can we run away together?" he whispered.

"Sure," she said. "After graduation."

Like last year, forums were held in the Harrington auditorium. It was August now, and even with the windows wide open, the room was hot and dead still. Cicadas droned in the trees. In the back of the room, third-years and first-years lounged together, whispering as they passed around honeydew slices, figs, and glasses of mint tea. The second-years gathered in quiet, anxious knots in the front rows, right behind the professors.

"Are you nervous?" I asked Yaya as we went to sit with the other second-years.

"About what?"

"I don't know. Failing."

Yaya frowned, as if she didn't even understand the question. "I'm not going to fail."

Diego hugged his stomach. He looked like he might throw up again.

Viktória was sitting at the end of the faculty row, next to M. Neptune. Her hair was twisted up into a strict high ponytail. She wasn't smiling.

Theo was at the end of the row in front of us. These days, I was always hyperaware of his presence, even if I could barely see him. I could just make out his fuzzy hair and neck. He was wearing his current favorite shirt, a bright teal polo with yellow buttons that Yaya had gotten him from the commissary. The shirt had a small rip in the sleeve. I couldn't see the rip now, but I knew it was there.

"Fig?" Yaya said. She had gathered a handful of them before sitting down. I took one of the sticky fruits from her palm.

The first presenter was a tiny blondish boy. He was a history concentrator focusing on black visual traditions, specifically zombies. In his dispassionate voice, he explained how the zombie myth traveled from Haiti and through the American imagination, how the superstition shifted as it moved across various cultures and times. I thought the presentation seemed fine, but his advisor kept asking for more and more details on various areas of research. The boy just repeated tonelessly, "Yes . . . Yes . . . Yes, I do plan to explore that further."

The next presenter was a small Indian girl who wanted to analyze the biology of a particular tulip pest. Her hands shook every time she moved to switch the transparency. When she finished, the biology professors spent half an hour barraging her with questions and criticizing her essential premises, suggesting she choose a different track or switch topics entirely. The girl's voice grew smaller and smaller as she tried to respond. When she finally sat down, her face was wet with tears.

Viktória held a notebook open on her lap, but she hadn't written anything down. She didn't move at all. Only her eyes followed the girl as she took her seat.

Theo was walking up to the stage. He flipped through his transparencies. He fitted one onto the projector.

"Please introduce yourself," M. David said as he scribbled something on his clipboard.

"My name is Theo Williams," he said. "I'm a new materials concentrator."

Theo stood motionless beside the projector. His face was empty.

"And the topic of your tutorial?" M. David said.

"I plan to perform a research study on plasm development in moss architecture from seed to bloom," he said.

"Excellent." M. David jotted down another note.

Theo clicked on the projector.

Theo flipped through moss photographs as he outlined what we already knew about plasm and flowerless plant growth. He presented a list of the available literature, most of which was already on site in the library, and the mosses that were available here in the garden and elsewhere around Catherine. He gave a list of specialists he might reach out to and critical texts he would order in. The paper would be theoretical in scope. It would be about one hundred pages long.

Yaya yawned. "Pinch me when it's my turn," she mumbled, slumping lower in her seat.

What was this? Where was Theo's real project? What was he doing?

Theo's advisor said nothing. Neither did M. Neptune, who sat still and firm, hands folded over his stomach.

Viktória tucked a stray strand of hair behind her ear. Her emerald ring flashed.

"Thanks," M. Neptune said as Theo removed the last transparency. "Sounds great. You can take your seat."

❧

In the morning room, I watched Theo pile his plate with wheat crackers and hard-boiled eggs, frowning as he tried to balance it all together. The slippery eggs kept sliding around the plate. He must have felt me watching him, though, because he looked up.

He stared back at me. Neither of us smiled.

I put down my yogurt spoon and started to stand, but he was already turning to walk out of the room.

I sat back down. I picked up my spoon.

❧

When I arrived at our next session, I felt like something was different.

I glanced around the hall. Yes, something had changed. The hall was emptier than usual. There were no first- or third-years in the hall, only second-years. We were spread around the room, as we usually were during session, but we were alone. We eyed each other in uneasy silence.

I folded my hands tightly together. My heart beat against my pressed palms.

Viktória stood with lowered eyes in her usual place by the window, her hair neatly brushed over her shoulder. I wished I were sitting close enough to see her face. But unlike our usual sessions, she wasn't the only administrator here; M. Neptune was sitting on the dais, a notebook and pen on the table in front of him.

It was the weird, in-between time of day when afternoon

became evening, the light in the hall turning gray and oblique. I felt like I couldn't see anyone's face clearly.

Viktória took a sip of water. Then she set down the glass and straightened.

"Welcome," she said, "to today."

She gestured in, toward her heart. "Come in closer," she said.

We looked around blankly at each other, then moved to sit at tables closer to her, by the windows. As we gathered, I had the sudden impression that I was at our coming in again, and didn't yet know anyone around me. That wasn't true, of course; a girl from one of my German classes was sitting on my right, and Anna was right there across the table, not meeting my eye. But somehow we all felt like strangers again, in some new place.

"My precious ones." Viktória smiled. "It's been a long time since it's been only us, together. And I know this time has not been easy. This school—this experience—is not right for everyone. Some of the students who first walked into this house two years ago are not here today. But all of you, everyone in this room, you have each spent these past years in total devotion to your studies, to one another, and to Catherine. You are all here now. And you are here magnificently."

Aides and a few new materials concentrators, M. Neptune's students, filed in from the kitchen with trays in their hands. I peered to get a better look as they set the trays on the edges of the tables. They were the same trays from our coming in, laden with the same cakes, clay cups of wine, and plasm pins.

"How wonderful this is," Viktória was saying. "How wonderful."

But we weren't really listening to her anymore. We were watching the concentrators. There was Burt, the girl with the braid, and the pretty blond one—all of M. Neptune's students except for Sandy, the one who never seemed to speak.

They had begun fitting the pins to our skulls. They approached us one by one, told us to lean forward, then lifted our shirts so they could fit the pins to our stomachs and backs. They pressed them into place.

We looked from one to another, then back at Viktória. It was all happening so quickly, I couldn't read anyone's expression. I could just make out Diego, on the other side of Viktória, sitting straight-backed and stone-faced, hands pressed together so tightly his knuckles had turned white. I tried to meet his eye; he wouldn't look at me. Theo was sitting far from me, on the opposite side of the table. I could feel him there. But I couldn't see his face.

M. Neptune peered down at us from the dais. His arms were folded and eyes narrowed.

Fine, I thought. You can study us. But I'm studying you, too.

Someone had come up behind me. A pair of cool hands touched my neck. It was my turn.

I let the concentrator fit the pins to my skull and belly one by one. The pressure against my body felt both familiar and strange. Soon the warm milk smell overcame me. I shivered.

Where was Gerald the mouse right now? Was he sleeping, curled with his tail around his fragile body, the pins still linking him to his teddy bear and mirror? Was he breathing deeply, calm and content, because he was fine, he was good, and he wasn't alone—never alone—but here, pinned into some infinite network?

I rested my hands on the table.

My hands were on the table. The table was in the house. I was in the house. I was in the house.

Viktória said, "Let us be quiet together."

I closed my eyes.

Some time passed in silence. I didn't know how long. I waited to feel something. I paid attention.

Clouds moved over the sinking sun. I breathed slowly, in and out, for minutes, maybe hours.

I opened my eyes. I closed my eyes.

Someone coughed.

I touched my scalp tentatively. The pins hadn't moved, of course.

I didn't feel anything. Did I?

The sun had set. The room grew colder.

Then we were chanting. I am in the house, I said. The house is in the woods. The woods . . .

We were quiet again.

It was true, I realized. I was here, in the house. My feet were on the stones. The stones were in the hall. The hall was filled with glass, and the glass was touched by light. I was filled with light. I was filled with everything. Everything.

Something bright rose up my throat.

Oh, I thought, *oh*. Then the thought was gone.

"You are here," Viktória was saying. Outside, the trees moved. "You've done well so far. But I want to touch you. I want to bring you further inside. I want you to feel it."

I opened my eyes.

It was nighttime in the great hall now. I couldn't make out anyone's faces in the dark. We were strangers again, but family, too, close and damp, like a litter of animals.

Viktória was sitting on the edge of a table. Cold moonlight crowned her head.

She said something, but I couldn't hear her.

A girl stood, then slowly walked to Viktória, who took the girl's hands in her own.

Viktória whispered something to the girl. The girl nodded, her face glistening with tears.

The girl returned to her seat.

A red-haired boy went up next. Then a girl from my Critical

Theory class. One by one, every student walked to Viktória and sat down again.

I glanced toward the dais. It was too dark for me to see M. Neptune anymore, but I still felt him there, watching, like a god.

I see you, I said. I see what you're doing.

I didn't know if I was speaking aloud or just thinking it, awake or asleep. I didn't know if I was surrounded by my friends or all alone. I didn't know who or where I was.

Yes, I did. I was here. In the woods. I was the house. I was the stairs. I was the curtains in the parlor brushing against the floor on a Tuesday morning. I was the smell of raspberry bread baking in the kitchen, inside.

My mouth was open, but no sound came out.

I was walking up to Viktória. I looked down at my feet. They were bare.

She took my hands in her own. She smiled. Her skin was white and cool.

"Ines," she said. "My precious girl."

"I'm precious for you," I said.

She squeezed my hands.

"Mother," I whispered, without knowing why.

She touched my cheek. I breathed.

"We are together," Viktória was saying, when I was sitting again. "We are here. In the house."

"In the house," we said.

"In the house," she said. "Inside, in the woods. We are not alive. We are not people. We are more than people. We are the infinite person. We are forever figures. We are an eternal moment, on an eternal surface, together with every other eternal object—everything here, inside this house."

Inside the house, I whispered.

I lifted up my hands. I closed my eyes.

"So," Viktória said.

I opened my eyes.

Viktória was smiling on us. A tiny rainbow refracted through the windows and flashed over her face.

"Let us eat," she said.

It was morning. A new day beamed through the great hall's windows. I felt as if I were seeing everyone for the first time after a long trip. There was Anna, dazed and blinking, and Yaya, who looked almost insulted as she cleared her throat and straightened in her seat, though I couldn't think why. The girl on my left was smiling shyly and eyeing everyone around her in girlish, embarrassed pleasure.

I didn't know how many hours—or how many days?—we had been sitting in the great hall. But I did know that I loved that girl, the one beside me. I loved her, and I loved Yaya, and I loved us all. I loved that we were all together, in our beautiful jeans and T-shirts, in the beautiful hall, by these beautiful golden windows, so beautiful, here.

I touched my head. The pins had been removed, but I could feel where they had been. The spots were tender. I pulled up my T-shirt. Yes, I could see the spots there, too. They had left funny orange bruises. I poked one. I hadn't noticed any after the coming in.

Aides filed in from the kitchen again, carrying trays. Not austere ceremonial trays this time, but gleaming silver platters filled with food. We cheered and stomped as they placed the platters on the tables, presenting us with our feast of sausage links and steaming baked oysters, grapes and olives and butter and breads, emerald glass carafes full of sweet wine.

Viktória poured herself a glass of wine as we continued to cheer. She raised it up.

"To today," she said over our noise, "the future forever."

We ate and drank. We laughed a lot. The girl next to me wouldn't stop babbling on about her pet cat. I couldn't understand what she was saying, but I rubbed her knee as I mopped up cream sauce with a hunk of bread. I was drunk. The room was pounding. The food kept coming. Meat cakes, fatty lamb chops, savory rice pudding by the bowl, and for dessert, ladyfingers, and snowy piles of vanilla cream, and plums, apricots, frosty black grapes.

When I reached for the grapes, I saw Theo.

Theo wasn't eating with us. He was up on the dais. He was with M. Neptune, watching.

I tried to stand, but I couldn't. The girl beside me was holding my elbow. I was too drunk. I couldn't move.

But I knew what I saw. Theo was there, whispering something in M. Neptune's ear. Then M. Neptune nodded, clasped Theo's arm, and whispered something back.

❧

The afternoon after I completed my last final, I walked out onto the yard. The atmosphere was dense and dark. I could smell nervous electricity in the air. An August storm was coming. No one else was out on the yard. I was alone.

Our class had passed the two last weeks of the semester, the weeks after the experiment, in a kind of trance. We didn't talk at breakfast or lunch and took long, drunken naps in our bathtubs. We went to bed early. We studied alone, if we studied at all. We skipped class and showed up late to our finals.

Now finals were over.

Lightning flashed, but I didn't hear any thunder.

I didn't know what had happened to me during the experiment. Some part of the night had slipped out of my memory and beyond my comprehension. I wasn't even sure how many hours I'd lost.

I didn't understand. But I wanted to.

I walked across the yard, over the paths to the west, through the garden wall. I walked through the rosebushes and over the bluebell hill, into the clearing by the fountain.

Theo was sitting there by the fountain, staring into the water.

"Hello," I said.

He looked up. "Hi."

I sat down next to him.

"It's going to rain," I said.

"I know."

The water in the fountain was calm and clear. I could smell the stone's mineral wetness.

"Theo," I said.

"Yeah?"

"What are you doing?"

He looked up at me.

I said, "You can trust me."

He shook his head.

I sniffled.

I'm your nice, sweet girl, I thought. *You like me. You will let me in.*

"I like the rain," I said.

I wiped my nose.

I said, "It reminds me of when I was a very little girl."

I shifted onto my hands.

"Before we moved here, back in the country," I said, "we had a house with a garden, and in the garden was a shed. A normal shed, you know, with garden tools and dark hiding places. I would play in that shed for hours, alone, and stare at it while I was going to sleep. I liked the shed. I thought that monsters lived there, big, big monsters. I thought the monsters were my real family." I cleared my throat. "Anyway. The rain—it smells like the shed."

Theo was breathing harder.

I sniffled again. I wiped the tears from my cheek.

"I've always felt," I said, "like I'm not here. Not in the shed, not in the country, not in the condo, after we moved. Not here, either. Like I'm floating, somewhere far away. Like your kite, remember? The sailboat kite. I'm bobbing somewhere up in the sky. I can see everyone else down below, all the little people. I can see their faces, I can see them smiling and laughing, I can see their mouths moving—but I can't hear what they're saying, and I don't get why they're laughing. Everyone is too far away."

I wiped my nose again.

Theo said, "Do you feel like that now?"

I turned to him. "No," I said.

He rubbed my jaw. When I kissed him, he tasted like the humidity, warm and electric.

❧

The next morning, I woke to the noise of birds chattering in the courtyard. I blinked my eyes open.

I'd already woken up several times in the strange, hot, shifting night, but made myself stay in bed. That was the nice thing to do. Now the light in Theo's bedroom was soft morning gray and I could see the fig tree branches pressed against his window, their leaves still wet from last night's rain.

I turned in the bed.

Theo lay facing the wall. His back rose and fell with each breath. He had a cluster of moles on his shoulder blade. I'd never seen them before.

What was I doing?

I took a deep breath, then slipped out of bed.

I stood naked in the middle of the room, considering.

I decided to start by looking behind the radiator, where he had kept the photograph of his grandmother. There was nothing there; even the picture was gone.

I looked through his bag, the one he carried to class each day. It only held two chemistry textbooks, three condoms, two stubby pencils, and a blue notebook. The notebook was filled with his tiny, neat handwriting and a lot of diagrams I didn't understand.

His handwriting reminded me of Baby's. I closed the notebook quickly.

I slid open Theo's desk drawers, but inside were only more pencils, condoms, lab notes, old graded reports, and erasers arranged in neat little rows. I flipped through the reports. None of them looked particularly interesting.

Theo shifted in bed and sighed. I froze. But his eyes were still shut, his mouth open and slack. I closed the desk drawers quietly.

I opened his dresser drawers next. But my hands hesitated over his clothes. His T-shirts were soft and human against my touch. When I pressed them to my nose, they didn't just smell like Catherine, but a little warm and lemony, too. Like Theo.

I started to put the shirts back. But as I did, my fingers brushed against something hard, there in the back of the drawer. I pulled it out.

A white keycard.

I held it up to the dim sunlight. The card was blank, completely unmarked. But I knew what it was.

I slipped it back into the drawer. I placed Theo's shirts over it.

I crawled back into the bed. Theo stirred sleepily, mumbled something, then reached for me. I slipped into his arms. I let him hold me.

Year Three

THE WEDDING

This," Diego said, "is our last September."

The two of us were bundled up in blankets on the Ashley terrace. We were supposed to be diagramming poetry for our Modern American Poetry class, but mostly we'd passed the time drinking pear cider, eating bananas, and watching the evening fall. Amber sunlight flashed through the pines and a brittle breeze tousled Diego's hair. The muss made him look younger than usual.

Diego pulled the blanket tighter around himself as he craned to get a better look at the yard. A group of first-years were down there, tossing a Frisbee. They yipped like puppies.

"They look like they're having fun," he said.

I took a bite of banana and said, as I chewed, "First-years are never having as much fun as they seem."

"You don't think they're really happy?"

"I wasn't happy," I said. "When I was them."

Diego picked at his cuticle. "I was happy," he said. "I loved being a first-year. I had this whole idea . . . I felt I could arrive at Catherine and be someone completely new. You know, like a new car, all shiny and modern and beautiful. That whole first year, I was so young. Young and drunk."

"Diego, we're still young."

Diego raised a shoulder in a half shrug. "I don't know. I don't feel that way anymore. And now we're going to graduate."

"Not soon."

"Soon enough. And I don't feel new like that. Not anymore."

A cool breeze stirred the pages of our textbooks. The breeze smelled like the woods. Like animals and dying leaves.

"Of course you don't get it," he said. "You and Yaya, you've always felt trapped here. But I don't want to graduate." He rolled a banana against the table with his palm. "I've spent my whole life reading beautiful books and watching beautiful movies, dreaming that there was some real place out there where I would fit in and be beautiful, too. And now I'm here. And I don't want to leave. I don't want to get an ugly job in an ugly office full of shit like staplers and fax machines. I don't want to write *memos*. I don't want us all to move far away from each other and grow up and forget to call. I don't want to get fat. I don't want to be tired. I don't know. I just . . . sometimes I can't imagine anything good happening to me. After Catherine."

He sipped his cider.

"But you can get a fun job, can't you?" I said. "There are a lot of jobs that aren't in offices. Maybe you'll teach art to kids in a pretty classroom. That would be nice. And you'll make new friends and sleep with new men. And you'll get to listen to the radio. Don't you want to hear what new songs have come out?"

"It'll be too late," he said. "I won't dance anymore."

"Grown-ups dance."

"Do they?"

"If they want to."

He picked up the banana with his slender fingers, eyeing it as if he'd never seen one before.

"Did you know," he said as he unpeeled it, "that I'm sleeping with M. Luther?"

I hadn't known, but it made sense. M. Luther was Diego's advisor, a slender, pale-eyed art history professor with tiny hands and a gentle voice. He'd taught my landscape course, and with that low voice I'd barely been able to hear a word he said and didn't really try. But Diego was always gushing about what a brilliant thinker he was, how his contributions to the field were so underappreciated. He went to all of M. Luther's office hours, and whenever he met us for dinner afterward, he would have the smuggest smile on his face. Yaya would nudge his shoulder and the two of them would giggle in that intimate way of theirs as they shared a bowl of clementine pudding.

"It's not just some dirty little affair," Diego said. "He loves me, and I love him. But I love him because he's brilliant, and he loves me because—because I'm young and raw. I'm not even that smart, I know. Just new. I make him newer. But I won't be new forever."

Diego was folding up his banana peel.

"It's not going to last," he said. "I'm not stupid. I know he has a wife. Soon he'll go teach at some college far away, and I'll graduate and dim and disappear into those staplers and fax machines. Here at Catherine—we're lovely, you know? Everyone and everything is lovely." He raised one shoulder in an elegant shrug. "I don't know. I'm scared that out there, someday I'll look around and realize forty years have passed and no one can see me. That I'm gone."

The first-years had moved farther across the yard. The neon Frisbee didn't make a sound as it arced through the air.

"You'll see," Diego said. "With Theo. You and him, everything is so good now. But when everything is good, everything's going so well, that's when you'll really start to freak. Because then you've got something to lose."

"Theo and I are just having fun," I said. "It's not serious."

"Sure," he said. "All right."

A chorus of cries rang out from the first-years. The Frisbee had gotten caught in a tree.

Everything really was good. Everything was going so well. I attended my classes. I studied. I finished my homework, and had long, ambling meetings with M. Owens where we drank peppermint tea and chatted about everything from astrology to orchids to children's schoolyard games. I slept easy. I put on clean clothes in the morning and made my bed. Even my appetite was good. I dreamed, like a queen, of rich foods, custards and tarts and bloody steaks. And I was with Theo.

Theo. Theo in the afternoon, in his bedroom, a slithery breeze running through the window and over my bare skin as he pulled up my T-shirt and bit my stomach. Or Theo at night, laughing as I flung open my door to pull him inside. Theo's hot breath. His fingers seizing my hair, his slick sweat. Morning, legs against legs and arms entwined, his hand stroking my throat. Because I was the thing he liked to touch. I was the thing he wanted to reach inside.

Mornings, we untangled ourselves to go eat big breakfasts of ham and puddings and gleaming eggs with runny yolks. We sat with our friends and laughed uncontrollably at the stupidest things. He rubbed me under the table. I went to class and paid attention, took notes, and answered questions, but I could still feel him inside me.

I was full. The days were big.

Evenings, I studied with Yaya in the music room, in the dark. She was memorizing passages from Homer. I listened to her with my head in my arms and looked out the window at the whirling starry sky. The Greeks had used those same stars to conquer the world. We were like them—gods and heroes.

"You're shaking," Theo whispered.

It was late afternoon. I was watching his face. His summer freckles were fading.

"No, I'm not," I said.

He squeezed my thigh. "You are."

"I'm cold." I shifted in the bed, pulling the sheet tighter.

His hand ran farther up my thigh. "I'm happy you're here."

"Where else would I be?"

"I don't know."

The features of his room—the jeans slung over the back of his chair and the papers bunched under his desk, his kicked-off sneakers, and on the dresser, a withering bunch of grapes—it all appeared to me with hyper-clarity. Before, his room had been so neat that it felt like a hotel room. Now it was his home. I liked it like this. I could feel him in everything: his jeans, his papers, his sneakers, his grapes.

"Let's stay here," he whispered against my ear. "Forever."

He didn't realize I knew about the keycard, and that he had been accepted to M. Neptune's lab. If I hadn't seen the card with my own eyes, I probably would never have guessed it. He was the same Theo as ever, the same relaxed, laughing kid. He didn't sit with M. Neptune's students in the great hall. And when he disappeared for hours at a time, he never told me where he went. "Just the lab," he would say if I asked.

I knew where he was really going. Because when he went to M. Neptune's lab, he came back smelling like warm milk.

In all those heady days and close, muggy nights, he never said anything to me about his studies. But I never felt he was keeping a secret. He would tell me when he was ready. I knew he would, because I knew Theo. Not just the obvious things, like his high-pitched laugh or his favorite card games, or how cranky he got when he was hungry. I knew his insides, too. I knew his private things. I knew the way he mumbled to himself when he was waking up in the morning. I knew the face he made when he lost control of his body. I knew his ugly secret parts. He was mine. He belonged to me.

So the keycard belonged to me, too. Sometimes when I touched him, I could feel it in his pocket. And when he was asleep, I would go to the drawer and feel it there, hidden beneath his clothes. I would run my fingers over its surface before moving his clothes back in place and slipping into bed.

Theo propped his head in his hand to peer closer at me. "What are you thinking about?"

"Nothing," I said. "You."

He kissed my nose.

❧

The projector clicked to a photograph of a doll. Not a pretty doll, but a grotesque little monster, two girl bottom halves fused together at one taut, bloated belly. The leg stumps fit into the body with deep articulated grooves, as if they could be repositioned and recombined. The two vulvas were swollen and hairless.

The Surrealism movement, our professor explained, was inspired by Freud's concept of the uncanny, the dreadful double. According to Freud, doubling creates meaning. Doubling turns sounds into words; a baby first speaks by turning *ma* into *mama*, *pa* into *papa*. But when a double appears uninvited—the buried object returns—it brings us into the realm of the uncanny. We watch dead things wake up. And we are afraid.

The class had ended. I poked Nick awake as the other students filed out of the room. He'd arrived late, wrapped in a long woolen coat and carrying a mug of wine, and slept through the second half of the lecture with his head on the table.

"Up." I poked him. "Dinnertime."

"Mmm." He rubbed his face. "Not yet. I'm still asleep."

I rubbed his back. He blinked at me like a lazy cat.

"I feel like I haven't seen you in a while," he murmured. "How've you been?"

"If you had been awake, you would have seen me." I pulled at one of his curls. "I'm good. Philosophy of Law might kill me. But I'm good."

"Yeah. And you've got the sickness."

"What sickness?"

"*You* know."

I put my chin in my hand. "God."

He patted my arm. "Don't worry. Enjoy it while you can."

His textbook was open to an Yves Tanguy landscape. Abstract alien figures cast long, silent shadows on the empty horizon.

"Ugly, isn't it?" Nick mumbled, staring at the image. "My grandma collected that kind of shit. Weird little paintings . . . and she was always smoking these nasty cigars that smelled like spearmint. God. I hated that apartment."

I didn't like the Surrealists, either. I hated that class. I didn't want to waste my time dissecting insipid German psychology and analyzing childish paintings. I just wanted to work on my tutorial.

Not that my tutorial was any easier. The critical theories of minimalism and abstract expressionism were impenetrable; I spent many hours bent over texts trying to understand stupid new meanings for words like *absorption* and *object-beholder*. But I didn't mind doing it for Agnes Martin. Agnes Martin's paintings were perfect. Her simple, large, plain canvases, each gridded into even shades of pale, were better than language, better than history. They were good. Holy, even.

One untitled Agnes Martin painting had been hanging in the gallery since October. I would go there in the morning and stare at it. Every day at around nine o'clock, pale sunlight radiated on the painting just so, and its surface would glow, weightless and pale and supernatural as sea-foam.

When I looked at the painting then, I thought: *This is it.* It wasn't gold that was the sublime material, the magic matter; it was the surface itself. The stuff in between. The birth of the world. I'd found it. It was here.

❧

Through the hall, down damp stone stairs, past a pavilion of windows. Down another hall, the one with green vine wallpaper, into the Harrington lounge, then the courtyard, where an October wind kicked up a whirl of wine-red leaves and a smell of black, humid soil. Into a Harrington parlor, then through a gray door.

The walls of the Harrington music room were lined with blue silk, as were its dark wood Edwardian chairs and tea tables. A low-backed crushed velvet settee sat beneath a window draped with gauze curtains, and in the middle of the room stood a grand piano, its lid lifted. The piano's mechanics—the endless recurrence of dampers and strings, the biomorphic twist of metal and wood—gleamed like the insides of a space machine.

I'd spent many afternoons in this room, cross-legged on carpet, listening to musical practices or poetry readings. Now the room was empty, and the piano stood silent.

I sat down on its bench. I ran a finger along its keys.

I wandered farther into Harrington, toward a billiards room filled with noise and bustle. I found Theo there with some of his Ashley chemistry friends, playing bid whist and eating cherry pie.

I glanced at Theo's cards as I sat beside him. He had a good hand. Mostly clubs.

He kissed the side of my mouth. "Play with us?" he whispered.

"No. I want to watch." I swiped a fingerful of his pie.

The night lengthened as they played. The others disappeared into libraries and bedrooms. Eventually we were alone.

I watched our hazy reflections in the window as Theo shuffled the cards.

"Let's make a pie together," I said.

"Okay. What kind?"

"Peach. Blueberry. Every kind."

"Rhubarb." He tapped the cards together. "My grandma used to make rhubarb pie."

"Let's do it. Now."

"Now?"

"I bet the kitchen has rhubarb. Apples, anyway. Maybe they'll let us use the oven."

"Mmm," he said. "Maybe. I should go study."

"Don't study."

He ran a hand through my hair.

"Everything about you is so beautiful," he whispered. He was staring at his fingers entwined in the ends of my hair. "Every part of you."

He lowered his hand. I took it in mine.

"I used to think that no one could be so beautiful," he said. "No one and nothing. But in here—I'm so happy." He looked up, smiling. "And you'll be beautiful forever."

I laughed a little. "I'll get old and ugly someday. Old, ugly, and ornery."

"No," he said. "You'll always be beautiful."

I squeezed his thigh.

"I should go study," he said again.

"Not yet."

"No," he said. "Not yet."

I didn't want him to study. I didn't want him to go anywhere. I wanted to be closer. I wanted us to hit each other. I wanted it to hurt.

He laid out the cards in a game of solitaire.

There were moments when I felt like Theo knew me exactly. Like he could read my brain, with all its dark ideas and affections, and still liked me. As if we were two faces of the same villain. It felt stunning.

Other times I wondered if he knew me at all. Sometimes, when he stared at me, I felt he was watching me from far away. Like I was a moon he dreamed of conquering.

I didn't care. I wanted to be that moon, that beautiful thing, as long as he kept looking at me.

Outside, as we walked through the courtyard, he drew me close and kissed me. I rubbed his cheek. His skin was rough, chilled by the autumn night. The stars blurred.

"Let's go," I said.

"Home?" he said. He glanced at the Molina door. "We are."

"No," I said. "I mean somewhere like the Great Barrier Reef. Or the Grand Canyon. Somewhere real."

"Man, the Grand Canyon's so hot. When you go, you're just in the car forever."

"You've been to the Grand Canyon?"

Theo shrugged.

He started walking again. I skipped to follow him. His profile shone in the moonlight.

I don't think I realized it until that moment: Theo didn't want to leave Catherine. And he didn't want me to leave, either.

Of course he didn't want to leave. Why would he? He had nothing out there, and at Catherine he had everything. He had friends. He had food. He had work. And he had me.

He squeezed my arm as we entered the house. "You know, I should probably stop by the lab and get some shit done," he said. "I'll come by after?"

"Yes," I said.

He gave me a little kiss before skipping down the stairs. He turned to the left, toward the Ashley basement.

One morning in late November, I dragged myself back to my bedroom after many long hours in the library to see that the tea trays had already been delivered. I found a white card tucked behind my teacup.

"You are cordially invited," the card read in florid script, "to the wedding of Diego Jimenez and Yaya Osmond."

"What on earth is this?" Anna said, waving an identical card as she padded toward me. She was wrapped in a towel and her skin was damp.

"Guess those crazy kids are finally making it official," I said.

She flipped over the invitation, but there was nothing on the other side. "Honestly," she said, squeezing her wet hair, "I don't know what you guys are going on about half the time."

I glanced back down at the invitation. The ceremony was scheduled for five o'clock in the Molina parlor. According to the program, I would be giving a poetry reading before the exchange of vows.

When I arrived at the parlor that afternoon, the room had been transformed from its usual dusty elegance. All the chairs and couches had been turned to face the fireplace, and dried roses clustered in vases at the end of the makeshift aisle. Scarves and fairy lights were draped over the windowsills. Curious first-years and second-years lounged toward the back. Theo, Anna, and Nick had gathered in the front seats.

"I still don't really get what's going on," Anna was saying as I sat down next to Theo.

"What don't you get?" Theo said. "The invitation was so clear."

Anna examined her cuticles. "This was all your plan, wasn't it?"

Theo held an affronted hand to his chest. "Me? I just made the cake."

"Excuse you," Nick said.

"Helped make the cake."

The cake, a mess of gloppy frosting and rainbow sprinkles, was stationed on the tea table. I now saw that Theo and Nick were covered with flour.

"I think you're wanted in the bridal suite," Anna said, poking me. "She's been calling for you all afternoon."

"The bridal suite?"

She nodded at the door to the bathroom.

I found Yaya leaning over the sink, eyes widened as she swiped on mascara. Her dress, a short white pouf made of tulle and sateen with a plastic lace collar and sleeves, fell open to the small of her back; she hadn't been able to reach the line of buttons. A teacup full of pink wine sat on the toilet tank.

"Oh, there you are," Yaya said, glancing at me in the mirror. "Close the door, quick. Can you do me up?"

I buttoned the dress, then sat on the toilet. "How long have you been planning this?"

"Oh, since about two, three in the morning. Last night."

"That's when you found the dress."

She twirled, hands arched back to keep makeup off the sateen. It shimmered. "Do you die?"

"Yes."

She bent closer to the mirror. "I have to share the most wonderful gossip with you," she said. "Do you remember Deandra? That nasty little second-year with the perfectly enormous breasts? Well. She won't be around much longer. She got *knocked up*."

"Really?"

"Really. By some idiot first-year who's also getting kicked out. She tried to cover it up, but the doctor found it, and that's that.

Yesterday, when you were at work, they came for her in the great hall and she started screaming like a demon. It was spectacular. Made me like her a lot more. Anyway, I've just been dying to tell you." She reached the blush. "My dear, what reading have you prepared for the ceremony?"

"A poem," I said.

"What poem?"

"'The Charge of the Light Brigade.'"

"Do you have it memorized?"

"No."

"I guess that's okay." She smiled wisely into the mirror. "On such a big occasion, with so many details to arrange, you just have to focus on what's really important. You'll see one day."

I took a sip from her teacup. "Where's Diego?"

"Writing his vows. He's such a nervous groom."

She gestured for the cup. I passed it to her, then kissed her on the cheek.

"You make a beautiful bride," I said.

She stroked the ends of my hair.

I went back to the main room and sat next to Theo. He put his arm around my shoulders.

The chandelier winked. The whole room smelled full of roses. I felt full of roses, too.

The door to the parlor opened and Diego strode in wearing a crisp white tuxedo. He'd slicked his hair back with severe efficiency. His expression, as he walked down the aisle, was rigid and solemn.

Watching Diego, in that moment, I had a sudden image of him as an older man, a renowned architect, maybe, crouched over his desk in an all-glass office, or a professor lecturing to a room full of students. Some things would be the same, probably; he would have the same smart eyes and graceful hands. But his skin would be tough and thick, his hair grayish, his stomach paunched. He would be a grown-up, like he'd said. He wouldn't do silly things anymore, like burlesque weddings on Thursday nights. Most nights he would go to bed early. We would all go to bed early.

Well, I thought, at least I would always remember him as young, stupid, and sweet.

Diego proceeded to the fireplace, which served as the altar. Nick, the officiant, gave him a beatific nod.

When Yaya walked in, the room fell silent. The only noise was her dress shushing against her legs. Her cheeks had a pretty, girlish flush, and her hair was braided into a garland around her head.

My throat hurt. She looked like the fairy bride from my book.

Yaya took Diego's hands as she met him at the altar. They stared at each other without smiling.

"What a blessing," Nick began, "to be here, now, in witness to such an auspicious occasion."

Theo's arm tightened around my shoulders. I wiped my eyes with the heel of my hand.

When the ceremony was over, we feasted on chicken salad, cake, and ice cream that Theo had stolen from the kitchen. We drank wine. We put a Duran Duran cassette in our rented stereo and stripped down to dance. We sang into our fists and jumped on the chairs.

It was a long time before we grew tired, but when we did, we slumped: Nick and Theo asleep, together, on the couch, Anna snoring, head on her arms. Yaya and I lay on the carpet, forking cake straight from the platter. The frosting was so sweet it made my gums ache.

"I really do love Diego, you know," Yaya said. "And he loves me, too. Not like, la-la, love-love. I'm not an idiot. But really, it's better than that. We have the most fabulous time together. And he's never going to break my heart."

"How do you know he won't break your heart?" I poked at the cake crumbs. "Maybe he'll change. Or you will. Maybe you won't be friends forever."

"Of course we're going to be friends forever. We're *married*." Yaya set down her fork and sat up. "Me and him, we have a plan, you know. When we graduate, we're going to Los Angeles. We're going to drink coconut-banana coladas and party on the beach and sleep with the most gorgeous men. And we're going to dance and sing and have a fabulous time."

"Diego doesn't sing," I said.

"Well. He'll play the piano for me. He'll adore it."

The room was spinning. I closed my eyes, but that made it worse. I opened them again.

"We're going to be stars," Yaya said. "Big, big stars."

❧

We spent two days camped out in the art studio creating our fall festival costumes. We mixed bowls of papier-mâché paste and crafted masks, cut out poster-board skirts and glued feathers onto headdresses. I had decided to be a mummy. I spent a lot of time wrapping bandage strips around my face and staring at myself in the mirror, getting used to the idea of seeing myself undead.

The night of the parade, Viktória visited us in the studio. We gathered around her and chanted.

We are in the studio, in the house.

Our hands are folded.

We are here.

We are here.

There was no experiment that night, there were no plasm pins. But somehow, I could still feel them in me. I could still feel everything.

As we chanted, aides cleared off the dirty, paint-splattered tables and set down platters of beef, buttered peas, and carafes of wine. We ate and drank as we helped each other into our costumes.

We started our parade in the studio. Then we roared, banging drums and blowing whistles, through the halls, past the lounges, and onto the frozen black yard. There, the gathered first- and second-years clapped and whooped as they threw candy at us. We let them touch us. We laughed.

We crossed through the courtyards, then back inside, through halls, parlors, and music rooms. We saw ourselves, happy spirits, reflected in the windows.

When we arrived in the ballroom antechamber, we pulled off our masks. We could hear the music pounding as we drank more wine and helped each other out of our costumes. Naked, we pushed into the ballroom.

The space was almost black, but a white light strobed somewhere. I didn't know where my body was. I wasn't sure if I was alive. I couldn't recognize anyone. No, I could, but it was as if I recognized their bodies and faces from some long-ago dream. Or was this the dream?

Light became music. Music beat in my heart.

I danced. I lifted up my arms. I felt the night, hot and divine, and felt myself as part of a boundless whole. I didn't just feel good. I felt full. Full of light and flowers, full of the whole world.

And when I found Theo—was it Theo?—I touched him, and I was gone.

I hadn't really understood plasm. I had thought of it as a substance, some kind of semi-liquid, or a subatomic particle essential in all things. I had thought, if you tried hard enough, you could almost touch it.

But right then, I understood. Plasm wasn't a substance; it was the beginning of substance. The fabric connecting all things and all people. The language that created me, the chandelier, the floorboards, the light. When I touched Theo, I could feel us together somewhere between now and tomorrow, this world and the next, on that eternal surface connecting everyone and everything. I felt him and myself and the glowing lamps and the courtyard's flagstones and a hundred yellow teacups and the sky and the planets, the whirling planets, a galaxy of things, and I was here. I was so wonderfully here, inside that infinite horizon, here—in love—forever, always.

❧

Long cold nights faded into strange cold days.

I stayed up for hours the night before my Philosophy of Law final. My study partner, a reedy girl with violent acne and red-rimmed eyes, sniffled constantly as we worked, reviewing study sheets and flipping through flash cards. She thought I was an idiot, I could tell. Whenever I got an answer wrong, she blinked at me with disgust.

I didn't mind her glares. I didn't mind anything. I didn't even mind studying. I wasn't going to get a good grade, but I could pass, at least. And it felt nice sitting here, wrapped in a snug blanket by the radiator, surrounded by the kind warmth of the library's lamps.

I fell asleep. And when I woke up, it was morning. The girl had disappeared.

I looked out of the window as I stretched. I could feel winter coming. The sunlight that morning was sharp white, and the specifics of the Molina courtyard—the stone boy in the fountain, the dead brown leaves tripping across the walk, a blue ribbon tied to a branch, fluttering in the breeze—all appeared super-precise. I didn't know how I had slept so well, but right then I felt very awake. I was seeing things very clearly.

Two figures bundled in sweaters walked across the courtyard. I recognized them as two of M. Neptune's plasm students, the angelic blond girl and the odd boy, Sandy. The girl was pulling an empty red wagon. Sandy followed slowly behind.

Sandy stopped in the path, suddenly frozen for some unseen reason. He turned to the library window—had he forgotten something here?—but he didn't turn around. He didn't move at all.

When the girl realized he wasn't following her anymore, she skipped after him and tugged on his sleeve with a huff and a sigh. He turned back. He kept following her.

But when he had turned to face me—eyes to the sun, chin out—I saw him. I saw him exactly.

I padded barefoot to the library reference room. The rug was nubby against my bare feet. I shivered as I ran my fingers along the scrapbook spines and pulled out the one from six years ago, the year the boy had died.

We hurt, Viktória had written, *because we miss him.*

I examined the photograph, as I had many times before. The dark curls. The mole next to his lip.

In the photograph, even frozen in stillness, the eyes shone with vibrancy. His eyes still shone—I remembered them flickering in the dining hall—but they shone with some stranger kind of life.

A life in suspended animation.

I closed the book and slipped it back on the shelf. I went to gather my philosophy notes. I couldn't be late to my final.

SOS

As fall descended into winter, I watched Sandy more closely. I watched him follow M. Neptune's students to class, then follow them back out again. I watched him wait for the blond girl outside the bathroom as she peed. I watched him hover by the dessert service, his hands held out with inhuman patience as Burt handed him apple slices one by one. I watched him follow Burt back to the table and sit when Burt told him to sit. He gathered food but never ate. He just stared at the apple slices or lemon custard pie or fatty, broken pieces of chicken without appearing to understand their function.

I was watching Sandy now. But M. Neptune's students watched him even closer. Everywhere he went, to class or the bathroom or dessert, one of them was there with him, shrewd eyes tracking his every movement. Sometimes they even jotted down notes. They pulled at his curls and examined his fingernails. They laughed when he tripped over his shoelaces.

He never laughed back.

Diego's words kept ringing in my brain: *M. Neptune is going to do whatever he can get away with. More, even.*

Sandy and M. Neptune were walking across the yard down below. The tiles were clouded white with an early frost. M. Neptune placed his hand on Sandy's shoulder. Sandy didn't react.

How many times had I looked at that photograph in the library and not recognized him? How could I have been so stupid? Wasn't it obvious?

Of course it was obvious. Of course M. Neptune would test his experiment out in the open, right before our eyes. That was the whole point, wasn't it? To create something so real that it could live seamlessly among us, its people and its objects?

I glanced at Anna. We were in one of Ashley's parlors, a crooked blue room, sitting with our books in the window seat. We were supposed to be studying, but Anna, like me, was staring down at the yard, watching Sandy and M. Neptune. I couldn't read her expression.

Did everyone else already know what was going on? Did anyone care?

"Anna," I said.

She turned to me, blinking.

"Are you hungry?"

"Not really," she said. "Are you? Tea should be soon."

"I don't want to wait." I got up. "I need to go."

She was already looking back down at her notes.

I went down the stairs, through the halls, across the Molina courtyard, to Theo's room. He wasn't there. I climbed into his bed still wearing my clothes. His bed smelled like sex and sweat. I pulled the blanket over my head.

Bitter December winds whistled through the courtyard. I could hear leaves skitter over the tiles, rattling like bones. I shivered.

Afternoon became evening. Time shifted. I couldn't move.

I opened my eyes, then closed them again. The heat wasn't on. The room was so cold I felt afraid.

I couldn't move. I couldn't move.

I tried to scream but no sound came out.

Help me, I wanted to say. Help me.

But no one could hear me. I wasn't there. I wasn't ever there.

Theo was shaking my shoulder. I opened my eyes.

"Hey," he was saying, "wake up."

His breath was warm on my face.

"Wake up," he said again. "Shh. Stop yelling. You're having a nightmare."

I sat up, kneading my palms against my eyes. It was night now. The sky through the windows was black and starless.

❧

Days passed. I did nothing, and nothing happened. Until the morning I received a notice with my tea tray.

Viktória wanted to have tea with me. Here in my room, the following afternoon.

I stared at the note until the words blurred. Then I folded it up and slipped it into my back pocket.

I hadn't had an official meeting with Viktória since my first year, when I'd almost failed out of Catherine. Was my tutorial going that badly?

Or was it something worse?

Would they send me to the tower again?

My hands were shaking. I clenched them into fists.

Before Viktória arrived, I spent two hours cleaning my room. I swept under the desks and used an old T-shirt to wipe down the windowsills. I folded my clothes. I even aired out and remade Baby's bed. I was running a hand over her coverlet when a knock sounded at the door.

Viktória's face, when I opened the door, was so close, so magnificent and large, that it startled me. Her eyelashes were thick and dark today, her cheeks china-pink. She was carrying a tea tray.

"My apologies. I'm a little late, I know." Her green raw silk dress shushed against her legs as she swept into the room in a haze of perfume. She set the tray on the tea table. "I got caught up in—well, it doesn't matter. Thank you for hosting on such short notice. I like to get out of the office."

"Hello," I breathed.

She glanced around the room. "How tidy."

"I cleaned."

Her eyes flashed on me. She smiled.

I watched her as she poured the tea. Her wrists were thin but strong and the skin of her inner arms was as luminous as I remembered. The porcelain chittered as she handed me my teacup.

"Beautiful," she said, after taking a sip from her own.

I sipped. It was jasmine tea. It tasted like the gardens in summer.

"So," she said, setting down her cup. "I hope you're not nervous, meeting me. I wanted to check in and see how you're progressing with your classes. I know from your professors, of course, how wonderfully your studies are going. But I thought it would be nice to hear from the girl herself."

She watched me with a soft smile.

"I thought," I said, "you were about to throw me out."

"Throw you out? Of Catherine?" She laughed lightly, touching my knee. "Ines," she said, "your professors, your advisor, your coworkers at the gallery—everyone can see that you've grown into quite a star."

That didn't make sense. My grades were better than when I first started at Catherine, but they still weren't great. And my boss at the gallery constantly corrected my work. I was not, as she said, a very *detail-oriented* girl.

"I'm doing okay?"

Viktória laughed. "More than okay. Your work these past semesters has been truly remarkable. And I know it hasn't been easy. I'm quite proud of you, really."

She smiled.

"Thanks," I said.

Viktória kept talking. She asked about my Great Exhibitions seminar, and Freud, critical theory, and my tutorial. It all sounded fascinating to her. And she loved Agnes Martin's paintings as much as I did. The abstract expressionists had been her favorite when she worked in the New York galleries "oh, a lifetime ago."

"And how about your friends?" She poured herself a third cup of tea. "You all seem very close."

"Yes."

"Your boyfriend," she said, "is quite a scholar. His projects have been remarkable."

"Theo?"

A quirk of a smile. "Yes. Theo."

I reached for a butter cookie.

"It's been wonderful to watch Theo come into himself," she said. "The new materials concentration is a unique field of study and requires unique skills of its students. But Theo's work has been quite impressive. I believe that one day he'll contribute to the field in a truly meaningful way."

"Yes." I took a bite of the cookie, chewed, and swallowed. Then I said, "He really is so smart, and he works really hard. I know he was disappointed when M. Neptune didn't choose him for his team."

She lowered her eyes. "Not everyone is suited for M. Neptune's lab," she said. "Even amongst plasm students. But Theo can always reapply. If he continues to work hard."

Viktória uncrossed her legs, then crossed them again.

I already know, I wanted to say. *You can stop this silly pretending.*

She put down the cup.

"You know," Viktória said, "you could be a plasm student."

It took me a moment to process the words. Then I shook my head and said, "I—I never took the required chemistry."

"No," she said, "and there are other perquisites you're missing as well. You would have to take them or be tested in. But you would make it. I know you would. You think the right way, Ines. You have the right kind of mind. You have the right . . . dynamism."

I set my teacup on the table. Someone was shouting down in the courtyard, but I couldn't hear what they were saying.

"I don't understand," I said.

"This is a serious offer, Ines," she said. "After you complete your studies in summer, instead of graduating, you could stay here and begin a new education. It would be a long time to be at Catherine, of course. Another three years, at least. But we want our students to serve the concentration that suits them best. I believe—and your professors believe—that the study of new materials could profoundly enrich your life. And you, in turn, with your skills, could enrich the new materials discipline. The most essential discipline there is."

She covered my hand with her own.

"You can stay," she said. "You can stay here."

The noise in the courtyard had stopped. The whole house was quiet.

"Why?" I said.

She cocked her head. "What do you mean?"

"Why are you offering this to me?" I raised my shoulders. "Do you think Theo's sleeping with me because I'm especially smart? Because he's not. And I'm not."

Her lips flickered into a smile, but I couldn't read her eyes.

"Theo has mentioned several times that he believes you're an exceptional young woman," she said. "And that you would be perfect for the concentration. But this isn't about Theo. This is about you. Ines, you and I both know that every student who comes to Catherine is in some way . . . extraordinary." Her eyes flickered at the word. "And most students graduate from Catherine into fruitful lives of accomplishment and reward. But a rare few others . . . well. They never quite fit into their lives before Catherine, and they won't fit in afterward. For them, Catherine is their home. It always was, and always will be."

Her hand was warm on mine.

"I said once that you remind me of myself when I was young," she said. "That is true. And to be honest, I wish . . ." Her voice grew soft. "I wish someone had given me this chance, then. A chance to stay."

"But you're Catherine's director," I said. "You have stayed."

She hesitated, then shook her head slightly. I didn't understand. But before I had a chance to ask anything more, she was clearing her throat and speaking again.

"Ines," she said, "in all my travels to conferences and panels and fund-raisers, I have the pleasure of meeting so many wonderful Catherine graduates. We are everywhere, you know, from the greatest halls of power to the most darling little houses. So many shining men and women who have everything. Everything, except they are no longer twenty years old. They are no longer here. They no longer have Catherine. Is that what you want? Or do you want to stay here, at home?"

Her breath, so close, smelled like the jasmine tea.

"Don't you want to be happy?" she said.

She was smiling.

"You don't have to answer me now," she said when I didn't respond. "You still need to finish up your tutorial and the rest of your art history classes. You have a couple of semesters to think about it. But do consider your options carefully. Because this is a real opportunity, Ines. An opportunity to become your truest, most exquisite self."

She squeezed my hand.

I went over to Theo's that night. He grabbed my T-shirt and pulled me into his room. He had been up all night studying and needed a bath. He smelled like an animal.

As I fucked him, I thought of Viktória's long, slender wrists. The pressure of her fingers around my hand.

Afterward, I held Theo's body close. A mean, freezing December rain pattered against his window, but I was inside, and Theo's body was warm.

Theo was staying here at Catherine. For as long as he worked for M. Neptune, Theo would be here.

"Do you still have your CDs?" I asked.

"What CDs?" He was tracing a slow circle around my knee. He had recently trimmed his fingernails and cut them too short. Dried blood beaded on his thumb.

"You know, that CD booklet you used to have, and the Discman."

His hand paused a moment, then kept tracing. "No. I got rid of those things."

"Did you really?"

"Yeah."

"When? Why?"

He shrugged. "Man, I don't know. A year ago? I shouldn't have had them in the first place."

"So you just threw them out? All of them?"

"Ines, you know that stuff's not good for us. Viktória's right—it messes with our concentration. It's not good for my work."

"But you loved that music."

"It was just music."

"If it was just music, why did you bother throwing it away?"

"Why are we fighting about this?"

I lay back down again. He grasped my hand and held it to his chest.

He had thrown out the Discman. And the photograph of his grandmother, the one he had sneaked past the gate and hidden so carefully. I'd thought he had stashed the photo somewhere else, but now I realized he'd probably trashed it. He had loved that photograph and those CDs. But he loved plasm more. And he'd do anything to keep working.

I stared at our hands clasped together on his chest.

I wished I could see Theo at work in M. Neptune's lab. I wanted to see the expression in his eyes as he bent over a plasm spindle or scribbled down a formula. I wanted to recognize his frown of concentration as he made those strange things happen. Because how bad could they be if he did them?

The rain had stopped. White mist drifted over his windows.

I shivered.

"Are you cold?" he said.

"A little."

He held me tighter. "How did your meeting with Viktória go?"

"Fine."

"What'd she want to talk about?"

"Just my tutorial," I said. "Wanted to make sure I'm on the right track."

Someone was walking down the hallway with light footsteps. They grew closer, then padded away.

"She says you're doing well in your studies," I said.

"Mmm. I try."

I stroked his arm, then his stomach, then lower.

A door slammed. The footsteps came close again.

❧

We celebrated finishing our midterms with wine, music, and Monopoly. None of us were good at the game, or remembered the rules at all, really, so it was hours before we realized that Nick had been embezzling funds from the bank the whole time. By then we didn't care. We were drunk, and on our fourth listen of the ABBA greatest hits cassette. Nick and Anna had made up an interpretive dance to "SOS" that involved several pillows and blankets. We cheered for show after show. Their fourth encore was disrupted when Nick realized it was time for cookies, and soon they were running off to the kitchen.

I closed my eyes and listened to them go, their voices growing smaller, and smaller, then gone.

"Sometimes," Yaya said, "I have this idea—a dream—of a room full of people. Everyone I've ever fucked, and everyone I will ever fuck. Men and women, young and not so young. They're all together, standing in, like, a ballroom, at a conference, and they're all talking about *me*. And it's fabulous." She turned to look at me. "Do you ever think about that?"

"Of course," I said. "I dream that exact thing all the time."

I poured myself more wine. We were drinking out of glass Winnie-the-Pooh mugs that Yaya had taken from the dock. As I lifted the mug to my lips, I saw the room through the glass, perverted. The Monopoly money, scattered on the rug, refracted into the fireplace, the lamps, and Yaya, who was lying on her back with her legs stretched along the wall. She was upside down. I didn't recognize her.

"I wonder what it will be like to shave my legs again when we leave." She ran her fingers lightly over her calf. Then she said, "I don't think I will."

I put down the glass.

"Did you know," I said, "Viktória offered to transfer me into the new materials concentration?"

Yaya twisted to look at me. Then she pulled down her legs and sat up.

"Wait," she said, "what?"

"Viktória offered to transfer me into the new materials concentration."

"No, I heard what you said." She leaned forward and peered at me with narrowed eyes. I couldn't tell if she was angry or confused. "Start all over? Stay for more years?"

"Yes."

"And you're thinking about doing it."

I shrugged.

"But you were never interested in plasm," Yaya said. "You never applied for the concentration in the first place."

"I know. I would have to take so many prerequisites. It would take a long time."

"But you could stay."

I licked wine off my lips.

"You just want to be with Theo," Yaya whispered. "Theo, who now has no other life than plasm. Plasm, and you."

The pipes clicked in the walls.

"You used to see this house for what it really was," Yaya said. "You knew why you were here and weren't fooled by all its glamorous bullshit. Now you're thinking of staying for you don't even know how long? Ines, don't you realize what we're missing, being in here? Don't you remember?"

"No," I said. "I don't remember."

I poured myself more wine.

"I never knew why I came here," I said. "To Catherine. I've never known why I did anything."

I stared at the wine without drinking it.

"But I do know how I feel now," I said. "Here. And I feel . . . like I could be getting better." I laughed. The sound echoed harshly around the room. "Honestly, Yaya. Don't you feel it? Like Catherine might be the only real place in the world?

"Ines," she said, "how can you think this place is *real?*"

I didn't respond. Even I wasn't sure what I meant.

Yaya shook her head slowly.

"I wouldn't have thought it would happen to you, too," Yaya said. Her eyes were dark. "But it did. You're all fucked up."

"I have nothing out there," I said. "Don't you get it?"

"No, don't *you* get it?" Yaya spat. "Don't you realize—" She shook her head. "*None* of us have anything out there. Like, take Nick. His family owns half of Philadelphia, but they're obviously evil. Catherine is his only chance to become someone different. Theo is brilliant, but he comes from shit. And Anna, well, you know how fucked up things are between her and her brother. She can't go home. None of us can go home. Come on, Ines, pay attention." Her voice had risen. "We all think we're so lucky to have ended up here, that we all got into Catherine despite whatever secrets or miseries we have in our past. But it's not *despite* these secrets that Catherine chose us, it's *because* of them. If we have nothing—nothing but some creativity and weird test scores—Catherine can become our everything. Our whole, drunk, happy everything."

I swirled the wine.

Was that true? About Nick and Theo and Anna?

And when Mr. González, beautiful Mr. González, had told Viktória that I was trying to disappear—did that only make her want me more?

"I have months to decide," I finally said, trying to remember what we had been talking about. "But if I decide to stay, you can't stop me."

"No," she whispered. "I can't."

Wind rattled the parlor windows.

"Can you just promise me one thing?" she said.

I sipped.

"Someday," Yaya said, "not today, but someday, I want you to seriously think about leaving Catherine. Because I don't think you have. You thought about coming here, running here from whatever you're running from. And now you're thinking about staying. But you've never really considered leaving."

"I've thought about graduation," I said. "The daisy garlands."

"Not the ceremony," she said. "I mean really *leaving* Catherine. Going away and not coming back. Moving on."

I chewed at my thumbnail.

"Will you consider it," she said, "when I ask you to?"

I said, "I'll try."

She looked down. "I don't want to talk about this anymore."

I didn't want to, either. I'd finished my glass of wine already. I poured myself another.

We played more Monopoly, just the two of us. Despite Nick's cheating, Yaya was winning, though I was pretty sure she had built some houses illegally. I added more and more hotels to Baltic Avenue, my one terrible property, and when Yaya finally landed on it, she laughed so hard she had to pee.

I rolled the dice. I skipped my thimble forward.

"This is where we can go," Yaya said suddenly. "When we leave."

"Where?"

Yaya pointed at the board.

"Atlantic City?"

"What?"

"The Monopoly board is Atlantic City."

"No, you doofus." She tapped insistently on the New York Avenue square. "New York."

"New York Avenue?"

"New York City."

"I don't think there's a New York Avenue in New York City," I said.

"Are you sure?"

"No."

"Let's find out someday."

"I thought you wanted to go to Los Angeles."

"New York has better clubs."

"Everyone wants to go to New York. We should go to Florida."

"No. I want to go where everyone is."

I lay down on the rug. I closed my eyes.

"I used to do this," Yaya said, "with my friends in middle school. Before everything got bad. Sleepovers, you know. Truth or Dare. Prank calls. Did you?"

"No," I said. "I didn't have friends."

She leaned back against the wall. "Truth or dare?"

"Dare."

"I dare you to finish your drink."

I did, gulping. It didn't hurt. I burped into my hand, then said, "Truth or dare?"

"Dare."

"I dare you to tell me something real."

"Girl, that's a truth," she said. "Anyway, I always say real things."

"No, you don't."

She burped into her hand, too. Then she said, "I love you. That's real. And the truth."

"I love you, too," I said. "Truth or dare?"

"It's my turn." She scratched her knee again. "Oh, but I can't think of one. Okay, dare."

I said, "I dare you to come to M. Neptune's lab with me."

Yaya glanced at me. Her eyelashes were caked with mascara.

"I would never study plasm," she said. "Even if Viktória lost her mind and offered me the concentration. No way."

"No, I don't mean switch concentrations. I mean come visit his lab. With me. Tonight."

Her eyes narrowed.

"Theo has the keycard," I said. "M. Neptune added him to his team months ago. Theo hasn't realized that I know. I'm not sure how long he wants to keep it secret. Maybe until graduation. But I know."

"Theo has the key," Yaya said. It wasn't a question.

"I need to see," I said, "before I decide whether or not I'm doing the concentration. I—" I bit my lip, then said, "I need to see it all and understand and be sure, the way Theo is sure. And the way Baby was sure. I need to know what they're doing in that lab. I'm going."

"You're going to steal the key and sneak into the lab."

"Come with me?"

"Child, are you insane?"

"I thought you wanted adventure."

"What I want is to *graduate*. You think there isn't security in there? Cameras? You could be thrown out."

"We'll be careful and quiet. We'll wear hoods over our faces."

"You are insane."

"So, you won't come."

"I wish you hadn't even told me you were going."

The door banged open. Nick and Anna came in, laughing, carrying a tray piled high with fig rolls and lemon bars.

"What did we miss?" Anna said as she sat down.

I reached for a fig roll. So did Yaya.

"Nothing," Yaya said as she broke off a bite.

I didn't go to the lab that night. I went weeks later, after our last session of the semester.

It had been a ruthlessly cold day, and as we chanted the sky darkened to black. I sat with my hands flat on the table, intoning as I had so many times before: *The house is in the woods. The woods are in the night. I am here, in the night. I am here. I am here.*

I was there. Not alone—*nothing and no one is alone*—but together in everything. I felt the night reverberate from this night into the next, then back again, into all the nights that came before and all the nights that would come after. Minutes mirrored themselves, occurring and recurring in infinite flux. I was there: an infinite object tessellating into the house's infinite architecture.

After session, Theo and I returned to his room. We touched and bit each other. I screamed.

When Theo finished, he fell asleep almost immediately. I stared at his profile in the blue moonlight, watching his chest rise and fall. I ran a finger over his nose. His breath was warm against my cupped hand.

I slid out of bed.

Theo's room was so cold my clothes felt damp as I pulled them on. I rubbed my arms and blinked against the dark before bending to rifle through the pockets of his jeans. Yes. There it was.

I slipped the keycard into my pocket. I grabbed one of his hoodies and pulled it over my head.

I glanced at my reflection in the window. With the hood down, I looked almost like Theo. We were the same height and had the same skinny shoulders. It made me smile.

As I walked through the dark halls with Theo's key in my pocket, I saw the whole house, as if in a cross section. The boys and girls fast asleep in their beds; the classrooms, empty now, blackboards wiped clean and projectors clicked off; the aides dancing to Motown as they cooked breakfast down in the kitchen. I even saw the professors in their tower. Some were sleeping, gently snoring, and others were stirring from their beds, wandering to the bathroom, falling asleep on the toilet.

My house. My beautiful house.

Past the art gallery, down the stairs. Into the hallway with the gold umbrella wallpaper.

Something whistled behind me. I turned, but no one was there.

I listened to myself breathe. My heartbeat was steady and low. I didn't feel nervous. I felt wonderful.

I swiped the card in front of the keypad. The keypad beeped and clicked. I turned the handle.

The lights in the lab were off, which was good, because I hadn't considered what I'd do if someone was still there, working late. The glow from the hallway briefly illuminated two long lab tables that recessed into gray space before I closed the door and the room fell to black.

I felt along the wall for a switch. I flicked it on.

The lab looked like a smaller version of the one upstairs. Long rubberized counters held a mess of ledgers and notepads, pen caps and pencil shavings, compasses, beakers, thermometers. One wall was lined with bins filled with plasm kits and rubber gloves. Another was lined with bright red cubbies all crammed with heaps of junk: broken teacups, computer mouse pads, a crushed-in lampshade, two dusty VCRs. I reached in to feel the insides of a cubby I couldn't see clearly. I found a netted bag of marbles.

My footsteps echoed against the tile as I walked farther into the room. The air had that familiar warm milk smell.

This could be my place. These could be my secrets.

The wall by the cubbies held a whiteboard scribbled over with incomprehensible equations and diagrams. Someone had doodled a silly, googly-eyed dragon in the corner.

A series of cages lined the wall on the other side of the whiteboard. I bent to peer into their recesses.

That's where the smell came from: more rabbits.

I unlatched one of the cages and reached inside. The rabbit barely reacted as I pulled it into my arms, but it was definitely alive. Its nose twitched as it nestled into the crook of my arm. Its fur smelled like urine and sawdust. I stroked the rabbit's soft, fine, fragile head. She looked like a girl bunny, I decided. An Amy.

"Hi," I whispered into the pink folds of Amy's ear.

"Hello," someone responded.

I whirled.

How long had Sandy been standing there? At the other end of the lab, near a tall black door.

He stepped forward into the light. His eyes had the same vague look they always did. As if he weren't quite focused on my face.

"Hello," I said back.

"What," he said, "are you doing?"

He moved closer, and closer. I had never stood this near to him before, not since I spoke to him a year ago in the great hall. He was wearing pajamas, and his curls were mussed, as if he had just gotten out of bed. In the dim light, I could barely see that his skull was covered with orange bruises.

I clutched Amy tighter.

"I'm no one," I said. "I'm not here. Okay?"

Amy's heart beat fast against my own.

"Okay," he said.

Sandy walked past me. I stepped back, but he didn't touch me. He sat in one of the chairs by the lab table.

And that was all he did. He rested his hands on his knees. He didn't look at me, or at anything. He just sat and stared ahead, blank-faced, incurious.

I watched Sandy for a few minutes more, my heart still thumping. But he didn't do anything else.

Amy's whiskers twitched against my hand.

I glanced back at the door Sandy had come from. There was a keypad next to the handle, like the one outside the lab.

I clutched Amy tighter as I swiped Theo's keycard in front of the box. It clicked.

As soon as the door closed behind me with a thud, I was lost. The room was perfectly black, a depthless void. I tried not to panic as I groped for a light switch. I don't know why I was scared. I'd never been afraid of the dark.

I finally found a switch, and the overhead lights flickered on, casting a low submarine-yellow glow. I blinked and rubbed my face. I felt like I was in a golden darkroom, or some mystic mermaid hollow.

At first I thought it was a small space. I noticed only one lab table. But on the right stood another table, a long surface with a series of cases arranged on top. That table receded into the dark farther than I could see.

Behind each case lay a binder of notes. The binders were all dated; the earliest one was from the year M. Neptune was hired.

Still petting Amy, I walked along the cases. They looked like they were made of black plastic. Some were small, no bigger than my hand. I thought I heard an insect-like buzz coming from a few of them. As I kept going, they grew progressively bigger.

I peered at the spine of one of the binders. Below the date, the label read, "Rabbit 2.14."

I clutched Amy tighter.

The case by the Rabbit 2.14 binder was fixed with a simple flip lock. I pushed it open.

A rabbit sat crouched inside. A real white rabbit, alive, just like Amy. No—not alive like Amy. As I opened the case, the rabbit sniffed and its whiskers twitched, but otherwise it didn't move at all.

It didn't move because plasm pins were connecting its skull to four perfect spools of thread. One spool in each corner of the case.

The rabbit's nose kept twitching.

I closed the lid carefully.

I rubbed Amy's ears as I stared out at the rest of the cases. They marched on to the end of the room. Cases and cases, all full of animals and objects networked into the suspended animation of Theo's plastic infinity.

On the other side of the room stood two much bigger cases, each about seven feet long. It was hard to see in the low light, but one of them looked like it was already opened, the other still closed.

A binder lay beside the closed case.

I squinted at its cover: BARBARA PEARCE. Beneath that, it listed her age and weight.

I walked closer, slowly.

I put my hand on the case.

I swallowed.

"Hi, Baby," I whispered.

I swallowed again.

I didn't know why, but in that moment I felt nothing. I felt nothing and thought nothing. The only thing in my head was a stupid scrap of lyric from that ABBA song we'd been singing weeks ago, echoing over and over as I tried to breathe. *It used to be so good. It used to be so good.*

I stared at my hand.

I could have opened the case. I could have seen what objects were there inside. Maybe Baby was pinned to her sister's old Brandeis T-shirt, or to a cold Master Lock, or some freshly sharpened pencils. Any of the silly little objects she really, really loved. Maybe she looked peaceful, like I'd always dreamed for her. And maybe, when her eyes roved toward mine, I wouldn't have been afraid. Maybe she would have touched my hand and I would have felt fine.

I don't know. I didn't open the case. I only stood there, my hand on the cold plastic, trying to imagine that I could feel something beneath my palm, some kind of human energy. But I couldn't, really. I couldn't feel anything.

I wiped my face. My cheeks were wet.

I returned the keycard to Theo's drawer that night, but I didn't stay in his bedroom; I went to Yaya's. I opened her door without knocking. The hallway light flashed onto her sleeping face. She was in bed, breathing steadily, her mouth relaxed into something like a smile.

I climbed in next to her. She made a small sleepy sound as her arm reflexively tightened around me. I curled into a tight ball, hugging myself.

I must have slept, because then I was waking up alone in Yaya's bed. The pillow was damp. Gray morning had dawned.

I ran a hand over the sheets wherc Yaya used to be. The bed smelled like her.

I wanted to call for her—I needed her—but couldn't. My throat ached.

I could hear Yaya's small, human noises in the bathroom on the other side of the wall. Water sloshing in the tub, her humming as she washed herself. Then the drain popped, water gurgled, and her damp feet padded against the tiles. She was brushing her teeth. She was getting ready for the day.

UNTITLED

I shifted my books to my other arm as I pushed open the door to the great hall. I felt stupid carrying my things all the way from my bedroom, but I needed to work on my tutorial, and I hated being in my room. I always found myself looking around, remembering all the little things of Baby's that used to be there but weren't anymore. Her hairbrush. Her notes. Her jacket. Her shoes. I wished her things were there. I wished, in the middle of the night, I could turn in my bed and whisper to her, Are you sure about this? Are you okay?

How could she be okay?

I couldn't be in the bedroom. And I couldn't go to one of the libraries, where I might run into Anna or Diego. I couldn't see anyone right now. I couldn't pretend to be fine.

Some days I was different. Some days my brain ran in abstract nightmare circles. I paced from one wall to the next. I took nervous shits. I couldn't be alone, so I ended up attending classes that weren't my own and lingering in the great hall after meals. I lounged for hours in the music room, hanging out with second-years I didn't like or even know. I wandered from bedroom to bedroom, lazing and gossiping and begging friends to tell me stories until I fell asleep. But I couldn't sleep. I just lay in my bed and stared at the black ceiling, wishing I could stop thinking, wishing I were dead.

Other days, days like today, I just wanted to be alone.

I dropped my books on one of the tables in the great hall.

The sky through the windows was anxious predawn ultramarine. Outside, on the yard, dirty snow melted into the soil and little creatures twitched and oozed awake. The night was warming into a grim March morning. But in here I was the only living thing. The tables stretched out long and empty. The chairs, which were usually scattered all over the room, were tucked neatly in place. The tapestries hung still. Nothing moved, and nothing made a sound.

I pulled out a chair. It screeched as it scraped against the stone floor. I sat down.

I stood up again. I walked to the ice cream case by the dessert service.

I scooped up a big ice cream cone. Two lumps of cherry chocolate chip.

"Oh," a voice called, "there you are."

Theo was loping toward me from across the hall. His hands were in his pockets. He was smiling.

The emptiness of the hall had distorted his voice. I almost didn't recognize it.

"Yaya thought you might be here," he said as he came closer. "Hi."

He gave my cheek a cheery kiss, then climbed up onto the table. He swung his legs.

"Go figure," he said, "I pull an all-nighter, and that's the only time I can catch you. You've been waking up so early."

I licked my palm. The ice cream was melting down my hand.

"Well?" He laughed a little. "How are you doing? I feel like I haven't seen you in forever."

"I've been studying," I said.

"Studying?"

"Yes. My advisor keeps giving me more revision notes on the first half of my tutorial essay."

"Shouldn't you be in the second half by now?"

"That's why I'm studying."

He ran a hand along my cheek.

"You're so pretty," he murmured. "I could look at you forever."

I stood very still as he touched me.

"Where are you coming from?" I said.

"The lab. This is like my third all-nighter this week. I'm getting better at them, though. I'm getting so strong." He made a bicep and mugged.

I threw the cone in the trash.

Three weeks had passed since my visit to M. Neptune's lab.

Theo rubbed my shoulders. "I miss you," he said.

I touched his waist. I missed him, too.

Make me better, I wanted to say. Say everything is all right. Say everything is fine.

I stepped between his legs. I ran my hands over his thighs.

"You know," he said, pulling at a lock of my hair, "sometimes I like to imagine you as a little girl. Scraped knees, climbing trees. Playing princess games."

"I never pretended to be a princess."

"Man, everyone pretended to be a princess. Even I pretended to be a princess."

"I never wanted to be a princess. And I didn't climb trees. I got into fights."

"I can just imagine you," he said, "like one of those magic story creatures. A child born under a leaf."

I stroked his fuzzy head. That wasn't me at all.

Noise had started to stir in the kitchen, pots banging against pots and porcelain scraping against porcelain. The aides were preparing lunch.

I bit Theo's neck. I pulled at his shirt. He got up and lifted me onto the table.

It almost felt good.

"Are you okay?" Theo said afterward.

I looked down. I was bleeding. I wiped between my legs.

"I'm fine," I said. I wasn't sure if it was my period or not.

"Sorry."

"Stop apologizing. I did it."

Theo grabbed a napkin from the dessert service and handed it to me. He kissed my hairline.

❧

The painting shone. I stared at it, my Agnes Martin notes limp and useless on my lap. Months of classes and theory and notes and drafts, and now I had less to say about this work than ever before. What could I say? What words could I use that were honest, the way the painting was honest? Words were silly human inventions; the painting was a vision. Its pattern of space and light and colors had a rhythm that was so arcane, so simple and true. What description could possibly contain it?

I used to think the painting's surface was beautiful. I used to think its material, the magic matter, was the stuff of divinity. But what if the space between this world and eternity wasn't a happy place? What if it was infinitely lonely and sad?

I went to my room. I closed the door and turned off the light. I looked down at the Molina courtyard.

No one was there. No one was there and nothing moved. I could smell, through the cracked window, a spring perfume of fester and growth.

Today was Friday. Soon, session would begin in the great hall. But I wasn't going. I hadn't been to any sessions since visiting the lab. It didn't matter that we weren't pinned during the ceremonies; I knew Viktória and M. Neptune had to be using them to experiment on us in some more oblique way. I didn't want to be there. I didn't want to feel the power of the house and its things.

I stared at my hand on the desk, like I had stared at it when I touched Baby's case in the lab.

How could I have left her?

I went to the bathroom, clutched the toilet, and heaved. Nothing came up.

I closed the lid and sat on it. I leaned against the cool, clammy wall.

It didn't matter if I was awake or asleep. Either way, I couldn't breathe.

Baby wanted this, I tried to remind myself. Baby wanted this. Baby believed in Catherine.

So why couldn't I? Why couldn't I believe?

I'd never been afraid of dying. Even after I saw the girl in the hotel. I'd hated myself and that room and everything, but I still wasn't afraid. I wasn't afraid of the dark. I was afraid of the light—the future. And now I could see them all, all the future days, smothering Baby's nose and mouth. And every object around me, from the pale tiles on the bathroom floor to the toilet pull, the mirror over the sink to the empty claw-foot tub, every detail that once blessed the house now seemed to damn us, me and Baby, here, to our world's double: a boundless hollow horror earth I hadn't recognized until now.

Rain slurred and smeared against the parlor window. We lingered over our tea, slouched in armchairs, prone on the floor, still hungover from the night before. There had been a party in the Ashley basement to celebrate the end of midterms. I had a blurry memory of a pair of blue-and-red roller skates unearthed from the bottom of some closet, a long stretch of hallway, the noise of plastic clattering against stone, and Yaya screaming, "I broke my arm! I broke my arm! Oh—did I? Oh—oh, it's fine." And me, laughing desperately.

"I want to die," Anna mumbled. She was lying on the rug, arm slung over her face. "They used to be better than this."

"Who did?" Diego said.

"Not who, what. Hangovers, I mean. They didn't used to hurt so much." She flopped her arm off her face. "And I already have another Phonetics test coming up. Have you started studying for it, Ines?"

"No."

"Do you know if Theo has his notes?"

"No. I don't know. Didn't you see him in class today?"

"He wasn't there. You haven't seen him lately?"

I sat up in my chair. "No."

"He hasn't been in his room in a while," Nick mumbled. He was munching on a pear, the only one of us who seemed to have recovered from the party in good spirits.

"He's probably been in the lab," Diego said. "You know their hours are insane."

Nick shrugged. He licked pear juice from his palm.

But Theo usually stopped at his room between classes. And I hadn't seen him there in days.

I stood up.

"Ines," Anna said, "where are you going?" But I was already pushing my way out of the parlor.

I went to Theo's room first. I knocked before opening the door, though I knew he wouldn't answer.

His bed was unmade and a half-full cup of tea sat on his desk, as if he'd dashed off to class in a hurry. But his books were all there, strewn across the floor. In his closet, I saw he was running low on clothes. He hadn't picked up his laundry, which he should have done yesterday.

I rifled through his dresser. The keycard wasn't there. So he could be in the lab. Or it could be in his pocket, and he could be anywhere.

My heart was beating fast as I left his room.

Down in the courtyard, the rain had stopped, but the leaves, tiles, and branches were still wet, their colors hyper-vibrant. I hugged my elbows as I walked over the slick stones onto the yard.

Theo was missing. He wasn't in my room. He wasn't in the courtyard, on the bench underneath the fig tree where he liked to study. He wasn't in the hallway, whistling his way to class. He wasn't in the Molina library, the Ashley library, the Harrington library. He wasn't in the garden. He wasn't here by the fountain.

I sat on the fountain bench.

Could I remember the last time I'd seen him? Yes. He was down on the yard and I was up above. I was leaving my Islamic Art class in the Ashley tower. As I'd packed up my books, I turned to the window and saw him on the bright grass below. He was wearing the blue nylon rain jacket he'd been loving lately. He was waving to someone—Nick, maybe?—and shouting something cheery, something like, *Wait, wait, I'm coming*. Then he was jogging to catch up. Then he was gone.

Now the sun was setting. Purple evening descended over the house.

I got up. I went across the yard to the professors' tower. I made my way through the halls to M. Donna's door.

"Come in," she said at my knock.

M. Donna was sitting at her desk, head bent over a page of tiny notes. She didn't look up as I entered.

"Hi, M. Donna," I said. "How are you doing today?"

She barely glanced away from her notes. "Hello, Ines," she muttered. "I'm fine, how are you?"

"I'm wonderful." I tapped my fingers against the doorjamb. "Can I ask, have you seen Theo lately?"

Now she looked straight at me, lowering her hands as she eyed me up and down.

"Theo Williams?" she said. She leaned back in her chair. "Why do you ask?"

"He's my partner on a project," I lied. "For Intro to Phonetics. It's due next week. But I haven't seen him for a couple days. You're his tutorial advisor, right? Do you know if he's been in the lab?"

M. Donna tapped her pen against the page. "Ah," she said.

I sat down. I crossed my legs.

M. Donna cleared her throat. Then she said, "Ines, Theo is in the Restoration Center. You know that."

She was still tapping her pen against the page.

"But he's a perfect student," I finally said. "He's perfect. Why—why is he in the tower?"

"No one's perfect, Ines," M. Donna snipped. "And the *Center* isn't a place of punishment, but improvement, which every student can use. You know that, too."

"What did he do?" I said.

"The affairs of other students are no business of your own," she said.

"You have to tell me."

She stood up.

"No," she said, "I don't. This is a matter between Theo and the administration. I can only recommend you speak with your Phonetics professor about arranging for a new project partner."

She gestured to the door.

I was taking a Greek art seminar that semester with a new materials concentrator, a black-haired boy with a pale, oblong, aristocratic face. His features were handsome from the front, but in profile you could see that he had an ugly overbite. Theo hated him. I didn't know why, but I could imagine. His name was George.

That afternoon, after class, I asked George if he wanted to cram for the midterm with me. He looked me over with a prissy smirk before responding, "Sure, whyever not?"

I met up with him after dinner in one of the Ashley libraries, a cramped, crooked, dusty room with blackwood walls and a low ceiling painted bronze. Tonight, the only other person there was a chubby first-year girl, napping over her notes. She drooled onto the pages.

I'd brought a jug of beer some Molina second-years had brewed. I sat close to George. As he flipped through our textbook rambling on about the texts, I made sure his glass was never empty. I watched the foam pop and fizzle. I didn't like looking at the sculptures, the ones photocopied into the texts. I didn't like their white, frozen faces.

It was going to be an easy midterm. The vocabulary list was short, and we only had to memorize the dates within one hundred years. George sighed every time I asked him a question. He didn't think I was very smart. That was what I wanted.

"What's contrapposto again?" I said.

"An asymmetrical pose," he said slowly, "with the weight on just one leg. A dynamic position. Makes the figure look both powerful and relaxed."

"Oh," I said. "Right." I poured him more beer.

"What's really cool," he said, pushing his glasses up on his nose, "is seeing the same pose appear thousands of years later, in

American Western film. Think John Wayne entering the saloon, leaning back on one leg. It's that same pose. Comfortable power. You know, the ideal man."

"Wow," I said. "Yeah."

His lip curled into a smirk.

"No," I said. "Really. You're right. That is cool."

I poured him more to drink. I swiped a lick of foam from his glass and sucked it off my finger.

I watched his Adam's apple bob as he drank.

"Can I ask you a question?" I said.

"Naturally."

"You're in the new materials concentration, right? You know Theo Williams?"

"Sure." George ran a hand through his hair. "You guys are dating, aren't you?"

"We used to. Not anymore." I rested my chin in my hand. "Anyway. He's in the tower, right?"

George took another big sip of the beer.

"Why?" I said.

He licked his lips. "Why, what?"

"Why is Theo in the tower?"

George hesitated. He glanced at me, then away. "Why do you care?" he said.

"I'm just curious."

"How curious are you?"

I ran a hand along his thigh.

"Tell me," I said.

He looked up.

"I'll fuck you," I said, "if you tell me."

He sneered. "You'll fuck anyone."

"That's not true," I said. "I usually only fuck people I like."

"Well, you must like an awful lot of people."

"I don't like *you*."

He lifted his chin and assessed me with his glacial blue eyes.

"You're really pretty, you know," he said. "Even with your weird teeth." He narrowed his eyes. "Well, maybe not pretty, exactly. But there's something about you."

He took a sip of his drink.

"You're right," he muttered. "No one likes me. I thought this school would be different. But nothing's ever different, really." He glanced back at me. "*You* wouldn't understand."

"No one likes you because you're a snob," I said.

"You think so?"

"Yes. You could have friends. If you really wanted them."

The napping girl snorted in her sleep.

George twisted his pencil between his fingers. His expression turned dark.

"George," I said.

He looked up again.

"Tell me," I whispered.

He kept twisting his pencil. "I don't even work with M. Neptune," he said. "What makes you think I know what's going on with Theo?"

"Do you?"

He gave a dramatic shrug. But after glancing at me one more time, he sighed and said, "Theo went into M. Neptune's lab outside of project work hours. That alone is a huge transgression. But he also, well. He released one of their test subjects."

"A test subject?"

"Yes. A rabbit." He was sneering again and talking slower, as if relishing the moment. "He took it out of the lab and set it loose out on the yard. Don't know why, really. Pretty dumb move for someone who's supposed to be such a genius."

A memory flashed of Amy's fur, gray as the moon in the night, as I set her down on the grass, kissed her head one last time, and hoped, really hoped, that she would be fine.

I didn't know why I had done it. I just couldn't put her back in the cage.

"But that doesn't sound so bad," I said. "It was only a rabbit."

"Sure. And they found it on the yard the next day. But it could have been much worse. I mean, it wasn't just any rabbit." George spoke even slower now. "It was a *test subject.* The department doesn't exactly want to lose those. Honestly, Theo fucked up. He should have been thrown in the tower weeks ago, but M. Neptune is so blind when it comes to his little wunderkind. Well, he used to be. I guess he's come to his senses now."

George took another sip.

"All right," I said. "But if it didn't happen during lab hours and no one was there, how did they know it was Theo?"

"The security footage showed him there."

I breathed out. "Really?"

"Sure. We all saw it. Looked just like him." He wiped the corner of his mouth. "And anyway, they looked at the log from the night and his keycard had swiped into the lab."

"The keys are different from each other?"

George glanced at me. "Of course they are. Anyway. Altogether, a pretty big series of mistakes." He was definitely enjoying the story now. "They'll probably throw him out of the concentration. If not out of Catherine."

I looked down at the page. An ancient Greek statue stood alone in a marble room. The god's lifeless eyes gazed back at me.

❧

I lay on my stomach on the floor of the music room, staring at one of the legs of a rococo armchair. I focused. This close, the leg's wood grain came into such detail that it abstracted. It didn't look like anything.

Theo was in the tower. Theo was gone.

"You're shaking," Ursula said. "You better hold still if you don't want me screwing this up."

I braced my arm against the rug. Pain pulsed through my shoulder.

When Yaya had heard there was a Molina first-year giving tattoos, she had immediately gotten herself on the wait list, and put mine and Anna's names on there, too. She hadn't bothered to ask if we wanted in. We did. And of course we had to get the same tattoo, the Catherine House insignia. In exchange for the tattoos, Yaya gave Ursula the faux-mink coat, the one she had worn all our first year. It made me sad to think of her giving it up. Yaya didn't care.

Ursula had frowned as she bent over each of their shoulders, examining the skin with a sharp eye, then sighing. She tucked her long, stiff black hair behind her ears. Her hands moved with reverent care over her kit of needles, colored ink bottles, a blue BIC lighter, and a hand towel embroidered with tiny strawberries. She ran the needle through the lighter's flame before crouching over Yaya, then Anna. She didn't talk and didn't smile. She just slowly pricked.

Now, lying on the rug with my arm outstretched, I could see Ursula's black eyes and stern brow, her deep widow's peak. I could feel her breath on the back of my neck.

Stay here, I wanted to say. Keep touching me and make it hurt. Make me forget.

But I couldn't forget. Because Theo was gone.

Anna stood before me. From here, I could see only her fuzzy blond ankles and bare feet, facing away from the mirror. She was probably craning to see her tattoo.

"Anna," I said.

"Mmm?"

"Is it pretty?"

The feet turned. I felt her consider me.

"My tattoo," I said.

"Oh, yeah," she said. "Gorgeous."

I closed my eyes and clenched my teeth. The pain in my shoulder blazed.

It felt like hours passed before Ursula finally said, "Done."

My knees creaked as I stood.

I twisted my neck to look over my shoulder into the mirror. The tattoo really was gorgeous: a little Catherine insignia, its tiny swoops and scrolls all flushed with blood.

"Thank you," I said to Ursula.

She nodded. She wiped her needle on a towel.

I lingered behind Anna and Yaya on our walk to dinner. Their shadows grew long as they skipped over the yard, holding hands and laughing. I couldn't hear what they were saying. A bandage swathed each of their left shoulders, just as one did mine.

Another shadow moved ahead of us, near the door to Harrington. I thought for a moment it might be someone waving to us, but it was only a trick of the light.

Theo had been in the tower for a week now, but I still saw him everywhere. I would be on my way to the bathroom and hear his footsteps behind me, but when I turned, it was only some first-year scurrying toward the commissary. A face in the great hall was him until it came into focus. Shadows through classroom windows were his until they weren't.

Theo was gone. And it was my fault he was in the tower, that his life was ruined, that things would never be the same between us. Mine. I was the one who had ruined everything. Of course I was.

Before Baby, I had never missed anyone. I didn't think I even understood the idea of missing a person or a thing or a place. But now I missed Baby, and Theo. And I missed me, too. I missed me, here at home.

"Ines," Yaya shouted. She was waving for me, holding open the door. A clover-scented breeze stirred the grass.

Daphne sat typing at her desk, lips pursed in peevish concentration as her fingers clattered over the keys. Every few minutes she cast a glare my way. Her hair was brushed into a pouf on top of her head, and she wore a bright red dress with a ruffled collar.

"You look very pretty today, Daphne," I said.

She glared at me again.

The clock ticked. I hugged my knees.

The door to Viktória's office creaked open, and I sat up straighter. But it was only M. Linus, the hunched gray professor I'd had for my Monuments and Memorials seminar. He slumped toward Daphne and murmured, "I'm on the calendar for next week, too, yes? Because—" before he saw me waiting.

"Oh," he said, "hello, Ines. Lovely, lovely to see you. Ah." He glanced at Daphne, then back at me. "Do you have an appointment with Viktória?"

"Yes," I said.

"No," Daphne said sharply, "she doesn't, and Viktória has meetings all afternoon, but she won't leave."

"I need to talk to Viktória," I said.

M. Linus glanced from one to the other of us, then bowed at Daphne again. "Thursday, yes?"

She penciled in the appointment. M. Linus slunk out without meeting my eye.

"Please," Daphne snapped at me, "*try* to sit with some decorum."

I put my feet on the floor. I was wearing the denim skirt Yaya had given to me last summer, one steamy July day on the dock. She had plucked it from a storage box, held it up to my legs, and said it would look so perfect. It would make my legs look so amazing.

"Really," Daphne said, "I don't know how long she will be."

"I can wait," I said.

The clock ticked. I needed to concentrate. I closed my eyes.

I am in the house. I am in Viktória's office. The computer is on the desk. The daisies are in the vase. The clock is ticking. It is three-twelve p.m. I am here.

Please. Please. Let me believe in this house. Let me stay.

Please. Please keep me here.

A loud laugh rang out in the hall. Then M. Neptune walked in, guiding a woman, the new English professor, by the small of her back.

"Oh, hello, Ines," the professor murmured. She looked me up and down as she slipped a sunny strand of hair behind her ear. "Oh, do you have an appointment with Viktória? Are we early?"

"She doesn't have an appointment," Daphne snapped.

M. Neptune turned to me, smiling. I don't think he had ever looked at me directly before. The power of his stare made my stomach twist.

"Hi," he said. "Ines."

"I need to talk to Viktória."

He gestured toward the professor at his side. "We have some schedules to go over with her. Can it wait?"

"You can go first," I said. "I'll speak to her after."

M. Neptune's eyes were so black I couldn't see his pupils.

M. Neptune touched the professor's elbow and muttered something in her ear. She nodded. Then he brightened as he turned back to me.

"Want to come to my office?" he said.

"I need to talk to Viktória."

He touched my shoulder. "It's just down this hall."

Daphne's face twisted as he led me out.

The furniture in M. Neptune's office was more modern than any I had seen at Catherine. His chair was made of ergonomic, adjustable vinyl mesh and his broad steel desk shone like an engine. Everything smelled leathery and expensive.

"Want a chocolate?" M. Neptune said, pushing a tray toward me. "They're from Ecuador."

I sat in an amoeba-shaped armchair. "No."

"Water?" He gestured toward a pitcher.

"No," I said again, then changed my mind and poured myself a glass.

"So," M. Neptune said, folding his hands over his stomach and rocking slightly in his chair. "What is it that you need to talk to Viktória about?"

"I was the one who let the rabbit out of the lab," I said. "Not Theo."

Nothing changed in M. Neptune's face. But he stopped rocking.

I'd never realized before—probably because I'd never seen him up close—that M. Neptune's face was completely unreadable. It was magnetic, dark, and powerful, but it didn't reveal the truth. It didn't reveal anything.

"I stole Theo's keycard," I said. "It wasn't his fault. He trusted me and he shouldn't have. I took the key while he was asleep and snuck in. I was wearing his clothes, so I looked like him. I didn't realize the keys were tagged. I didn't know he would get in trouble."

M. Neptune tapped his fingers together over his stomach. I reached for a chocolate.

"Why?" M. Neptune said after a long pause. "Why did you do it?"

I swallowed the chocolate. "I don't know," I said. "Rabbits should be hopping around on the grass. Not locked in cages."

"No," he said, "I mean, why did you steal the key? Why did you break into my lab?"

"Oh." I shrugged. "Because I needed to know," I said. "I needed to know what the house was doing. I needed to know everything."

M. Neptune tapped his fingers against the table. He stared as I folded the chocolate wrapper into little squares.

"So," he said, still staring. "You saw my lab."

"Yes," I said.

"How far did you go?"

I looked up.

M. Neptune was smiling.

"You saw my projects," he said. It wasn't a question.

The chocolate had gummed up my teeth. I hadn't realized there was caramel inside.

He was still tapping his fingers.

"And what did you think?" he said.

I blinked.

"I don't know," I said. "I don't know."

He was still smiling.

"I don't," I said.

I was crying again. I wished I didn't keep crying.

"I just want—I just want them to be okay, Baby and the boy. I can't stop worrying about them." I sniffled. "Baby has a sister. Did you know that?" I sniffled again. "I keep having this dream of Baby being somewhere, doing something, anything. Like, ordering cold cuts at a deli, maybe, or waiting for the bus. And then her sister runs into her. And her sister—she taps Baby on the shoulder, laughing and so excited, like oh my God, she can't believe they're randomly running into each other like this. But Baby turns around and just blinks. She doesn't recognize her own sister. And I wake up sad. I'm so sad."

I wiped my nose.

"I know I should be excited about your work, like Theo is," I said. "But ever since I saw your lab, I've felt so . . . sick."

I looked up again.

"I'm messed up," I said. "I've always been wrong inside. These past couple of years, I've tried to be better, and it almost worked. I was almost happy here. But now I'm fucked up again."

M. Neptune glanced at the clock.

"Please," I whispered. "Help me."

He picked up the phone. He dialed four numbers.

"Please," I said again. He was focused on the phone.

"Hey, Maria," he was saying. "Could you send over an aide? Yeah, right now would be great. Yes, thanks."

M. Neptune hung up. He leaned back in his chair again and folded his hands on top of his head as he considered me.

It wasn't long before I heard the click of footsteps on the other side of the door.

"Thank you," I said as the door opened.

Hours later, I was standing by the bare light bulb in front of the tower door. I could hear the aides inside talking in low, lazy voices. They weren't in a rush. They were gossiping about me.

While I waited, I played a game: I pressed my back and hands hard against the door, as hard as I could, for as long as I could. Then I stepped forward.

My hands rose, weightless, up and up, into the sky.

The yard smelled like sap, mulch, and sweet grass. Sunset

beams flashed through the pines. I couldn't see the sun itself, though, only a bank of plummy dark clouds and four diamond stars.

Right now, in the house, students were studying in the library or playing piano in the music room or getting drunk with their roommates. They were in the parlor playing cards and braiding each other's hair. Dinner tonight would be tomato salad and whitefish and big bowls of vanilla ice cream. And after everyone grew tired of studying, finished their games, washed their faces, and brushed their hair and teeth, they would all go to bed. They would get cozy underneath their blankets and close their eyes. They would fall asleep, warm and fed, comfortable and clean.

An aide, a reedy red-haired girl, stepped out of the tower. She glared at me but said nothing. Then she walked off into the grass. She crossed over the yard, toward the house, without looking back.

"You can come in," the other aide called.

Walking back into the tower felt like returning to a dream. There were the wood-paneled walls and rolltop desk, the armoire and shelves shrouded by blue latex curtains. There was the yellow door. The aide was different, but everything else was the same. Two years later and nothing had changed.

This aide had long, smooth chestnut hair and warm eyes. She was eyeing me with curiosity.

"You know what to do," she said. "Strip."

"Is Viktória coming?"

"No."

I unbuttoned my jeans.

The aide chewed on her lip as she folded my T-shirt and jeans and placed them in the armoire. She reminded me of a girl I'd read about in a book once, one who played with boys and rode unruly horses. I couldn't remember its title. I hadn't thought about that book in a long time.

She removed my bracelet. It was just a bit of string Yaya had tied there months ago. Her hair fell over my wrist as she did it.

"They let Theo go," I whispered. "This afternoon?"

She glanced up at me before nodding. "About an hour ago."

I let out a breath.

"So," the aide said, "I guess he was right all along."

"Right about what?"

She shrugged. "Theo kept arguing with M. Neptune, saying you were the one who did it. He didn't know how. But he always knew there was something wrong with you." She glanced up again. "Isn't that funny?"

A clock ticked somewhere I couldn't see.

"My tutorial," I said. "I have a draft due next week."

What had the aide said last time? Something about classwork being suspended until I was out of the tower. Something about making it up later.

This aide only straightened, stared at me with an expression I couldn't quite read, and said nothing as she opened the yellow door.

Pity. That was the expression I saw in her eyes.

Light from the antechamber lit up the room. As I stepped inside, I got a vague impression of the bed along the wall, the bookcase, the tea table. Then the door closed, and I was alone in the dark.

GLO

Was I alive?

Yes. I was in the tower. I was lying on the bed. My eyes were open, but everything I saw was gray. The ceiling was gray, the bed was gray, the rug and table and bookshelves were gray. My gray hand rested on my naked gray chest. The gray walls receded, as if they weren't there at all.

I moved my hand from my chest. I hated the sound of my heart beating.

I closed my eyes. Time must have passed, but I didn't feel it. Because I wasn't there, in the tower. I was in the Harrington library. I had an American Poetry midterm tomorrow, and I really needed to study. I was having trouble concentrating. The textbook's words swam before my eyes.

I pressed my hands over my ears. No, I was in the tower. I had been asleep. And now I was waking up again.

The room was dense with heat, and the window, when I'd tried to open it, it was locked. So I lay there sweating. I rotted and sweetened.

One night, and another night. And another.

There must have been days, too. Someone brought me trays of food, as they had the first time I was in the tower. But no one brought any plasm pins, and the days folded into the nights, and in the night, I wasn't a girl. I was only a crazy, twisted brain, draining on the bed. I was dying. I was dead.

What was happening back in the house? Did my friends miss me? Were they horrified that I was locked in here? Or had they always known I would fuck things up?

I turned to face the wall.

Theo had known. He'd seen me for what I was.

I stroked the peeling plaster wall. It felt so cool and heartless beneath my fingers.

Baby had been here. In this room, touching this wall, feeling like this: so seized by sadness, so violently alone.

Did she feel better now?

Or did she feel nothing?

I slept with my mouth open. My lips cracked and bled.

I didn't know if it was many nights later, or many weeks, when I sat up and looked around the room as if seeing it for the first time.

An English dictionary and a science fiction book stood on the bookshelf. The thriller from last time, *The Second Lady*, wasn't there anymore. I wished it were. But there was the same elephant figurine with its trunk lifted. And on the other side of the room was the same back door and the tea table with its packet of cards.

The curtain to the toilet was pushed aside. It smelled like shit. I must have forgotten to flush.

Somewhere over the yard, up the stairs and through the hall, was my beautiful little bedroom. My window was open, a summer breeze rustling through the notes that littered my desktop. I was putting my books in my bag and munching on a slice of cantaloupe I'd taken from the morning room. I was licking its juice from my palm.

Someone was turning the tower doorknob. It was the aide. It was time for my weekly shower.

The aide let me out the back door to a shower situated over a plastic drain on the lawn. I shivered as she hunted for the spigot.

The sky was a clear, brutal blue. A chubby bee hovered over the grass, then drifted over the yard and down the hill. There, past the hills, I could see the silos and the loading dock. I'd never seen the dock from this angle before.

The shower puttered on. The sudden cold water shocked me.

The aide was sorry, she had forgotten to bring a washcloth. That was fine. I didn't mind. I rubbed the bar of soap all over my body.

"Hurry up," she said.

I scrubbed harder.

❧

When did I realize that Catherine would never let me go?

❧

Rain echoed against the roof. I was waking up. I opened my eyes.

Viktória was sitting on the edge of the bed.

"Hello," she said.

I sat up. Then, remembering I was naked, I pulled the sheet to my chin.

A smile twitched her lip. Her skin was damp, and a long black umbrella stood propped against the door, dripping onto the floor. A pair of high-heeled pumps dangled from her finger. Her slender feet were bare and muddy but the shoes were clean.

"These silly things," she said, following my gaze to the pumps. "I just came in from a conference. I forgot I would be walking across the yard. But the grass under your feet, even in the rain—it feels good, doesn't it?"

She smelled like grass and dark, sultry soil.

I sank lower in the bed.

"You shouldn't have gone to the lab," she said. "It wasn't time."

"I know," I whispered.

She ran a hand over my head.

"You really were a wonderful student," she said, brushing my hair away from my face. "Unlike any other I've known. I read through your tutorial essay draft. Sixty pages describing an off-white canvas. Indecipherable." She shook her head. "It's as if you never learned the most basic analytical habits, so you never had to unlearn them. You see the world sideways, like a stranger. Yes, you were lazy. And you never learned to study well. But you had an interesting mind."

I sneezed.

She lowered her hand. "Bless you."

I sniffed.

Viktória leaned back against the wall, uncrossed her legs, then crossed them again.

"I came here," she said, "because I thought you might have some questions for me, and I'd like to answer them for you."

She stared at me with kind but austere eyes. The rain slushed harder.

I said, "Do my professors know where I am?"

"Yes."

"Do my friends?"

"Yes."

I scratched my knee.

"Baby," I whispered. I swallowed, took a breath, then tried again. "Baby, in the end—did she choose . . . that? Did she choose to be an experiment?"

"Yes," Viktória said. "She did. And so did Alexander."

I nodded. I nodded again.

"Ines," she said. "We are not cruel. You understand that. If you'd really thought Baby were being held against her will, you could have done something. You could have disturbed the experiment or told a professor. Anything. But you didn't. You trust

Baby, and you trust Catherine. You do—you trust us. Even if there are some who don't."

Viktória bent to arrange her high heels on the floor, lining them up neatly beside the bed. I stared at them—the empty ghost shoes—suddenly sickened, though I couldn't have said why. She leaned back against the wall.

"Listen to me," she said. "I'm quite familiar with the reactionaries' arguments against our work. Of course I am. I was witness at M. Shiner's trials, and I heard every silly, misguided invective tossed his way. Believe me, I remember how many people out there weren't ready to see how far we had come, and how much further we were ready to go. Because they were small people with small imaginations."

She shrugged.

"For those small people," she said, "the world is fine. Years go by, they watch their bodies shrivel and shrink and their brains warp, and they don't care. They say goodbye to their friends and families, to themselves, and to their realities. And still they don't care. Because they have some delusion that to be human and perishable is to be divine. But here in Catherine, we know differently. We know that the divine is the object. The supernatural matter." She touched my ankle. "You understand. You do. You've felt it."

She smiled.

"I'm proud of Barbara," she said. "I'm proud of Alexander, too. He was our first, did you know that? Our first human." She shook her head, impressed. "He's done so much better than expected, especially since M. Neptune decided to set him free in the house. Braiding Alexander's body into Catherine, our operations, and our objects—it's made all the difference, really."

Her hand, on my ankle, was damp and cool.

"I've seen—before I came here," I whispered. "I saw a dead person. I stared her in the face."

"Yes," Viktória said. Her voice was sweet. "That must have been terrible for you. Awful, really. Things like that should never happen to such young, lovely girls."

I couldn't keep my thoughts straight.

"Sandy—Alexander," I finally said. "With our sessions and the coming in and all the experiments . . . have we been helping him stay? Have we been keeping him here?"

Viktória shrugged. "M. Neptune's reports indicate that this is all a very inexact science," she said. "But I'm sure everything helps."

I shook my head.

"And all of us students, we've been going along with everything," I whispered. "Without any questions."

"My dear, you would have asked questions," Viktória said. "If you wanted to know."

I hugged my stomach.

"It's a stunning project," she said. "But yes, it is a project Barbara and Alexander believe in. A project for which they gave everything of themselves. Not for a perfect today or a perfect future, but for a perfect object forever."

She was still smiling.

"But you don't know what it's really like," I said. "I don't know about . . . Alexander. But Baby was a sad person. She was so unhappy." I squeezed my stomach tighter. "She gave herself to you because you were the only thing she ever believed in. You and your plasm, your perfect object forever. She was desperate. You don't know what it's really like, being that way. What if it's terrible? What if it hurts? Or what if it doesn't feel like anything, anything at all, and it's really forever? I've looked into Sandy's eyes." My voice was rising. "He's wandering around, right in the open, like some kind of pet. He's not alive."

"No," Viktória said. "He's not. Isn't that wonderful? Living, that's what hurts. Don't you understand? We saved him."

Her smile grew bigger. I had never noticed how her teeth were girlishly crooked.

"And isn't he a beautiful thing?" She said. "And Baby will be, too, someday. Such a beautiful thing."

"She won't be beautiful," I said. "She won't be real."

Viktória laughed, shaking her head. "She will be real. We are not."

I sneezed again.

Viktória stroked the ends of my hair. She examined my split ends with a disinterested eye.

"I try so hard," she said, "to make this house a home. To pull you in and hold you close. Nothing in the universe matters more to me than you, my sweet children. But what if I could give you even more than Catherine? Can you imagine how it would feel?" Her voice grew softer. "This house was founded on the idea that there is some strange, extraordinary, beautiful power inherent to every one of us. That power is real. But we've since learned that we are not singular beings. We are each facets of some larger infinite truth. What if I could teach you that truth?" I could barely hear her now. "What if I could make you at home, forever—not merely in one house but a whole world? Can you imagine?"

"No," I said. "I can't imagine."

Viktória hesitated, then burst out laughing. I jumped at the noise of it. "No," she said. "I suppose I can't, either." She inclined her head. "But I wish I could."

She stroked my hair slower and slower.

"You said I was the only thing Baby ever believed in," Viktória said. "That's true. Me and my plasm. New material for a new world." She dropped her hand. "I was very proud of her for that. She saw the truth. And someday, the rest of the world will see it, too. Not yet, of course. Even our graduates aren't ready to see how far we've come. It's not time yet. But Catherine's truth will come out. Catherine's exquisite truth."

The rain had stopped. Droplets beaded on the window, suspended.

"So," she said, "do you want to do it?"

At first I didn't understand the question. Then I realized what she meant.

I didn't know how I hadn't heard the voices before. The tower aide was speaking with someone on the other side of the door. Now that I was listening carefully, I realized it was one of M. Neptune's students. Burt, probably.

And they were fiddling with something. I heard plastic clicking against plastic. Wheels creaking against wood.

I said, "No."

"You said you didn't want to be sick anymore," Viktória said. "This is how you become better. This is how you get all your poison out."

I whispered again, "No."

Viktória shrugged. "If you're not ready, that is fine. Of course it is fine. We won't make you do anything you don't want to do." She was touching my ankle again. "But please, Ines. Remember: I know who you were before Catherine. I know who you were and how you ended up here."

She rubbed her thumb against my skin.

"You wouldn't have gone to prison," she said. "Of course not. You could hardly be implicated in that girl's death. But that doesn't matter. What matters is how easily you presumed your guilt. Because you were ashamed. Ashamed and alone. No one cares about you out there, Ines. No one. And no one will notice if you're gone. There's nothing for you in that world. There never was and never will be." She touched my ear now. "My little sideways girl."

I slunk down in the bed. I thought of bringing up Mr. González, but knew that was stupid. He'd never really cared about me, either.

"When you offered me the concentration," I said, "those months ago—was this what you meant?"

Viktória kept smiling.

"I want to go home," I said.

"This is your home."

"I mean my room. I want to go back to my room."

She inclined her head slightly. "You're not going back to your room."

"I want to finish my tutorial," I said. "And see my friends. I won't tell. I promise. I won't tell anyone about anything."

"No," Viktória said. "You won't."

She stood. She loomed over me.

"I'll give you some time to think," she said. "I do hope, Ines—I hope you will make the right decision."

She picked up her shoes. She padded her way to the door.

"Wait," I said.

She turned, her hand on the knob.

"Does Theo know," I whispered, "what you want to do to me?"

She smiled. "Of course. He was the one who suggested it."

As she opened the door, I caught a glimpse of the case. It was just my size.

Then the door closed, and I was alone again.

❧

I dreamed it was nighttime, and I was walking down the hallway, sucking on a cough drop. I was laughing and swinging Anna's hand. Cool blue moonlight shifted over her features. We were on our way to the pool. As we came closer, I smelled chlorine.

Another dream: I was in Baby's bed, hugging her close. The

smell of her almond blossom hair cream filled my mouth. I was whispering into her ear over and over, I'm sorry, I'm sorry, I'm sorry.

Then another: I was in the music room. A girl was hunched over the piano, playing a languid Beethoven sonata. The curtains were shifting. Something was moving behind them. Someone was there.

I woke up.

I was still in the tower. Every day and every night, I was still in the tower.

Viktória didn't return.

Was she waiting for me to do something? Give some signal that I was ready?

My throat clenched at the thought. I wasn't ready.

Would I ever be ready?

I pressed my cheek against the cool window. I could almost hear something out there, far away. A mechanical creaking, maybe, and kids laughing and screaming together.

Was today the Founders' Festival? I imagined Yaya in the bouncy house, jumping up and down, giggling and drunk, and Nick lying on the grass with a big grin. His teeth were stained red with wine. He'd said something funny, and Anna was laughing, laughing so hard she couldn't breathe.

But Theo? Where was Theo?

I sank to the floor. I hugged my knees.

When had Theo realized I could be used for their project? When I learned how to ride the bike? When I kissed him by the fountain? That night in the abandoned office, when we watched *Bye Bye Birdie* together? No, it couldn't have been that night; that was before he was working with M. Neptune, before he knew what was going on. It must have been sometime after his forum presentation. Some specific, precious, crucial moment when he turned to me and realized I was perfect. But when?

I pressed the heels of my hands into my eyes.

You'll always be beautiful, Theo had said to me once. That's all he wanted for me: to be beautiful and real, forever, like Baby. He just wanted me to be happy. He wanted us to be happy.

Why couldn't I be happy?

I shouldn't be thinking of myself. I should be thinking of Catherine. I needed to try harder.

I squeezed my eyes shut tighter.

But then I wanted to laugh. It suddenly hit me: after all this time, I still didn't understand plasm at all.

I'm in the house, I tried to say. I'm at the edge of the woods. I'm here. I'm here. I'm here, and everything's going to be fine.

But no matter how many times I said it, it didn't feel true.

Many nights passed—days, weeks maybe—before the aide was opening the door and saying, "You have a visitor."

My eyes darted up, but it wasn't Viktória. It was Yaya, wearing braided rope wedges and a long, royal purple jersey dress that twisted between her breasts and fell to the floor in folds. Her hair was puffed up like a halo on top of her head.

I had been bundled in a sheet at the tea table, playing solitaire. I tightened the fabric around my shoulders.

"Oh, Ines," she breathed. The dress floated around her legs as she came toward me. She sat in the chair next to mine and touched my shoulder. Then she hugged me.

I let her hold me. I tried to hug her back. She smelled like I remembered, like roses and nuts.

"Oh," she said again, squeezing me tighter.

The aide, the same one who had admitted me, stood blank-faced by the door, her arms folded.

Yaya held me at arm's length. "You're so skinny."

"How are you?" I said.

She looked me up and down. I wished she wouldn't. I wished she couldn't see me.

She glanced down at my game of solitaire. I'd scattered the deck in frustration.

"Oh," she said. "You've lost."

I burst out laughing.

But Yaya wasn't laughing. Her eyes were welling up with tears. I'd never seen her cry before. Her face didn't move as they streamed down her cheeks.

"Yaya," I said, "don't be sad."

She wiped her face as she settled back into the chair. "You look just awful," she gasped.

"Sorry."

"We've missed you." She wiped her face again. "We all miss you."

"We're together now."

She fiddled with a silver ring she always wore around her pinkie. "We're graduating," she said. "Tomorrow."

I nodded. So it had been a full semester.

I shifted on my seat. "How's everyone?"

"Okay. Good. We finished our tutorials and took our finals. We all passed, if you can believe it. Though Diego lost his mind for a while there. Remember how he was sleeping with what's his name—his advisor?"

"Yes."

"Well, he's been, like, sobbing all night at the thought of leaving him. Apparently Diego thinks they're actually in *love*. He's lost, like, ten pounds that he did not need to lose." She shook her head. "Anyway. We did it. We're graduating."

"How about Theo? Is he doing okay?"

Yaya's mouth hardened. "He's fine."

She must know by now that Theo was staying. That he was on M. Neptune's team and wasn't going to be graduating with everyone else. But Yaya said nothing more about it.

"Anyway," she said, "everyone misses you, but I was the only one who had enough points to come here. So. Everyone says hi. Especially Diego. He misses having someone to sneak to the kitchen with."

That wasn't true, about the points. I knew Theo had earned many and was miserly with them, like he was with food. He could do whatever he wanted.

Maybe Yaya had sensed my thoughts, because suddenly she spat out, "Theo thinks this is good for you. Being here."

I fiddled with a playing card.

"Fifteen more minutes," the aide said.

Yaya glanced at her. Her throat pulsed. Her eyes were watering up again.

"Want to play gin?" I said.

Yaya sighed. She nodded.

I dealt out the cards. I won the first hand with three beautiful spreads. Then Yaya won, twice in a row, both with rows of hearts. She clapped her hands with delight as I moaned.

"Ha," she said. "Ha."

"Just deal," I said.

She started to deal the next hands.

When the aide glanced at her watch, Yaya slipped something out of her bra and played it into the cards.

I studied her face, but she wouldn't meet my eye.

I picked up my hand. One of the cards felt different. Something was taped to its underside.

I slipped the new card into the folds of my bedsheet.

Yaya played a hand of spades. Then she touched my hand.

"Remember," Yaya whispered, "I told you when it would be time to think. To really consider something."

The aide coughed.

"It's time," Yaya said.

I whispered, "I can't."

"Yes," Yaya said, "you can."

I drew another card.

"All right," the aide said. "Come on."

After Yaya had left, the aide disappeared, and I was alone again, I pulled Yaya's card out from the sheet.

It was a Monopoly property. New York Avenue.

Yaya had scribbled a note on the card. I didn't read it at first, just turned it over to find the tools taped to the front: the wrench and lockpick from Baby's kit.

I ripped the wrench off the card and held it up to the window. The metal glinted in the sunlight.

❧

One day, my first spring at Catherine, Theo and I spent the afternoon playing dominoes. He had found them in some obscure Ashley parlor, nestled at the bottom of a trunk filled with Latin textbooks and silk scarves. There were several domino kits scattered around the house, but this one was special; the tiles were painted Egyptian-blue and the pips were shaped like stars.

I ran my finger along the stars. They felt exquisite beneath my touch. Theo laughed at how entranced I was, but I didn't mind him making fun. I liked the sound of his laugh.

We were playing in one of the Harrington parlors, near the great hall. It was a tiny room outfitted with a tea table, two chairs, yellow silk wallpaper, and a glass cabinet full of books. The ceiling was decorated with a mosaic, a gaping goldfish with coruscating orange scales. We were alone. Through the open window, I could smell lilac trees blooming.

Theo and I didn't know each other well back then. We were new friends. We didn't know what would happen.

Theo clicked down a tile. I laid one down, too.

There was a noise on the other side of the wall. Footsteps, jostling bodies, a loud voice—Nick, shouting, "Oh my God, Yaya, don't you dare," then a burst of laughter.

Theo hesitated with his next tile. He glanced at me.

"Should we follow them?" Theo said, nodding toward the door. "They're probably going to dinner."

"Let's stay here," I said.

A cloud moved as he set down the tile. The goldfish in the ceiling scintillated.

For some reason, in that moment, I thought for the first time: I might be happy here. I might be very, very happy.

Theo and I stayed there together as the sun set. Then we turned on the lights.

❧

It was time for my hour of exercise. I hadn't been let outside during my first stay in the tower, but now I was taken out once a day.

The aide shimmied a pale dress over my head, fiddled with the knob on the back door, and pushed me out into the glaring sun.

I shaded my eyes with my hand. I took four deep breaths.

The yard rolled away into a bank of dark maple trees, ferns, and bushes. Summer haze warped the horizon. The gate was somewhere ahead among the trees, too far away to make out. The loading dock and silos peeked out over the cluster of dry bushes on the left. Otherwise, there was nothing to see.

I ran in circles. It felt good to move my legs; the weeks in the cramped tower had made my body creaky and weak. I ran until my heart stung and my whole body was damp with sweat. I ran until I thought I might die. Then I collapsed, panting.

The grass, this close against my face, could be any grass, anywhere. I squinted. The grass blurred into hazy green.

I poked a hole in the ground with a stick. I dug deeper. A pink worm pulsed against my fingers. I shaped my pile of dirt into a wigwam.

While I played, the aide sat in a white wire chair, knitting. She liked knitting scarves. This was her third scarf since I'd been here.

I lay down again and stared at my wigwam. It looked like a nice little home for a nice little creature.

A bird tweeped in the trees.

I wiped my mouth. I was drooling.

Today was graduation day. Everyone was lining up in the bluebell field with their white dresses, blue and yellow sashes, and pretty daisy crowns. Their skin was fresh as milk, their cheeks flushed with joy. They were clapping and cheering for each other. They were all so glad. They had all done such a good job.

Now they were packing their few personal items into suitcases long forgotten at the tops of our closets and under our beds. They were lugging them down the stairs, hugging friends in hallways, and scribbling down home addresses. Because they would definitely stay in touch. Of course they'd stay in touch.

They were boarding the shuttles in shifts. They were playing road trip games, games like I Spy and Twenty Questions, and napping with their heads against the bus windows. They were passing around one last bottle of Catherine wine and telling stories about the time Henry Vu threw up in the middle of Linear Algebra.

Then they were getting off the bus, kissing each other, and they were gone.

They were gone. They were all gone.

How could they do it? How could they let Catherine go? I didn't understand. Because I could tell already: I would never stop missing the house. I would always be missing here.

I ran a hand through the cool grass.

Wind hushed through the trees.

I love you, I thought. I love you forever.

"Hey," the aide was calling, "that's it. Come on. Let's go."

I waved a bee away from my face.

I wiped my hands on my legs as I stood. My palms were red, my knees stained a raw, gory green.

❧

The elephant figurine's howdah was painted bright circus blue and red, and its trunk was cleverly articulated to dip with the press of a finger. I had spent many days and nights in the tower marching him across the bedspread, imagining the beautiful stories Yaya would have thought up for him.

Now he was still.

I turned in the bed. I'd counted the passing days according to the instructions in Yaya's note, but I had no idea what time it was, except that the sun had set hours ago. That would have to be enough.

Something lurched in my guts, and I thought, *Now.*

I climbed out of bed.

I stood naked in the middle of the room for one silly moment, glancing over the bedsheets, tea table, and bookcase as if wondering what I should pack. But none of it was mine. It had never been mine. I wasn't waiting for anything.

I'd hidden Yaya's note and the lock kit under the mattress. I fetched them and knelt by the back door.

Moonlight gleamed on its simple knob. I'd never opened one

before, but Baby said they were easy, once you could do Master Locks.

I could do this. Baby's voice from our lessons echoed in my head. *Just feel for each pin, one by one, and then let them fall. Be sensitive. Let each one go when it wants to.*

I inserted the tension wrench, then the hook. I stroked, feeling for the pins.

None of them fell.

Panic squeezed my stomach. I could feel the heads of the pins but they were loose already. What was I doing wrong?

I stepped back. I jiggled the knob. It rattled in my hand.

I stood and twisted the knob fully. The door creaked open.

I sucked in a breath.

The yard was vast and dark. The sky, the great sky above, was violet and cloudless, fragrant, and sublime with stars.

I closed my eyes. I breathed again.

Had the door never been locked? I didn't know. But I couldn't think about that now. I had to go.

I took one step, then another. The night air slipped cool against my naked skin. I grabbed a towel I found by the shower and wrapped it around myself before walking quickly across the yard, down the sloping grass, past the bushes, toward the loading dock.

I wanted to turn my head for one last sight of Catherine: the house, the lights, the millions of rooms and windows and doors. My home in the woods. But I knew if I looked back, I might never leave.

The truck was already at the loading dock. Bunny stood smoking a cigarette by the lift.

"Bunny," I whispered as I came close to him. "Hi."

He tossed the cigarette to the ground, stomped it out with his heel. He looked me up and down.

"You don't look nervous," he said.

"I'm not," I said. "Nervous," I added. I was something, but I wasn't sure what yet.

He kept grinding at the cigarette.

"How about you?" I said. "Are you nervous?"

He shrugged. "I've worked at Catherine for twenty-seven years. I don't want to be here anymore, either. Anyway, they won't think it's me. They don't know I can think that far."

He chewed his lip.

"I love Yaya, too," I said.

He kicked the cigarette away.

I whispered, "Thank you."

He shrugged again.

I walked around to the front of the truck.

Glo sat in the driver's seat, her hair twisted up with a pencil and fingernails painted fire-truck-red. She was reading a newspaper. She didn't look at me as she said, "Hey, chica. We're all packed. You ready?"

"Yes." I hesitated. "How far can you take me?"

"Mmm. Probably somewhere off I-81. Then you should go off-road. They check the truck at destination."

She folded the newspaper, then peered down at me.

"All that studying you did—no degree?" she said. "All for nothing?"

"All for nothing," I said.

She shook her head. "Man."

Bunny was watching me from the dock, his hand on his belly.

"Well"—Glo nodded toward the back—"get on in. 'Fraid you're riding back there."

I climbed into the truck. In the gloom, I could just make out an old couch, a stack of mattresses, and boxes of discarded clothes and supplies. But something else was glinting there against the wall. Something metal. I ran my hand along its familiar body.

The bicycle. The one we had found in the attic all those months ago.

Bunny loomed in front of the truck's opening. He was holding a folded bundle of clothing.

"Ready?" he said.

"Yes."

He handed me the clothing. "You can put these on."

He turned. I dropped the towel and unfolded a soft, careworn Hard Rock Café T-shirt and black sweatpants. They smelled like Tide detergent. I'd almost forgotten that smell.

"You can turn around," I said as I tightened the sweatpants' drawstring. They were much too big on me.

He did.

"How do I look?" I said. "Cool?"

He nodded, smiling a little. "Oh," he said, "and . . . here." He rooted through his jacket pockets, then handed me something wrapped in wax paper.

I turned it over in my hands, but I couldn't tell what it was.

"Ham sandwich," he said.

I hugged it to my stomach. "Thank you."

He closed the truck with a clang. I was plunged into pure black.

I crept against the truck floor, feeling my way among the boxes, until I found the stack of mattresses and climbed on top of them. I unwrapped the sandwich and took a big bite.

❧

We traveled for hours. I lay spread-eagled on the mattress, blinking at the stale hot black air and trying not to be sick. I wasn't used to the road anymore, to the way trucks lurched and trundled. We were going fast. We were going very far away.

I should have peed before I left the tower. I could feel my bladder pressing down, not letting me sleep. Every time my mind slipped into the unreal—I was on a ship on my way to Alaska; I was a star, soaring through the Milky Way—something jostled me back to reality.

There was a crack at the top of the truck's door. I watched the sliver of night sky shimmer and shake.

Sometime in the night, I got up to stretch my legs. I reached my arms up and out, twisting from side to side. I touched my toes.

I made my way over to the bicycle. I ran a hand over the leather seat.

In a few hours, I would get on this bike. I wouldn't have anything except the other half of the ham sandwich, but it would be enough. I would go, go, go. I would travel over side roads and hide in secret rooms. I would become a new person in a new place. I could do it. I'd done it before. I was running before I came to Catherine, and now I was running again. This time I wouldn't stop.

I tried to feel sad about it. But I already felt nothing.

The truck slowed, then parked. Glo shuffled around in the cab. The door slammed and I heard her limp around the truck. Soon I smelled gasoline.

We were at a gas station. A normal place for normal people. Inside the station there was a coffeemaker with bad coffee and a cash register filled with soft dollar bills. The racks were crammed with chips, pretzels, glossy gossip magazines, and bundles of newspapers that sold for just three quarters each.

I sat back down on the mattress. I picked at the dirt underneath my nails.

Nick had climbed the beech tree the day before our summer finals, at the end of our first year. Or was it our second year? I wasn't sure anymore. But I did remember that it was a drowsy late afternoon, the breeze brushing through the grass smelled sweet and lush, and we were far out, near the gate, lying in the tree's shade. We had finished reviewing our German flash cards for the second time when Nick said, "How high do you think I can get?"

I'd looked up into the tree's rich, luminous leaves, branches dappled with honey-yellow sunlight.

"Don't," Anna said. "You'll break your arm."

"Dare me?" Nick said.

"I dare you to *study*," she said.

But Nick was already standing and brushing off his jeans. He squinted at the tree before grabbing at a low branch. The veins pulsed in his arms. He swung up.

Anna watched him with her hand on her throat. I don't know why she was scared. He was strong and nimble as a boy hero. He was going higher and higher.

Soon he was small, abstracted in the leaves.

I called to him, "See anything?"

He lifted a hand to shield his eyes against the sun.

❧

As the truck rocked, I finally dreamed. I dreamed that it was many, many years in the future and I had been running for a long time. I'd changed my name. I'd changed my body. I'd become good and bad women and earned good and bad money.

But through it all, I could never tell if I was happy. Even when something nice happened to me, something I deserved—a new deal closed, a new house, a new girl waiting for me on a banquette in some throbbing, neon club—I didn't feel anything. I didn't care. I sat on the subway and watched teenage boys smile into each other's eyes, or a girl in a pink tank top giggle at a text, and wondered: Are they kidding? Do they really feel something? Are they here? Are they alive?

I blinked against the dark of the truck.

I hugged my stomach. I curled up tighter.

I used to believe the house was haunted. Really, it was the other way around; the house haunted me. Butter cookies on the tea tray, the weight of a doorknob beneath my hand, a pattern of golden leaves on the courtyard flagstones—every detail reappeared. And I knew that someday I would be frying up dinner or rushing past a perfume store or kissing the inner wrist of a pretty girl, and I would suddenly catch the scent of damp soil or floral baby shampoo—and I would be in the gardens, Catherine's soft gardens, and I would be tender and new, and I would be home.

Then I would be, again, gone.

I closed my eyes.

Viktória probably wouldn't even try to find me, once she realized I'd run. She knew I wouldn't tell her secrets. I didn't need to. Because one day the whole dark world would know Catherine's truth. But for now, the house was mine. Lovely and mine.

❧

The truck was stopping again. I opened my eyes.

The sky, through the gap in the door, flickered pale morning blue.

I rubbed my face. I had been asleep, deep asleep. I hadn't realized how tired I was. All night long the engine had rumbled and my brain had whirred, but now there was only quiet.

I still needed to pee.

The front door slammed and footsteps crunched against gravel. I rubbed my face again. The footsteps, closer now, were brisk, precise, and even.

I stood to gather up my trash and the sandwich. While I was squeezing the empty wax paper into a ball, the truck door rolled open with a great crank.

I turned, raising my arm. I blinked against the light.

ACKNOWLEDGMENTS

Thank you to the whole team at HarperCollins, with particular gratitude for my sharp, steady, lion-hearted editor, Jessica Williams. Thank you also to Amy Perkins and Tinder Press for pushing me to dream bigger.

Thank you to all at the Friedrich Agency, especially my warrior of an agent, Kent D. Wolf. Thank you for believing in this story.

Thank you to all my educators and mentors, particularly those at the Brooklyn New School, the Berkeley Carroll School, Yale University, and The Museum of Modern Art, who taught me to take my daydreams seriously.

Thank you to my many communities of friends: the X-Plex, the Complex, Shaftmates, Gail Benjamin and Bob Miele, Schuyler and the Grant family, and Maryse Pearce. This story is dedicated to you; you save my life every day.

And of course, thank you to my family, especially my parents, Kevin Thomas and JoAnne McFarland, and my brother, Stephen Thomas. I love you forever.

ABOUT THE AUTHOR

ELISABETH THOMAS grew up in Brooklyn, where she still lives and now writes. She graduated from Yale University and currently works as an archivist for a modern art museum. This is her first novel.